Escaping Paradise

BY

JUG BROWN

Dear CARY —
I hope You & TAMARA
enJoy The Newest
Excursion —
Love, Andy
11/21

Escaping Paradise

BY

JUG BROWN

Cover Design by
Ben Perkins
deviantart.com/brattyben/gallery

Copyright © 2021

Dedication

The Jug Brown writing team of Andrew Levine and Rik Huhtanen would like to first of all thank Darlene Mea with the only words that truly apply to your contribution: Your assistance made this a better book.

There were others who contributed so much to this project. The first among them is Dianne Rux, who meticulously edited the book, and put all of the pieces in final order. She was invaluable at just the right time, and for that we are eternally thankful for her patience with us.

Ben Perkins, artist, www.deviantart.com/brattyben/gallery took our rough idea for a book cover and created a terrific design for us.

Tom Foster, wake7997@yahoo.com, gave us valuable editing and organizational advice, and also helped us punch up the prose in The Fountain of Scams.

Artist Jeremiah Kalleck@jjkalleck, who created such a fabulous cover for our last book, *Solly's Pinch*, referred us to artist, Ben Perkins, and for that we are grateful.

And to our families who generously give us the time and support it takes so that we can step away from our responsibilities and create a wild and happy writing space, we are awed by your amazing gift.

Escaping Paradise

by Jug Brown

Wily Odysseus, the Lord of Lies, answered...
Where can I start? Where can I end?
The gods have given me so much to cry about.
The Odyssey, Homer

Cassius: Oh ye gods, ye gods! Must I endure all this?
Marcus Brutus: All this! Aye, more!
Fret till your proud heart breaks!
Julius Caesar, Act IV, scene III, Shakespeare

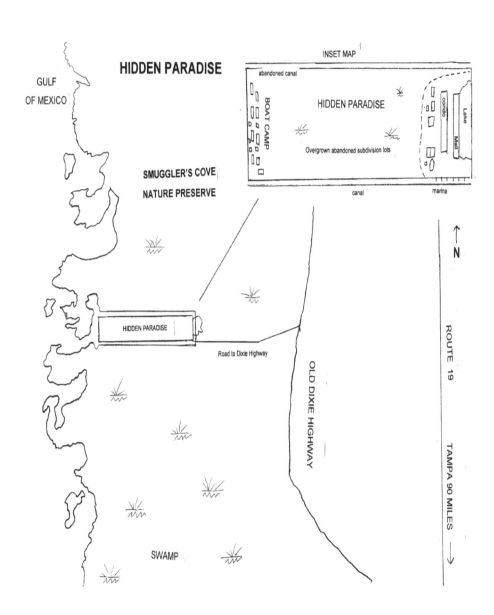

HIDDEN PARADISE

GULF
OF MEXICO

INSET MAP

abandoned canal

HIDDEN PARADISE

BOAT CAMP

Overgrown abandoned subdivision lots

condo

Lake

Mall

canal

marina

SMUGGLER'S COVE

NATURE PRESERVE

HIDDEN PARADISE

Road to Dixie Highway

OLD DIXIE HIGHWAY

SWAMP

N

ROUTE 19

TAMPA 90 MILES

Chapter 1

Like every other morning, Marie started work at the bakery at 4am before the birds began to chirp. Her life ticked like a clock, any interruptions were impositions.

On this particular morning when Marie's hands were in the dough, the phone rang. *No one ever calls this early, it's not even sunrise yet, must be family,* she muttered to herself. Scraping the thick dough from her hands, grabbing the phone from the wall, Marie answered abruptly, "DiCarlo Bakery."

"Marie, it's Santo." It was her brother's voice on the other end.

"Santo, everything okay? Who died? Why're you calling so early?"

Her face twisted in worry awaiting an answer.

"C'mon I'm at work, I got rolls here that need my attention. Tell me before they dry up, what's going on?" Santo rarely called. Impatiently, Marie covered the dough and waited for the 'news' and checked her timer.

Marie had stayed away from her NYC family for years. Even before she left the city she barely spoke with her brother. Santo kept his distance, never called unless he needed something, and he never asked for money.

'Deep Pockets' was his middle name and wheeling and dealing was his game.

For Marie, Santo's requests were always challenging and required a piece of her soul. And today, Marie had little soul to give her egotistic brother, especially during her morning baking schedule.

Santo's interruption, even if it were life or death, was in her way. But when family called, she answered.

"So, I take it no one died. Can you make this quick then

please, I'm making rolls."

There was silence.

"Helloooo Santo? The doors open soon and I've got a lot on my plate here; ciabatta, cannolis, and sweet buns, but NO time for silent chit chat right now. How about we talk this afternoon, could that work for you brother dear?" Marie looked at her timer, watching every second tick.

"I'm sending Marco to visit. He's gonna work for you. Don't worry Marie, I'll pay his wages, I set him up good for you. Nothing to worry about, it's just for a while. He needs a little attitude adjustment, you know what I mean? And... he's in a little trouble up here."

"No way Santo. Absolutely not! DO NOT do this. Please. I haven't seen Marco in what, eight, ten years? And I don't need any help. What are you thinking, Santo? This is Hidden Paradise. Do you even know what you're saying? You really want to send your son here?"

Marie's blood started to rise.

"Look," Marie continued as the tension in her voice rose. "Here's what I'm thinking... NO! Marco should not come here, not even for a visit. What is he, twenty-seven now? Hidden Paradise is no place for him, there's nothing here for him. It's no place for me either, and I'm old already, my life doesn't have much promise left. Marco must be in bad trouble for you to want to send him here."

She glanced down, grabbed a hunk of dough and automatically began rolling it between her palms. The phone was pinched between her ear and shoulder as she placed each raw roll on a tray methodically, still listening in great frustration.

"It's not *that bad* in Hidden Paradise is it? You know I wouldn't ask if I didn't need this. It's for Marco, Marie. He seems to be wandering aimlessly like he's lost all direction in life. I think he needs some new perspective, I think it'll toughen him up. And he'll be with you Marie, a woman who's not a girlfriend. If anyone can help him it's you, you're his auntie, you can help him get his life kick-started."

"You're pouring this on thicker than Nana's gravy, Santo," Marie interjected.

Santo continued with the sob story. "I know you're working hard at the bakery, you can teach him to be a baker. My son the Baker, I love the sound of it."

"Nooo Santo, you don't understand. There's no place in Hidden Paradise for Marco. Besides, I have NO time and NO patience to teach him to become a baker. I'm old, set in my ways and he's young, he'll be so bored. Don't you have a plan B?" Marie pleaded for reprieve knowing that if it's for 'the family,' 'yes' will be the only acceptable answer.

"You're our only option, there's no plan B Marie. I'll send you money and you pay him, like a salary. He won't know it's from me. I told him you needed somebody to help at the bakery. You can teach him. You're the best baker in the world." Santo continued relentlessly.

"Remember when you had trouble back when Arthur was around and needed help? Who helped you sweetheart? It was me! So please, you gotta give him a chance, it's what we do for family, we're here for each other no matter what."

Yeah, do it for the family, no matter what. That's always been the problem. Marie thought about the possibilities while coating most of the phone with her doughy hands. Then, while shaking her head 'no' she looked around the small room, it could use a good cleaning and a paint job, and maybe, she thought, I could bake more items if someone was at the front taking care of customers. She remembered the requests she had for pizza, real pizza, not that soggy chain store stuff that took an hour to get here. She thought about selling real New York Pizza. It could be great for business. Marco's young, good looking, and he's family. *This could be the answer I've been praying for... maybe it could be a good thing?*

"Okay Santo, I'm gonna do this for the both of you. You go ahead and send him, okay... I could use a little help. Maybe we grow the business together, Marco and I. He better not be any trouble for me Santo, or you'll hear about it after I bop him on the head. Where's he gonna live? He can't stay with me, my place is too small and he's big now, he's a man. He needs a place of his own."

"Sure Marie of course, we can do that. We put him up in the same place you live, what's it called, Hidden Paradise or something? What's so hidden? Something you're not telling me? Well, whatever it is, he'll figure things out, he's a bright kid, got our DNA you know? Get him a place where you are, a little paradise never hurt anyone."

"You got no idea about this place Santo," Marie responded, as she reluctantly agreed. "He must be in some kind of trouble, that's all I can say. Whatever I need to do... do I have a choice?"

Marie wiped sweat from her face with her dough covered hands, put the first tray of rolls into the proofing drawer, and with the second tray in front of her, began forming rolls.

Santo continued with his instructions. She thought, *'no matter where I move, even here, it's impossible to get far enough away from the 'familia.'*

"Let me know when he's coming?"

"He's on his way Marie. He left yesterday, called me from North Carolina last night, said he could be there as early as today, maybe tomorrow. He's got your number and address."

"You had this whole thing planned out without even asking? My permission means nothing to you? I'm telling you, Santo, Marco coming here is a bad idea. Why don't you send him to Miami?" Marie shook her head disappointed. But, that's how things worked, 'the familia' always sticks together. When someone really needed help they assumed it would be there without question.

"Of course Marie, that's why I called, to get your permission," Santo laughed.

And Marie bit back, "Santo, you must promise never to come here to visit Marco, he needs time away from you. You always smothered that boy. That was the problem all along. Leave him alone. Maybe he can be himself, breathe a little bit, grow up." She remembered Marco as a child, handsome, charming, mischievous and lazy. He always got his way.

"Ok, Marie. I know. I have to let him go. I won't visit. It's his turn to grow up for real. He always respected you and I'm gonna trust you with my son. I'll put cash into your account today."

"Wait, you know my account information?"

"C'mon Marie, you think I don't know how you got to where you are? The Karlowski Family that you married into? They've got no secrets from me. Their grandfather knew pop-pop when he came over from the old country. I know you had your own world, the Art Students League, the NYU crowd, living in the village, all that bohemian stuff. I know all about the Karlowskis."

"I don't have anything to do with any Karlowskis."

Santo paused for a moment and continued, "C'mon that's bullshit. How blind do you think I am? You're still in with them, and I knew Arthur Karlowski wasn't good for you. He was bad news and I'm glad he's gone. I thought it was a godsend when you were baking years ago in Brooklyn. But then, you disappeared to Florida. Big mystery, all hush hush. I put two and two together. He left you, and you got a bakery, be your own person, make a life for yourself. Good for you, but don't try to tell me you left the Karlowski Family. That didn't happen. It's how come you're at the bakery."

"Why didn't I see all this coming? Can't you just leave me alone?" Maria spoke despairingly while she completed the second tray and put it into the proofing oven.

"It doesn't matter Marie. I'm your brother. It's my job to watch over the family. It's what I do, and I'm happy I can do it. I love you." There was a moment of silence. Feelings coalesced briefly before she spoke.

"Yeah, yeah. Listen, thank you for taking care of us all. If I have to, I can do something to help Marco. He better not be a punk. It'll be good to see him again, maybe this could be okay, we'll see. But now, I gotta finish the rolls. Gotta go Santo."

"I love you Marie. Thank you."

Marie hung up the dough-caked phone feeling sick with worry in her stomach. What might happen with Marco here in

Hidden Paradise, how will he survive this place? She checked her watch as always and went on to the third tray of rolls.

Chapter 2

At 8pm there was a knock at the door. Marie had her feet up, sipping wine, watching her favorite series on TV. Interrupting her shows never went well. It made her grumpy. She paused the TV and slowly rose. Her days of baking gave her tired feet and her first few steps toward the door were awkward and slightly off balance. She hit her stride before she grabbed the door knob.

"Auntie Marie! Hello hello, it's been so long." Marco dropped his bag and stepped into a hug.

"Look at you Marco, you're so big and handsome, Oh My God." She held him at arm's length and took a long look at him. He had a tall slender athletic frame and rich black hair. His toothy smile was magnetic. She beamed with pride at him and gave him another hug.

"Oh God, it's been so long and little Marco is all grown up now. It must be nine years, I think. Come in, come in, sit down, Marco, I've got dinner if you're hungry. Lemme heat it up."

"You know Aunt Marie, I'm so tired I can just fall right to sleep. Maybe I could have it for breakfast instead. I just need to lay down."

"Of course, of course sweetheart. Please, here..." she dragged him to the bathroom and gave him a fresh towel. "Take a shower if you want, here's the guest room." She gestured to the room.

"It's kind of beautiful here, isn't it? But, I'm just gonna pass out. I can't even think straight." They embraced at the door to the bedroom and Marie stood for a moment gazing at him with a smile.

Get a good rest, big day tomorrow." "I'm gonna wake you up at a quarter to four. Set out your work clothes and we can get started." She patted his shoulder and turned to leave, closing the door on her way out. As soon as her show was over she'd go to bed. She sat down with a loving glow and returned to her favorite series.

Collapsing onto the bed, Marco took a deep breath and sighed, *out of the city at last.* The balmy sea air filtered through the open window. It was cooler along the coast of Florida.

Reviewing the last years of his life in a blur, Marco thought about the girls he'd left behind and about his undistinguished glide through Staten Island's own Silverhill University, 'college lite,' he called it. His mind sifted through his memories: his times as a bartender, valet, tennis coach, lifeguard, golfer and groundskeeper.

Marco was also the handsome, indifferent young man who showed homes when he felt like it, and met clients occasionally during the brief period of time he worked at his wealthy father's real estate firm. The hundred million dollar consortium that managed to fill hundreds of condos with tenants, and sold customized Long Island mansions to politicians and musicians. Marco hated every second of it.

His father's sister, aunt Marie, baked from childhood and worked in bakeries on and off. She met Arthur Karlowski while she was baking at a small pastry place in Brooklyn. His love of her small almond cookies connected them. Her light touch with the dough was superb and unusual for someone who was self-taught. They got married.

As Arthur's crime-connected family beckoned him closer to the fold, their marriage became unbearable and divorce was the only solution. As part of their divorce settlement, Marie accepted part ownership of DiCarlo Bakery located in an obscure Floridian housing development, Hidden Paradise. Here in the warm vacation land of Florida, Marie was guaranteed to have appreciative clients year round. The divorce agreement included a place for her to live, a monthly alimony check and freedom from Arthur, which for Marie, was the icing on the cake.

After eight years at the DiCarlo Bakery, Marie knew everyone and everything about the area. Hidden Paradise was located off the old Dixie Highway north of Tampa, down an obscure, untraveled exit. DiCarlo Bakery was in Smuggler's Cove Mall which was built on piers over a freshwater lake, in a large, swampy nature preserve. The poorly dug drainage ditches became estuaries for wildlife including mouthy alligators. Gators could be seen looking for a place to submerge and find food. Sometimes, all that was visible were dark eyes and a snout above the surface.

Smuggler's Cove Mall was a complex of a dozen stores. Everything was here from a dry cleaner to a gourmet specialty store. It was a quaint semi-circle of shops surrounding an outdoor, shade covered seating area. Customers could idly watch and feed the gators, who knowingly hung around for just that reason.

Occasionally, hungry, belligerent gators managed to get through the metal fence that surrounded the mall and condominium area giving everyone a thrill. Needless to say, they were unwelcome and ultimately were chased away.

Marie fell asleep in front of the TV realizing she had missed part of her series. Slightly peeved, she decided to go to bed. In what seemed to be only minutes, her alarm went off and it was time for another big day.

Chapter 3

Marco was bleary eyed as they walked to the bakery. In front of him, Marie had her head down determined to keep tempo with her daily routine. She knew if she got behind because of Marco, it would be a terrible day. They said two words: "Good morning."

The coffee maker perked and sputtered as the sun started to come up. Marie set up the rolls.

"What can I do Aunt Marie. How can I help?"

"You can start with the floor and the window sills. The cleaning supplies are in the closet over there." She pointed. Her morning had always been her own. She didn't want to share it with anyone. She enjoyed the silence and having to talk was starting to dampen her mood.

Marco swept and mopped the floors while yawning. After the rolls were put into the proofing drawer, they stopped for a coffee break.

"Here, try these...left over from yesterday." Marco grabbed a couple of small almond cookies to have with his coffee.

"Wow, these are great."

"It's why Arthur married me." She looked at Marco with a proud smile. She turned away and looked at the list on the white board and then back at her watch.

Baking demanded exactitude and timing. With only a few minutes to direct Marco and get him out of her hair, Marie grabbed a paper and pen and proceeded to make a list of what she wanted done. She directed him by pointing around the shop. It was a long list of things she couldn't get around to; clean the windows inside and out, scrub the door and window sills, clean out the fridge, re-stack the flour bags and check the mouse traps. The list ended with, detail the mixing machine and the exhaust hood.

"You see that area?" She pointed. "I always wanted to make this place into a deli and pizza place, you know, sandwiches, maybe a lasagna. You can get all those chairs cleaned, and clean the floor in there too. Then set 'em on the tables until we figure out how to arrange the place." Marie checked her watch again.

"You get started on that, I gotta make a call and start the pastries. I'm a little behind, I can't talk now, I'll catch up with you in a while. I wanna know why you had to leave the city, but not right now. You finish your coffee and have as many cookies you want. There's some other kinds of cookies in the bags behind the counter, help yourself."

She went into the back work area and returned to her well trodden path. The timer bell was her signal to switch tasks which she moved throughout the day. Her life swept by like a second hand. The only interruptions she enjoyed were the occasional songs on the radio to which she sang along with passion. Marco's presence, though helpful, was annoying to her on a visceral level. Marie was used to her own space. *I need to get him into his own place, asap*, she thought.

She called Shepp, the building manager and let him know she had to find an apartment for Marco. She knew there were plenty of apartments available. Many were furnished. Shepp agreed to see Marco and said he would clean up a place for him. Marie thanked him and got back to her rolls quickly.

As the baking alarm bell rang, Marie confirmed she was on-time with her rolls and reset the timer before putting the rolls into the oven. She went to the white board and crossed off a few more items. Her methodical process continued without stopping for a second to look over at Marco. Marco perused the page of tasks. He was exhausted already.

The day ground on. The morning rush had come and gone. The rush was followed by packaging special orders for pick up.

"This is good Marco, let's stop for lunch now, have some leftover spaghetti and meatballs." Marco sat down and in a minute the food was on the table in front of him.

"Aunt Marie, this is great."

"Thank you, Marco."

"Aren't you going to have some with me?"

"No, I have my tea now," she checked her watch again, and looked at the back tables.

"Thank goodness we have a few minutes Marco, good time to chat." Marie sat dunking her lady finger cookies in milky tea. Marco had a cautious look on his face. He knew he had to tell Marie what happened.

"So tell me Marco, what gives, how come you need to come here with me? Are you running from something? This is a little strange, you know, what's all the trouble?"

Her tight lips turned down in a moment of worry. She loved him. He was family.

Marco dipped bread into the sauce while he thought about how to tell her. He had learned to play it close to the vest all his life; no one had to know his business. But in this case, Marco cleared his throat, wiped his mouth and told the truth. "Well it's a long story auntie." He paused for several seconds, picturing the details.

"Please," Marie said, inviting his tale.

"Well, you know the love game, right auntie? You fall for someone, they become your everything and then, one day, they become everything you hate. They become everything that hurts you deeply and sometimes they become the one that forces you to change the course of your life, even if that was never your intention." Staring straight into Marie's eyes, Marco continued, "and you know what happens when you're crazy head over heels with someone and you see them kissing someone else?" Marco's head dropped, voice quivering from deep sadness. "That's right auntie, you lose it. You lose your mind, your common sense, and your next move may not be your best. Well, that's what I did, totally lost it on both of them. I couldn't help myself auntie, it was like I blanked out, completely lost it." Marco paused. Silence seemed to last forever.

"So what happened, what'd you do? You didn't...?"

"No I didn't kill anybody...but, I did mess him up quite a bit and I scared the shit out of her. I don't think she'll ever cheat on anyone ever again."

Marco bit into the bread, gazing forward. He found it easier to tell the truth than he thought.

"...And there's more. What I didn't know was that both their parents were invested with dad. They're all in a real estate moguls group, beau coup bucks, heavily invested and connected big time at city hall and with the 'families'." Marco sipped coffee and let out a sigh.

"So, they went to dad out of courtesy and told him I needed to get out of town or I'd get seriously hurt or worse. Dad knew they meant it. They would have done me great harm or even murdered me."

He joked out of fear, "no more pretty face, right auntie? So, dad said I needed to leave before I couldn't. So, here I am all in one piece, ready for my default life thanks to flying off the handle over a girlfriend. Next time, I'll walk away from the girl and not my life."

Marco wasn't happy about it, he wished it were some other way, but unfortunately it wasn't.

"Anyway, I guess it's time to find my own way out from under my dad's rule, and my past mistakes. Time to start over, find some kind of new life. So, here I am." His tone of voice dropped. It signified his reluctant acquiescence to change. He felt some real fear, worry and a deep reaching out from inside himself. Marco knew he wouldn't be seeing his old pals for a while and there wouldn't be no escape valve for him. He had to go it alone in a way he had never done before.

"Well, that's a sad story," said Marie. "It's too bad all that happened. I know how love can break your heart and change your life. It's unexpected, but it's part of growing up. It hurts, but it's a good thing. It means you're starting to get the hang of life and how it works. Now I understand what's going on with you, and I'm happy you're out here with me. Thanks for telling me about it." She looked at her watch and let out a breath.

"Let's get back to work now, we got things to do." Giving Marco a loving smile and a squeeze of his hands as if to tell him 'it's going to be okay dear.' Marie headed back to her work table and Marco chuckled to himself as he looked down at his chore list.

Marco worked harder that day than he had in years. He hated it and at the same time his talk with Marie made him feel grateful and calm. He felt the freedom of his escape from NYC and at the same time he thought about a future of menial labor or learning to bake and knew it wasn't for him.

I'm in the prime of my life. I need to live, have adventures, his thoughts raced as he lost himself in the broom. Florida was as good a place to start as any, but not in a bakery.

At five o'clock, Marie came out from her work room. "It's five o'clock. I want you to go to the first house right behind the condo and ask for Shepp. He's the building manager. He's got an apartment for you. He's gonna open my place so you can get your things. I need my own place back, you understand I'm sure. I'm glad to help you, but I have a hard time being interrupted when I'm watching my shows. You go see him and get settled in. Don't say anything to his wife, she don't like me. She thinks I'm after Shepp, but I'm not. So, I'll see you tomorrow at 4am. You go now sonny, you're making a new life for yourself and Shepp's gonna help you." Marie pinched him on the cheek, handing Marco a little booklet.

"Here, you be sure to read this."

"Why?" he bristled.

"Please, just read it."

Marco was tired from hard work and the lack of a full night's sleep. Marie's bossiness had just crossed a line for him. He took the booklet and as soon as he left the bakery he tossed it in the trash.

Chapter 4

Standing alone outside the Hidden Paradise Condominium in the late afternoon, Marco was dirty, sweaty, irritated and not at all pleased with his first day of working for his prickly, nosy, demanding aunt Marie. He thought about escaping right then, going back north, stopping off in Daytona Beach or Myrtle Beach to play on the way back to New York City. He'd visit Paul and Dougie. They'd let him crash at their place. Ridgeview Country Club would take him back in a second as an assistant golf or tennis pro. Anything would be better than repeating today's slave labor. His car was still packed. He could sleep in it and just leave whenever he woke up.

As he walked to his car, he yawned. He felt his tee shirt sticking to his back. He was crusty. He needed a shower. He was tired. He made a snap decision to play along a little longer and act interested in staying, but only in order to get clean and have a good night's sleep.

Heading towards the house directly behind the condo, Marco took a shortcut by walking under the open first floor of the condo. The first floor was odd. He noticed the open ground floor was a parking area for golf carts with extremely low ceilings. At 6'1," Marco's head cleared the girders above by only a couple of inches. Oddly, to reach the elevator, one had to descend a ramp. As he walked behind the condo building he found the manager's house, and knocked. It was answered by a slim, light-skinned African-American woman in her 50's with inquisitive eyes.

"I'm here to see Shepp about an apartment."

"Shepp, someone to see you." She gestured Marco into the house.

The living room was sparsely furnished with exquisite, matched pieces. His eyes were drawn to an abstract watercolor painting above the couch.

"This is lovely. I can't stop looking at it," he said, pointing.

"Thanks. I'm Carol," she said, sitting in a Swedish leather chair, holding a book.

A dark skinned African-American man walked into the room. He noticed Marco admiring the art.

"I'm Shepp. That painting is one of Carol's own and it's my favorite. She's an art professor at the community college." He held out a hand and shook with Marco showing a practiced warm and friendly smile, effectively camouflaging his well-trained suspicious eyes.

Shepp gave Marco a quick once over. His eyes were as perceptive today as they were when he was chasing fugitives as an undercover US Marshal, before he retired. Now in his mid 50's, of medium height, Shepp was trim and looked exactly like the ideal US Marine he had once been: squared away, direct, no nonsense, and tough, but not mean.

"I'm Marco Cavallo. My aunt Marie sent me to see you about getting an apartment."

"Ah yes, we talked."

Carol looked up from her book and her eyes narrowed into a dark look which quickly disappeared as she looked back down.

"I have a nice efficiency apartment next to your aunt's if you'd like. It's clean and ready.

Marco shuddered at being so close to domineering aunt Marie.

"How about something higher up?"

Shepp shook his head. "There's no elevator to the fourth or fifth floors. Nobody lives there. Everyone lives on the second and third floor."

"I don't mind taking the stairs. I prefer it for exercise. Are the apartments nice on the fifth floor?"

"Sure. But nobody has wanted to live there for years. Everyone wanted an elevator. You can take a look, be my guest." Shepp went to a drawer and pulled out a key.

"Here's the master key to the fourth and fifth floor. If you see something you like, let me know. Any furniture you find in any of the apartments, you can use. It's all yours."

Marco was thrilled by the thought of having his own place. He had never been out on his own without friends or a city full of distractions. It was a new world. The prospect of making his own way in the world was starting to feel exciting.

"I'd love to check out the fourth or fifth floors. I'll bet it has great views. Thank you Shepp. Can I ask you a question?"

"Sure."

"Your last name is Shepp. Are you by chance any relation to my favorite tenor sax player, Archie Shepp?"

Shepp's face darkened into an angry scowl. Carol saw this and suddenly looked furious. Marco stopped breathing. His mouth dropped open.

Very quietly, in a measured, menacing tone, Shepp said, "Let me get this straight. Because my name is Shepp, and there happens to be some musician whose name is Shepp, and because I'm black, then I'm supposed to be related to him? I'm supposed to know him? Like maybe you think all black people know each other? Is that how you think?"

Marco stammered "Uh no, no, I'm…."

Carol and Shepp drilled Marco with their angry stares for several seconds while Marco stood paralyzed in his tracks. Carol cracked up first. She looked at Marco and howled with laughter. Shepp joined in. He doubled over with booming laughter. When he straightened up there were tears rolling down his face.

"Did you see the look on his face?" Carol scrunched up her face and imitated the terrified Marco.

"No, it was more like this." Shepp did his own exaggerated imitation, pointing at Marco and laughing heartily.

"Sorry kid, you gave me an opportunity, I had to take it! And the answer to your question is, I might be related to Archie Shepp. Archie's family's from Florida, like mine, but I'm not sure. I've never looked into it. His music is great though, isn't it kid?"

Marco smiled broadly, laughed and shook his head. "You got

me, Shepp." Marco was relieved. It was comforting to find someone with a good sense of humor in the hinterlands of Florida.

"Okay kid, that was funny, Carol and I enjoyed the laugh. Before you head out to your new place, I have something for you." Shepp handed Marco a copy of the same thin booklet Marie had insisted her read, the same one he had thrown away.

"You need to read this." Shepp handed Marco the little booklet. He put his hand on Marco's shoulder and guided him towards the door. Marco took the key and heard renewed peals of merriment as he left.

Chapter 5

Marco was still laughing to himself about being ambushed by Shepp when he reached the fifth floor. *Too bad Dougie and Paul weren't here. They'd love it.* Wanting to share with them, made Marco miss his friends.

The open walkway to the apartment doors faced east toward the lake and the strip mall. Marco opened the first apartment door. The place was piled high with old furniture. It smelled musty. He closed the door and tried the next eight apartments, which were similarly dismal.

At this point he was resigned to sleeping in his car and forgetting a shower. Past a "Roof Access" door was the last apartment. He opened the door to apartment 590 and instead of it being filled with the stored junk, the apartment was well furnished and ready for occupancy.

All the couches, chairs, tables and paintings on the walls were covered with sheets. The place was lovely, albeit a little dusty. He walked past the foyer, through an open kitchen with an impressive marble counter top and custom built cabinets. The living room was filled with light from wall to wall panoramic picture windows, facing west. Two miles away he could see the expanse of the Gulf of Mexico at the edge of the mangrove swamp that surrounded Hidden Paradise.

He opened a sliding glass door to a long balcony fronting the entire apartment. He took a deep breath. *This feels like home, maybe I found paradise at last.*

"I can do this," Marco yelled into infinity from the edge of the balcony of his new home in Hidden Paradise, "thank you life, Dad, Auntie, Shepp, I can do this for sure... whoo hooo!"

At that moment Marco reconfigured his entire decision to leave the next morning. With renewed excitement and intent he explored the apartment. There was a small guest bedroom and bath, and a grand master bedroom. He walked through the bedroom and turned on the lights to an oversized bathroom. It had a lovely walk-in tiled shower, and a deep jetted tub. There were bath towels and washcloths in a large walk-in closet.

Tossing the booklet onto a table, Marco paused and thought, *I'll read the pamphlet at some point, not today. Maybe it's important, but right now, a shower is what I need.* Marco tossed his clothes on the floor and ran the water. He was excited about his new pad in the sky. When he jumped in he found a fresh bar of expensive soap and some designer shampoo. *I wonder who lived here?* Maybe it was some megabucks rock star's hideaway. He stuck his head under the water. *Thanks Dad.*

When he finished, he left to explore. Next to his new apartment was a locked door to the roof. His master key opened it. He climbed the stairs to discover an astonishing 360 degree rooftop view. *I'm in paradise here.*

Marco panned the rooftop. It was covered by a thick black membrane and had a 4 foot wall around it. In the corner nearest him was a storage building that held electrical panels, shelving, boxes of spare parts and other odds and ends. At the end of the storage room, a door led to a toilet and sink. *Okay, good to know*, he thought.

On the north side corner, Marco saw a window washing platform on davits. The motor and cables were covered with heavy tarps. He walked around the perimeter of the roof and saw a chain link fence surrounding the entire Hidden Paradise and the strip mall. *Kind of odd,* he thought. Looking east, onto the Old Dixie Highway past the strip mall and the lake, he could barely see evidence of civilization.

On the south side, he saw the only access road to Hidden Paradise with more chain link fencing running along the lake side for a few hundred yards. From there, the access road ran west directly next to a pleasant marina and a wide boat canal leading to the Gulf far away. Looking directly down on the south side, Marco saw a large swimming pool, two tennis courts, a clubhouse, and about 15 upscale fishing boats in the marina.

On the west side, he saw a couple of industrial metal storage buildings and 4 houses inside the chain link fence, one of them was Shepp's house. Outside the chain link fence, looking toward the Gulf, there was overgrown scrub jungle and a few collapsing abandoned houses.

Strange landscape, an incredible 360 view of chain link fences and abandoned homes. Where the fuck am I? Well, wherever I am, this is incredible for me. Up here on the roof, with this view, is bad ass. I love being on top and alone, peaceful, away from the hectic bullshit of New York. Free from my family's expectations. This is it. I'm gonna rent this place and fix up the roof, it's all mine. It was nearly sunset when he ran down to Shepp's house and knocked on the door. Shepp let him in, still smiling, and directed him to the table. Carol wasn't home.

"Well, what do you think? You want the efficiency unit next to Marie's place?"

"Actually, I was wondering if I could rent apartment 590."

"Huh? You like it up there? No elevator you know."

"I'm ok with that. It's the only place I liked."

"The rent on it is $400 a month." Marco was shocked by the low price.

"I'll take it. Also, I was wondering, could I rent the rooftop too?"

"Well, maybe. I already promised the roof to the groundskeeper, Reimundo, some time back. But, if you could make a deal with him, I'm ok with it. Why don't you go see Rei right away, he lives next door. You'll like him. He's a great guy. He might help you fix up your place. He can build or fix anything."

"Super."

"One thing you need to know. Rei got burned very bad in a boat fire. His arms and face mostly. He's pretty rough to look at, but don't let it put you off, he's a great guy. Go see him. If you want the roof, it's his call."

"How much for the roof, if I can make a deal with Rei?"

Shepp thought for a minute and said, "How about if I make you a work trade deal for renting the roof. If you and Rei can work it out, I'll let you have the roof for free in exchange for taking care of the pool."

Marco agreed with a nod.

"The pool takes about 15 minutes every night. You backwash the filters, skim for debris, check the ph and mow the strip of grass. All work has to be done after 7pm. The tenants don't want work going on when they're using the pool. Once a month I've got a service that comes in to drain it and clean it. You won't have to worry about that."

"I was a lifeguard at a country club. I know all about filters."
"Great," Shepp replied. Turning, he found a binder on a shelf. "Here are the manuals and the log for the chemicals, plenty of supplies in the closet down there for at least three months. You can start tomorrow night, I'll take care of it tonight. Come back in the morning and tell me what you and Rei decide. You can sign the lease then."

Chapter 6

Marco walked next door to a pleasant single story house, light brown with a well maintained yard of fruit trees and flowering shrubs.

Knocking on the door somewhat apprehensively in preparation of Shepp's warning, a horribly burned man answered. Even though Shepp had warned him, Reimundo's appearance was shocking. The right side of his face was covered with white, shiny pink and parchment brown skin, with the texture of crumpled paper, incompletely flattened. His right ear was a stub with no hair on that side of his face, and no eyebrow. The right side sagged a bit. But the left side of his face was intact, which made his appearance even more grotesque. He had full thick dark hair over a little less than half his head. Yet, somehow he smiled warmly with his lopsided loose, swollen, blubbery lips.

"Hi. I'm Marco Cavallo. I'm renting the apartment on the top corner of the fifth floor. I'd like to rent the roof, so Shepp said I should meet with you and work out a deal." Marco had a hard time not staring. He didn't want to make the man uncomfortable.

Reimundo's one eyebrow rose and his lopsided smile broadened. "Yes. Yes. Call me Rei. Come in."

Rei pointed to a teak kitchen table in his spotless, well furnished house. They sat.

"Coffee, or something to drink?"

"No thanks, I'm good."

"Ok." With his strong accent, and some diminished facial muscle control, it came out sounding like 'hokay.'

"Very good. Welcome. So, you're renting that nice apartment on the top floor?"

"I am." Marco felt welcomed by Rei. He could feel the man's sincerity as if it were physical.

"Very good. I know that apartment well. If you need help

fixing it up, I can help. I have free time now. I can fix or build whatever you need. I was an engineer in Cuba. I take care of the grounds here. There is not much for me to do. Also, there is lots of very nice furniture in the big storage building. It was salvaged after the hurricane just collecting dust now. Don't use the old mattress in that apartment. Buy a new one. That apartment has been closed for years. The kitchen appliances are good, but maybe some need to be replaced. There are some kitchen appliances in the storage building too, but most are old, from the hurricane."

"Thanks, I guess I'll figure it out once I move in.
What about the roof?"

"Ah, the roof. What do you want to do with it?"

"I just think it would be a great place to hang out. Put a barbecue up there, a picnic table, a couple of chairs. Nothing big. I thought about putting a platform on the north side to make a driving range, so I can hit golf balls into the swamp."

Rei nodded, pleased with this plan.

"What would you like to do with the roof?" asked Marco.

"Simple. A rooftop garden. Fruit trees, fresh vegetables."

"I like that. Let's do it."

Rei's face became grave and serious. "One thing. If we do this, the roof is only for you and me. Shepp can come up, but nobody else who lives in the condo. Nobody else! You must agree or I refuse."

"Why?"

"The tenants don't like me. They don't want me in the building. They call me monster, ghoul, Quasimodo, Freddie Krueger, Frankenstein or worse names. To my face they say this! Many years ago, the tenants voted to keep me from coming around the pool. They voted to keep me out of the condo, except when I am invited by a tenant to fix something. Then they voted to keep me from going to the restaurant. I once washed the windows of the condo but they voted to stop me because they did not want to see me outside their apartments. They don't like me. So, if they find out we have a wonderful roof garden, they will vote to exclude me, and keep it for themselves."

"That's awful," said Marco. "It's terrible. I agree with you. If I lease the roof, then it's just for us, nobody else allowed. I'll make sure it's in the lease that you can come and go freely." Marco felt good that he was making the roof safe for Rei, protecting him from the awful treatment by the tenants. He liked Rei.

Marco and Rei shook hands on the deal.

"We can bring up lumber for the garden boxes, soil, furniture for your apartment, using the window cleaning platform."

"That works?"

"Sure. It works very well. It came off an 18 story building in Tampa. I rebuilt the motor. Very powerful. The cable is barely used. It'll be our private elevator to the roof."

"Great. I'm excited Rel, let's do this."

Rei stood and smiled warmly. "Come see me tomorrow. We can get started."

As he ran up the stairs Marco realized he wasn't going to be leaving Hidden Paradise in the morning, and he wasn't going to be working at 4am for Marie either. The idea of having his own quiet place and chilling for a while felt like what he needed. On the way back to his new space, Marco remembered seeing some lawn furniture in one of the apartments. He found the apartment, and brought a chaise lounge with a thick cushion up to the roof.

The sun was going down, a spectacular sunset was brewing over the gulf. A few isolated thunderheads in the distance gave off an occasional bolt of lightning. Marco felt exhausted and pleased after his long day. He laid back on the chaise lounge, feeling the pleasant gulf breeze on his face. *I love my life,* he sighed out loud. With the distant rumbling of thunder in the background, Marco was lulled into sweet slumber.

Chapter 7

Excited by possibilities, Marco was up by 8am, stretched, showered and off to check out his new rooftop playground. He was eager to take a good look around his new apartment, but, not just yet. Down the stairs and out he went to knock on Shepp's door. Shepp answered, wearing a Hawaiian shirt, shorts and flip-flops. He offered Marco coffee and one of Marie's excellent cinnamon rolls.

"I want to rent apartment 590. Rei and I made an arrangement, so I can rent the roof too. We need to be sure our lease includes a statement that says Rei is allowed to come up anytime, and the lease must exclude anyone else, except you, of course."

Shepp nodded. "Good. Rei's alright. In fact, I prefer him to just about everyone here. Many of the tenants hate him, just because of his abnormalities."

"That's so wrong."

Shepp took out a lease, added the stipulations. Marco signed and paid, and Shepp made a copy for him.

"Welcome to Hidden Paradise," Shepp said, extending his hand.

"I do have one question. Why is the ceiling so low on the ground floor? That can't be up to code."

"Ah. The short answer is that the entire condominium is sinking. Fortunately, it's sinking evenly, at about 1/8 of an inch a year. That ceiling was once about nine feet tall."

"Wow. How did that happen?"

"Some greedy idiots did it. The footings were designed for a three story building, and the owners added two more floors in the 1960's without improving the footings. So, it's slowly sinking."

"That's crazy."

"Yep. Crazy and crooked is par for the course around here.

The history of this subdivision is rich. Did you read the booklet I gave you?"

Marco got up. "Nah, not yet, but I will for sure. Right now, I gotta go see my aunt, catch her up on what's going on. Shepp, thanks for everything." They shook hands and Marco left.

Chapter 8

Marie was behind the counter arranging baked goods in the display case when Marco walked in. An instant scowl came over her face when she saw him. It was already 10:30am.

"Sorry I'm late," he said brightly, just to see her reaction to his obvious tardiness. She put down the tray of rolls and stared at him.

"It's time for you to get back in your car and go home. You hear? I told Santo not to send you. I begged him not to let you come here. It was a terrible idea." She waved her hand towards the door. "Go ahead. Leave. This is not a good place for you."

"I already rented an apartment. I'm staying."

She shook her head sadly. "No. Please go. Don't stay. I'm serious. Just drive away."

Marco shrugged. "Maybe I'm going to like it here Aunt Marie. I could give tennis lessons, do odd jobs. I think I'll check it out."

Marie had an odd look that was both crestfallen and angry. She shook her head sadly, and looked at Marco like he was a stupid, stubborn child.

"Could you pay me for yesterday's work?" He asked.

"What?" She shook her finger at him. "You want me to pay you? I wanted some help fixing up this place. You couldn't handle one day of work. No. I'm not paying you."

Marco had a slight smile on his face.

"We both know my father's paying my salary."

"So what? I'm keeping your salary. You don't get any of it."

"Well," Marco said mildly, "I'll just call dad and tell him I'm not working for you. Then neither of us will get anything." He turned to leave.

"Wait a minute."

Marco turned back.

"Maybe we can make a deal."

"Yeah?"

"What if I tell Santo you're doing great here, and you tell him the same story. We can split your salary, 60/40."

"I get the 60%?"

"No. You're the pain in the ass. You get the 40%."

"No deal. 50/50 or I tell my father."

She humphed and thought for a moment.

"Ok. Deal."

Marco smiled.

"Ok, deal. And by the way, I have someone to help you fix your dining room up and I'll help him."

"Who's gonna fix it up? It's been a mess for 2 years."

"This guy named Reimundo, who lives behind the condo."

"No way. Not him. He can't come in here. Nope."

"What's the matter with you, aunt Marie?"

"Rei's alright. But, my customers don't want to see him around the shopping center. I'll lose business."

"That's awful. What's wrong with these people? Well, if that's the way you feel, I'm not helping you fix it up either." He started to walk out. He didn't need his aunt messing with his life. He could do whatever he pleased and he wasn't beholden to her.

"Wait. Wait. Marco. Damn. You're so touchy, just like your father." Marco turned back.

"What if Rei only worked after hours, at night?" She said, understanding the crazy prejudices of the condo tenants.

"That might work. I'll see if he'll go for it. If so, we'll fix your place up nice, just the way you'd like. You'll be serving pizza in no time."

Marie stood still, thinking. "Okay Marco. But, since I have to pay all this extra money to Rei, I'm telling Santo that I'm giving you a big raise."

Marco smiled a big lopsided grin. He felt kinship with his aunt; they were both happy to bilk money from Santo.

"You'll see, I'm worth every penny of it."

Chapter 9

In the days that followed, Marco cleaned and aired out 10 years of musky vacancy until his new apartment smelled fresh as ocean air. And with the help of Rei, they sorted through every apartment hauling whatever pieces of furniture Marco liked into his spacious pad.

As they searched the apartments they found a few puzzling things. The best example was that one abandoned apartment's living room featured a semi circular row of eight reclining chairs four feet away from a makeshift stage. In a windowed nook was a large octagonal card table with chairs. The bedroom had a mirrored ceiling with customized lighting surrounding an oversized super king bed. Marco had found someone's pleasure palace.

"Rei, give me a hand with this please? I want one of these La-Z-Boys."

"Oh sure. I'll take one to my place too." They removed the window, hoisted the chair out and took it down on the window washing platform to Rei's place.

Together, they made a super team of high speed movers. Within no time Marco created his cozy, comfortable place with spectacular views of the coastline through the wall to wall windows. It was beautiful. He couldn't think of a place he'd rather be. Compared to New York City, the sound of water and breezes were far superior to the traffic, horns and sirens that echoed between stone and steel high-rises. It was restful and safe in the arms of nature.

This is paradise, Marco felt, breathing a sigh of relief. *Finally I can relax.* His stress level was dropping away by the day. He felt safe.

Rei and Marco built several rows of raised garden beds, filling them with rich soil. In short order they were creating a restful rooftop space that included a substantial garden. Hours of toil everyday in the hot sun were followed by rest on the lounge chairs and a few cold brews. Rei was a good companion and partner in the rooftop garden. Although he often appeared sad, he was quickly becoming a resourceful friend.

Looking around at their accomplishments, Marco felt inspired. The rooftop was the ultimate setting for a private party. Marco was happy no one else was invited or allowed into his private paradise besides Rei. He hadn't met anyone, and didn't feel like he needed to, if they were as prejudiced towards Rei as he described.

It was a delightful undertaking. The constant daily hard work ended with Marco and Rei toasting their cold brews and going through plant catalogs to find more exotic fruit trees and flowering plants. Within two weeks, they had created a paradise in the making. And for the first time since he stepped foot in Hidden Paradise, Marco was feeling inspired and productive. *I think I'll stay at least long enough to see this garden give us some veggies, maybe I've found my new home*, he thought.

Marco's pool work was his final ritual each day. The sun was setting without a soul around. It was a restful time to focus and move through his tasks in a methodical rhythmic fashion. It was his time to reflect. I like my daily rhythm, it's soul satisfying and nourishing. I'm calm and relaxed. This is good, this is home. Marco was lost in his own peaceful bliss.

The sun began to drop into the ocean. The warm breeze dried his skin as he dozed on the lounge chair, until a voice woke him up.

"Hey Marco, can you help me?"

"Sure Rei." Marco smiled.

Marco was happy to have an uncomplicated friend who asked for help. It was comforting, and he was grateful.

Chapter 10

The next morning Marco decided to take the day off from his projects. He strolled to DiCarlo Bakery around noon to get paid.

"Aunt Marie, how're you doing?"

"I'm okay, sonny. You want your pay, right? I know you're not coming over here just to give me a hug and a kiss." She turned around with a dour expression and pulled money out of the cash drawer and handed him several hundred dollars.

"Don't ask for more until next week. That's it."

"Thanks Marie. I'm sorry things didn't work out. I'm just not cut out to be a baker, but I did promise to help and I'm gonna make good on my promise. We're gonna paint and set up the front of the bakery for you, just like you want. It's gonna be beautiful. You're gonna love it. What color do you want? How about a pale blue."

"I don't believe you Marco, you're not gonna do a thing. You say this, but you're gonna go home or swim at the pool. You're lazy like my relatives. Always taking a day off, you don't know what hard work is. Always the easy way. I know who you are. Don't think I don't." She shook her finger at him and scowled.

"You don't care for anybody else but you." She turned away from him and spoke. "I don't really care what you do with your life, sonny, just don't lie to me. I've known you since you were a baby. Go have a coffee and take some pastries. They're gonna get hard overnight. Eat something, please."

"I mean it aunt Marie, you tell me the color, we'll take care of it."

She turned looking straight into his eyes, searching for truth.

"You really gonna do this for me Marco, don't lie to me, now." Marie had grown up in a place where lying was a way of life.

"Really aunt Marie. We're gonna make it better than you can imagine." He shined a charming warm smile at her and she melted.

"Okay Mr. Helper. You make it blue, like this apron. And make the trim dark blue like that sign there." She pointed at a menu sign.

"You gonna clean too? All the stuff around the pizza oven, inside and out, right Marco? It hasn't been used in years. It needs to be deep cleaned and arranged. And don't forget the windows too, right?"

"Everything, Aunt Marie. We're gonna do everything, and we're starting tonight. We'll be in here when you close at 4. I'll go buy the paint right now, and you know what Aunt Marie, I'm paying for it just to show how much I really do appreciate you."

"No, no, you don't buy the paint. I'm gonna give you the money for it and for your helpers." Marie handed Marco $1200 dollars from an old wallet in her apron pocket.

"You get whatever you need Marco, all I want are blue walls with red and white checkered tablecloths on the tables." Marie walked over to a cabinet and pulled out a stack of brand new tablecloths and handed them to Marco.

"It's gonna look great. I'm off and running. Back at 4 with Rei."

"Wait one minute sonny." Marie scooped up a pile of pastries and cookies and put them in a box, "these are not gonna sell today, share them with Rei."

Marie handed over a box of pastries and a spare door key. "Marco, maybe you can find someone to help me out in the bakery when I start making pizza? But, they have to live in the condo."

"I don't know anyone yet, lemme ask around. You can't do this all by yourself auntie."

"C'mere," Marie walked from behind the counter and gave Marco a big hug. "I know you're family. You come through for me, I'll remember. But, when I come in tomorrow, it better be beautiful." Shaking her fist at him, looking at him and loving him completely, while pretending to threaten.

"Don't you worry, we've got this for you, You're gonna love it auntie."

Marco walked out with a bag of goodies and headed straight for Rei's place.

Chapter 11

"Rei? You here?" Marco knocked on Rei's front door. Rei came out, fresh from a shower.

"I brought something for you," handing Rei the large box filled with Marie's delicious pastries.

"What's this?"

"My aunt gave 'em to me, for us. She said they were day-old and couldn't sell them, but it's kind of a bribe, Rei."

"What do you mean?"

"She wants to start serving sandwiches and pizza so she wants us to paint, clean and set up her bakery for her.

"So, what's **us** about that?"

"That's you and me. We, Rei." Marco flashed his charming smile. "I thought maybe you'd help me get this done." Marco looked knowingly at Rei for his 'yes'.

"Is she gonna pay me?"

"Of course she's gonna pay you Rei. But, I'm thinking, we may need a third person. Know anyone who could help us?"

"I know a Vietnamese kid. Hard worker, lives by the boats. He's got nothing to do really. He tends his garden and sells stuff off the boat sometimes. Let me ask." With that, Rei picked up his phone and made the call.

"Thiem, you want to work tonight? I've got some painting and clean-up to do, but we can only work at night."

Marco listened to Rei's one sided conversation and gleaned the answer was yes. The kid rode his bike to the fence within a few minutes. Rei and Marco met up with him and off to the bakery they went.

Marie's pizza cafe was undeveloped but her pastries and specialties were the perfect combination to keep the guys content and engaged while Marco described what needed to be done. Then Marco did what he learned best from his dad, he offered them a price they couldn't refuse. Within moments of 'Yes,' they were off to town for paint and supplies before the stores closed. In a little over a flash, they were back, ready to fulfill aunt Marie's wishes.

As promised, they were at the bakery by five thirty sharp.

"Okay guys we've got a plan and we're completing it tonight. Piece of cake, right? Or in this case a slice of pizza," laughed Marco, encouraging the guys.

Soon the tables were emptied from the front of the shop while Thiem cleaned the back to a spotless glow, scrubbed floors, dumped garbage and removed mounds of useless stuff that had been collecting dust for years. Rei and Marco worked diligently prepping and painting. By 1am the cafe was painted, immaculately clean and the tables were set with checkered cloths. Marco fired up the pizza oven and got it up to 700 degrees without issue. At that moment, Marco looked around and considered his debt to aunt Marie complete, everything looked great and Marie would be happy.

"Mission accomplished guys," Marco offered more of his aunt's leftover cookies. "Great job, really, my Aunt is going to love it, hope it's okay to pay you in cookies?" Both their faces went from happiness to perplexed anger.

"Only kidding guys." Marco handed a generous sum of money to each of them.

"Say Thiem, maybe you want to work making pizza for my aunt."

"I don't know how, but I can learn. I will work very hard. I'm not making money now. I need to make money, so I want to work." He spouted eagerly. They exchanged contact info.

"I'm happy to work. She's not mean, is she?" Thiem continued.

Marco laughed "Not really. She's demanding, intimidating, but harmless."

"Okay, I'll give it a try. I work hard, I'm a good worker. I need to make money now, so thank you Marco."

Like clockwork, it was 4:30am when Marie arrived at

DiCarlo's. The first thing she saw was a light left on. Initially she was upset thinking Marco was wasting electricity. But, as she peered through the glistening windows she could see the super clean and shiny floor, the fresh blue paint on the wall, and the checkered cloth table tops. It made her heart flutter, Marco came through. It confirmed she had real family nearby, family that wouldn't let her down, family that actually cared, family that would be there for her. Marie began to cry.

The morning crowd rolled in and there was a roar of compliments and comments. Marie talked with everyone about 'real pizza' coming soon. "How soon?" They wanted to know.

At noon, when the store was quiet, Marco arrived with Thiem. Marie was instantly reluctant.

"Aunt Marie, he cleaned the entire shop while we did the painting!"

Marie looked at Thiem differently. Despite her demand for cleanliness, she herself had never done a good job cleaning the shop. She looked around. Every corner had been attended to.

"By yourself? Where do you live?"

"At Boat Camp. I cook at home, not pizza, but I can learn from you. I can learn quickly. You'll see," Thiem offered eagerly.

"Sorry, I can't hire anyone from Boat Camp. You should know the rules here, Thiem. I'm not even supposed to let you inside the chain link fence. The council says no Boat Camp people working in the mall–period. It's not my decision."

She pulled out a wad of cash and paid Thiem. Thiem was surprised because he had already been paid by Marco. He didn't object. He smiled and thanked her.

"I wish I could hire you. Good luck." She turned and gave Marco money to pay Rei. Marco took the money readily, knowing that he was double-dipping: Marie had already given Marco enough money to pay for the work and the paint.

"By the way, Marco, did you read that booklet?"

"Yeah, yeah, I'll get to it." Marco was getting tired of Marie making demands.

He left without a word, motioning for Thiem to follow. Marco was disgusted. He phoned Rei and together they escorted Thiem and his bicycle back through the gate and said goodbye. He shared some of Marie's extra money with Rei letting him know what Marie had said about not hiring Thiem. Rei shook his head sadly. Rei knew the rules and knew it was a long shot that Thiem could be hired.

Marco decided to take the rest of the day off. The discrimination didn't make any sense. Why would Marie go along with the rules? How could these people be so bigoted?

Chapter 12

Still bothered by the discrimination against Rei and Thiem, Marco had a sleepless night replaying an elaborate fantasy of standing up to small minded bigots. He felt sad and disgusted about how people could be so unjust to others for no reason. This would never happen in NYC, New Yorkers come in all shapes, sizes and attitudes. Judge me on my merits, not how I look or dress. Marco was exasperated.

The morning sun was covered by passing clouds in Hidden Paradise. It was almost noon, and the clouds were a break from the blazing white brilliance of the tropical sun. Marco headed for the pool to try to swim off his feelings of frustration. *Why do people do the things they do?* With only a few sunbathers around, Marco laid back on a chaise, shut his eyes, and quickly fell asleep.

Startled by sprays of cold water over his entire body, Marco opened his eyes to see a lovely dark haired woman splashing in the pool nearby. What is this beauty doing here? Who is she? Immediately Marco was drawn to her. He looked toward the pool where she was swimming. She peered at him from just above the water. Her dark brown eyes were like those of a seal, playful, cautious and thoroughly natural in their curiosity.

Holding his glance as she swam along the edge of the pool going in the direction of the other folks gathered there, Marco watched as she climbed the ladder. The muscles in her thighs and arms twinged as she got out of the pool. She was attractive. He followed her with his eyes back to her chair. She grabbed a towel and sensuously wiped off the excess water, all while sending a series of coy looks towards Marco.

What Marco didn't notice was her husband, a much older man, short and hairy, sitting nearby in a chair with an umbrella shading him. When Marco did see the man, he heard him say to his lovely wife, with scorn, "Don't even think about it!"

Marco turned his eyes away and closed them. He fell asleep again as the heat of the day came out from behind the clouds. Again, he was awakened suddenly, this time by a strong nudge to his shoulder. He noticed the pool area was filled with people.

"What?" Marco said.

Now standing over him was the husband of the lovely woman he was already hot for. He was in his 60's or early 70's. She couldn't have been more than 30.

"I just want to introduce myself. I haven't seen you here before, have I? What's your name?"

"I'm Marco. My aunt is Marie from DiCarlo Bakery. I came down to give her a hand."

"We lived here for a long time. Sometimes I go on vacations, on my boat," he jutted his chin toward the harbor dock. "I'm Niccolo Barare. That's my wife, Mysti." He looked back at the playboy-model-attractive woman whom Marco had been magnetized by. Niccolo jutted his angry chin out at her. Marco had met guys like this in New York. Friends of his father. They were friendly on the surface but had a threatening aspect just underneath the pleasantries and banter.

"Well, it's a great place to live. Very private. Quiet. I like it." Marco replied.

"C'mon" Barare gestured, "Let me introduce you to some of these folks around here. If you have any problems at all, let me know. I'm pretty much in charge here." Barare nodded with a sinister smile.

Marco took the cue and stood to follow him. The names and handshakes passed quickly. Almost all of the men were in their 60's, 70's or 80's. Many were heavyset, strong and guarded in their disposition. He forgot most of their names, but took notice of their faces. There were a few women among them who emphatically appeared to be taking a back seat to their husbands; nodding when introduced, suppressed and dominated as if some awful stifling agreement had been made and enacted regarding their limited self-expression and obedience.

Standing in the midst of the people by the pool, Nicolo Barare said, "There's a little book around here. I'm sure your aunt has some copies. Did you read it?" Suddenly angry, Marco thought, *That damn book again! What's with the fuckin' book?*

Marco knew these were the bigots who discriminated against his friend Rei. Somebody had to take a stand.

"No Barare, I didn't read the damn book. I'm sick of people suggesting it. In fact, I think I'm gonna be the only person here who will never, ever, ever read that book. How about that?! Never. Does **never** work for you?" Marco was talking so loudly anyone could hear. The entire pool area went quiet. Everyone stood perfectly still. Marco didn't care.

One of the men shook his head and said softly, "Don't do a Haney, kid."

Another man added, "It's too late, he did a Haney."

"Yep. I guess so. You can't put the Haney back in the bottle."

"But he's more like a Bertram, though. He's like a Bertram doing a Haney."

"Yeah, I can see that."

See what? Marco thought, *What's a Haney?* Marco was tired of this nonsense and decided he didn't want to mingle anymore. He excused himself abruptly and returned to rest on his chaise under the sunny sky. As soon as he laid down, another short, heavyset man with thinning gray hair who looked to be in his 60's approached and stood over him.

Marco looked up and noticed the man's big belly under a Hawaiian shirt, his skinny legs, the broken blood vessels on his bulbous nose and upper cheeks. He was carrying a plastic bottle of Downy Fabric softener, which he opened and drank from.

"Hi. I'm Leo DiCarlo, I'm the bakery owner. You're Marco, right?" He held out the Downy bottle. "Want a pull?"

"Uh, no thanks Leo and yeah, I'm Marco, nice to meet you."

Leo shook the bottle. Marco could hear ice tinkling.

"Come on. It's good. Have some. You'll like it."

"Nah. I'm good." *These people were obnoxious.*

Leo shrugged and frowned. He stood there for several moments, looking past Marco.

"Do you like to fish, Marco?"

"Sure."

"What do you say we go out on my boat tomorrow. There's some great fishing out in those Gulf waters."

Marco thought for a quick moment. "Sure. Sounds like an adventure. I'm in."

Leo smiled what looked like a well practiced, predatory salesman's smile.

"Great. We'll need to leave early, be at the dock, 5am sharp?"

"I'm already there!" Marco replied, smiling wide. "Nice to meet you, Leo."

Leo walked away. Marco lay back, closed his eyes and ignored everyone. After a while they all left and Marco stood at the quiet pool to perform his daily cleaning routine. Inhaling deeply he dove in for his end of day swim. It was a peaceful completion to another rather odd day in Hidden Paradise. *Who are all these awful people? Why do the men seem brash while the women are so meek? What kind of place is this?*

Climbing out of the pool, drying with the sun's warmth, Marco looked around wondering why everyone behaved so strangely. *I'll give it some time, see what comes up. That's what grandpa used to say: give it time, give it time. 'Tomorrow, fishing in the gulf, with aunt Marie's baking partner, Leo DiCarlo. What's with the Downy bottle filled with booze?*

Chapter 13

The dark pre-dawn morning was perfectly still when Marco found his way to the marina. It was deserted except for Leo DiCarlo who was stashing fishing tackle on board an expensive aluminum boat. It featured a small shade cabin and a solid 225HP outboard engine.

"Good morning to you, Leo." Marco greeted as he noticed the name of the boat, "Soft and Fresh."

Leo offered his wolf-like smile.

"Good morning Marco. Let's go catch some fish! Why don't you cast us off?" Marco undid the ropes, jumped aboard, while Leo started the powerful engine. Throttling down, they moved slowly away from the marina, down the wide canal towards the Gulf of Mexico. A flock of sandhill cranes stood like ghostly sentinels in the shallow water on the side of the canal. Marco sat in the back end of the boat on one of the cushioned seats running along both sides. Leo stood at the controls. A solitary fishing chair bolted to the deck was equipped with a pole holder and straps for tying the in fishermen. The water was peaceful like glass, and the air, cool, refreshing and perfectly comfortable. *Gonna be a sweet day*, Marco thought to himself, smiling big.

Two miles down the canal, Marco saw lights up ahead. Two men were unloading an untidy commercial fishing boat, painted matte black. Behind them, a row of ramshackle buildings. Marco heard a diesel generator. The men on the boat stopped working for a moment, and waved to Leo. He waved back.

"Looks like they caught some fish last night Marco."

"What is this place?" Marco asked.

"We call it Boat Camp." DiCarlo commented, "They're squatters. They took over this end of the property after the hurricane came through about 35 years ago. They come and go, move around to different places all over the Gulf coast. Some work in fishing, some are part-timers on the oil rigs, there are rumors some do a little smuggling. It's a big loose group. They've been on the property for a long time. They're like gypsies."

"Really? So this is Boat Camp. I didn't see a road. How do they get here?" Marco looked perplexed.

"No roads. The only access is by boat."

"Isn't this private property? Nobody chases them off?"

"I guess it's private, but nobody in the condo wants the hassle, that would bring in the law. Boat Camp folks keep to themselves. We insist on it. And they keep an eye on the canal here, so it gives us a little security. Live and let live, we say."

Leo's boat cleared the canal and entered the flat Gulf. He opened up the engine and they took off at high speed across the glassy surface. The warm wind blew in Marcos's face and through his hair. He was thrilled.

Leo slowed down and stopped once he got out to the point where land was barely visible.

"You wanna drive?"

"You bet." Marco responded without hesitation and headed over to the wheel. Leo grabbed his Downy bottle and showed Marco the throttle and compass.

"Keep us on a heading of 265 degrees, straight out."

"Aye aye, Captain."

Marco fed the engine some gas and got the feel for its power right away. Opening the throttle to full speed while skimming the top of the water, he felt the rush of energy and wind as the boat seemed to fly. It was exhilarating.

Leo took another swig from the Downy bottle and settled into a chair sheltered from the wind under the hard shell canopy. He turned on the surround sound system and blasted classic rock tunes from the 70's and 80's. This didn't bother Marco a bit. *What a great place*, he thought. How lucky he felt to live at Hidden Paradise. *What a great decision it was to come to Florida.*

Leo lit a cigarette and smiled, enjoying Marco's pleasure.

20 minutes later, with no sight of land Leo told Marco to

stop the boat. He took over the controls and turned off the engine. Marco, still excited, went to his seat in the back of the boat.

Leo quickly retreated into the tiny cabin. When he stepped out, Marco's breath stopped at what he saw... Leo was holding a nickel-plated 45 caliber automatic pistol, pointing it unmistakably in Marco's direction. He sat down, lit a new cigarette and took a drink from the Downy bottle.

"Want a drink?"

Marco shook his head slightly. He couldn't take his eyes off the shiny gun now resting in Leo's lap, still pointed in his direction. Marco's body felt like cast iron, he couldn't breathe, his mouth went dry like it was filled with cotton.

"You don't want to drink with me?"

Marco shook his head. The idea of drinking from the Downy bottle was worse than the gun in his face for some reason.

"Oh well. You and me now, we need to have a little talk."

"Ok," said Marco, in a dry whisper.

"How much do you know about Hidden Paradise?"

Marco didn't answer.

Leo picked up the gun and shook it.

"Answer me."

"Nothing. I don't know anything about Hidden Paradise."

"You didn't read the fucking booklet? Marie didn't tell you anything?"

"No."

Leo gave Marco his predatory smile.

"Wonderful lady, Marie." He held the gun in his lap sucking down even more smoke from his cigarette.

"It's time for your education. Too bad you came here. Your father's a dip-shit first of all, you know?"

"You know my dad?"

"Of course I do. I was at your parent's wedding. I brought Marie down here. I own her bakery. She was married to my worthless brother Arthur for a while. I never liked your father. He's a self-important fool with more money than brains. You take after him. He always thought he was better than me, better than everyone else. Just like you. He never should've sent you down here. Marie tried to stop him." Leo paused for a moment. "But now that you're here, you need to know the score."

Marco was transfixed by the gun.

"You ever hear of the witness protection program?"

In his tiny, breathless voice, Marco replied, "Yes."

"Well, Marco, everyone at Hidden Paradise except your aunt and a couple of other people are all in federal witness protection. We've all committed crimes, bad ones. We all got caught. We all provided evidence against higher up people, and those other people went away to prison. Now we're all in hiding from our former friends, here in witness protection. The stupid feds put us all together in this condo. They won't move us. Since we're here, we just want to be left alone. But, now you're here, you dumb arrogant shit. That's a problem, one that I might have to fix today. Do you see our dilemma? What are we going to do with you, Marco?"

Marco was stunned even more. *Witness protection? Criminals?* He looked across the empty water. *Was he going overboard? Was this blue sky and endless expanse of water the last thing he'd experience?*

Leo lifted the gun from his lap. "I have a choice to make. We're 10 miles out in the Gulf. I could simply shoot you, tie an anchor around your neck, toss you overboard, hose down the blood and tell everyone you had an unfortunate accident on the water. I might even manage a few tears. You fell overboard, hit your head and drowned, it happens. I did everything I could. I'll cry to your father and mother. Nobody would question the story. Not even Marie. The people at Hidden Paradise will understand, *it had to be done.* They'd thank me for it. I'd be a hero. No more Marco problem." He took another drag of his cigarette.

"I'm leaning towards making this choice right now. It's the safe thing to do." Marco sat there, already lifeless. *I knew there was something weird about this place, I should always trust my feelings, now look at the position I'm in with this killer. Oh my God, why didn't my dad or even my aunt warn me - or tell me anything.* Marco's head was racing. *How do I get out of this?*

"But, there is another choice, and it's yours to make," Marco heard Leo while watching him pause for a few more moments to take another drink and gaze out at the water. Was he thinking deeply or was he dazed and nearly drunk at 7am?

"If you can convince me that you'll keep this secret of what Hidden Paradise really is and not tell anybody, E-V-E-R, then maybe I can let you live."

"I will never tell anyone, ever, ever, ever. I promise Leo."

"Huh? I don't believe you. I think you're a punk, an asshole and a creep just like your father. You believe you're better than me, right?"

"No sir, I swear, I don't think I'm better than you. I won't tell. Why should I?"

Leo sat there pondering his choices. He stared at Marco for endless minutes, in an eternity of silence. Marco sat there barely breathing, unable to even conjure another thought. Finally, Leo started up the motor.

"I'm going to take a big chance. You get to live, but only for today. I run Hidden Paradise. Don't ever forget that. If you have an issue about anything, if you want permission for anything, you come to me. Got that punk?"

"Yes, got it. I'll come to you sir."

"You get one chance. I'll be watching." Leo sneered.

"Don't worry, you can trust me Leo, I promise." As Marco spoke he noticed he was feeling smaller than he'd ever felt.

"Yeah, we'll see, kid. Apples don't fall far from the tree you know. For now, I don't feel like fishing with a runt like you." Leo put the gun in a drawer by the wheel, did a quick turn around and headed back home at top speed. The sun was up, shining bright as they pulled back into the canal. Despite his overpowering fear, the scenery was spectacular. In his heightened state, he noticed the scraggly grey beards of Spanish moss hanging from giant cypress trees on both sides of the canal amid tangled mangrove roots.

Tropical birds were singing from everywhere, but Marco couldn't think straight, his mind was overwhelmed with panic.

When they came abreast of Boat Camp, Leo waved to a gangly, shirtless white man who was hosing down the fishing boat. The man reached down into a cooler and brought up a large fish. Using hand signs, Leo signaled that he would buy it and the price he would pay.

"You want a fresh fish, shitbird?"

Marco shook his head, no.

Leo shrugged. "Suit yourself."

The man on the boat handed the fish to a mixed race child with a dirty, wild, reddish afro. The kid jumped into a homemade dugout canoe, paddled furiously out to Leo's boat, exchanged the fish for money and paddled hard back. Leo's boat moved up the canal towards the marina. As they went inland the huge cypress and twisted mangrove gave way to an impenetrable mass of saw grass, palmetto scrub, skinny pine trees and spindly live oaks. When they got to the docks Marco jumped out and tied up the boat.

"Do you need any help?" He asked Leo.

Leo shook his head no. Marco walked away, numb, drained, like a condemned man walking to the gallows.

Chapter 14

As Marco was making his way back home he realized it was only 9am and he'd already had what felt like a full day in less than 3 hours. He opened the door to his apartment and stood there momentarily saddened. He went from joyful acceptance and the rich possibilities of a happy life to the angst of being under the coercive scrutiny of penned up criminals. He was determined to leave Paradise as soon as possible, no matter how beautiful things looked on the surface.

He was about to close the door, start packing and leave forever when he heard the sound of banging from up on the roof. It was Rei, working on the rooftop garden. He wanted to see Rei one last time and say goodbye to his only friend at Hidden Paradise. He left his apartment. When he reached the roof, Rei gave him a broad smile. He pointed to his project.

"Look, I am almost finished with your driving range platform. And here..." he said pointing to a stuffed duffel bag, "a bag of old range golf balls, hundreds of them. I got them from my friend who's a groundskeeper at a golf course."

Marco barely looked at the driving range platform he had dreamed about. It now seemed like a stupid idea. All his dreams were crushed to dust forever. He tried to talk, but his cottonmouth made it impossible. Marco grabbed water from the fridge and downed the bottle in one long gulp. He sat at the picnic table under the umbrella. Shoulders down, defeated, staring into space, exhausted, confused and scared.

Rei put down his hammer and sat opposite Marco. "What's up with you, looks like the air has been sucked right out of you. What's the matter?"

"I just found out about this place. Leo DiCarlo pointed a gun at my face."

"Oh" said Rei softly, nodding his head in sympathy. "That's

no good. Wanna tell me about it?"

Marco told him everything, including how time slowed to a stop the moment he believed he was going to die.

"Rei, I have to leave, today."

"I am so sorry," said Rei.

"Are you in witness protection, Rei?"

"No. But, I came here with a very bad man named Manuel Gonzalez. I guess I should tell you my story." Grabbing a bottle of water, Rei sat back down.

"My boss was in witness protection. When I left Cuba, the old overcrowded boat caught on fire. My wife and daughter drowned. I got burned in the fire. I found some floating wreckage, hung on and came ashore. I was barely alive. I wanted to die. My family was gone. My burns looked much worse than today, if you can believe it. My face was always bleeding and oozing, it was terrible. Nobody would look at me, nobody would hire me. The only work I could get was as a janitor cleaning toilets for a drug lord named El Pincho. He said he owned me. He found out I was a skilled engineer in Cuba and that I could fix anything, so I started doing skilled work for El Pincho. When his young nephew Manuel Gonzalez got married, El Pincho gave me to Manuel as a wedding gift, like a slave. Manuel was so happy. He called me El Monstruo, the monster. He never called me by my name ever, only perro, a dog or monster. He told everyone at Hidden Paradise my name was monster." Rei took a deep breath.

"We came here to Paradise because Manuel was careless. He started dealing white powder and he got careless. He was busted shipping 1,500 pounds of pure coke across the Keys. Instead of doing time, he made a deal with the Feds and turned informant on El Pincho. El Pincho ended up going to prison for 30 years or something like that, and Manuel went into witness protection here, at Hidden Paradise. He brought his new wife of course, and me, the monster servant. I had to live in a corner of the warehouse while I fixed up his apartment, which was the best in this building. He used to say, 'I own you forever, monster. I will never let you go'."

Rei paused. "Your apartment, Marco, was Manuel's apartment. I built everything there for him. I did my best work."

Marco was stunned. "Where is Manuel?"

"Gone. Nobody here liked him. They hated him. He tried to run this place, to be the big boss. One night, he and his wife just disappeared. Their car disappeared, and that was it."

"Maybe he ran into hiding."

"No, no no no," said Rei, smiling. "He would never leave without taking me, his slave, esclavo. He loved having a monster servant. No no. He is dead. He was fed to the alligators or something. He's definitely gone."

"Who do you think killed him?"

"Somebody here killed him, that is for sure. I don't know who. I don't want to know. There's a lot of very bad people here who could have killed him. The meanest of all, the one they call 'Sicko Fonseca' is gone. He left a year ago. Whoever killed Manuel left me alone. I don't know why. The federal agent living here at the time was replaced. He retired right after that. The disappearance was too much for him. After that, Shepp moved in to manage things for the government 10 years ago. The government was going to shut the place down, but they decided they would just never add any new residents. The police never investigated. Nobody called them. Everyone started saying that Manuel and his wife left one night on their own." Rei paused. "We all know better."

"Shepp works for the government?"

"Yes, of course. He is the federal marshal here, running the witness protection program."

Marco shook his head. It was all too much.

"Rei, I have to leave today. I can't stay. I promised Leo I wouldn't say anything, and I won't, but I've gotta leave. I didn't sign up for this."

Rei shook his head, sadly, "No, Marco. You can't leave. Please, do not leave. They will follow you AND they will kill you... Then they'll kill your family." Rei stood up, beckoning to Marco to follow. "We must go now to see Shepp. You have to tell him everything."

Chapter 15

Shepp answered the door, stepping aside for Rei and Marco to enter. Carol was sitting at the table, grading papers from her college class.

"He knows," said Rei, "and he wants to run."

Shepp shook his head sadly.

"Oh no. Sit down Marco," Shepp said pointing towards the table. Carol cleared her school papers and the four sat. Marco slumped forward finding it difficult to look into their eyes.

"I guess you didn't read the booklet? Tell us everything," said Shepp softly.

Marco told the entire story again, starting with what he had said to everyone at the pool, and DiCarlo approaching him afterwards. When he was done, they all sat still for a minute, absorbing Marco's fearful experience.

"He kept trying to get me to drink from his Downy bottle."

Carol leapt to her feet and stared at Marco, "Tell me you didn't drink it. That nasty, drunken pig. You didn't drink from his bottle, did you?"

Repulsed, she did an exaggerated full body shiver.

"Ewwwwwwwwwww." She stopped her shiver and shook her head, like she was trying to cleanse her mind of an image she couldn't unsee.

"I didn't drink from the bottle, I thought getting shot was preferable."

Carol was relieved. "Thank God. Good for you." She breathed an exaggerated sigh of relief. Shepp smiled at Marco's response and his wife's theatrics.

Now Carol turned to Shepp. "Downy has a gun? They let a piece of garbage like him have a gun? Can he even shoot it? I'm surprised that nasty ass clown hasn't shot his dick off." She pointed a finger at Shepp. "You let a person like that have a gun, Shepp, really? Leo? Of all people?"

Shepp raised his hands, palms up next to his head. He raised his voice a notch, sounding every bit like the exasperated husband he was, "This is Florida! Everybody has a gun! If I take his gun, he'll just get another one. Give me a break, please!"

Carol sat down, after one final "Ugh." They sat in silence for a few long moments, each one lost in thought. Finally, Shepp spoke.

"You know Marco, you probably could have avoided the whole ordeal with Downy if you had simply drunk from his bottle when he first offered it to you by the pool. And... if you had read the booklet, you would've known."

"Come on Shepp," said Carol. "Marco had to find out sooner or later about this place."

"Yes of course. Reading the book would have been easier. So, here we are."

Marco was feeling a bit better, knowing that Shepp, Carol and Rei were on his side.

"How did this place come about, an entire community of criminals in witness protection, living together?"

"Ah ha, very good question," Shepp responded, getting to his feet. He went to the bookshelf, and handed Marco another copy of the booklet. "Read it." Marco opened the book to the first page and read the title: *The Fountain of Scams: Greed, folly, murder and the history of Hidden Paradise subdivision, 1991,* by Caspar Melton, former Resident of Hidden Paradise 1988 to 1992.

Shepp pointed to the binder. "This was written by one of the first people to live here in the witness protection program back in the late 80's. Caspar Melton was his assumed name. I don't know his real name but I know he was a mob guy from Brooklyn. He fixed horse races and ran scams. He got interested in Florida history when he moved here and wrote this while he was bored. Once his book was complete he got pancreatic cancer and died."

He pushed the booklet towards Marco. "You want to know how Hidden Paradise came to be Federal witness protection? Read it. There's lots of copies floating around the condo. Apparently,

Caspar ordered hundreds of them. People use them to light barbecues and clean windows. The book answers some of your questions. Carol and I have been here for 10 years. We came right after your boss went missing. Right, Rei?"

Rei nodded in agreement.

"Read it. But first, we have much more important things to discuss than history," looking at Marco to make sure he had his attention, Shepp continued. "You need to learn some survival rules Marco. Are you listening? Your life and family's lives back home depend on your learning and practicing these rules. Your friend's lives depend on this too. Do you understand this is very serious? Don't toss this to the side again, read it like your life depends on it, and we can move forward." He paused for a moment to let this sink in.

Marco nodded earnestly, as if his life did depend on it.

"First of all Marco, you can't leave, I know you want to, but you can't. You can't go home. You can't run. And, in less than a day everybody living here will know the story of what happened on Downy's boat. Downy is already bragging to everybody he runs into. If you run now, the most paranoid of the very worst people here will believe you're a threat to their anonymity, to their personal safety and they'll start hunting you. Every single one of them has a price on his head. They've all sent bigger criminals to prison. Some are stone cold killers. If you run, they'll hire people to follow you. They'll follow your family and your friends. They'll send you violent messages, or they'll simply kill you, your family and your friends. So, leaving is not an option for you. Got it, Marco?."

Marco went back into shock.

"It's not all bad news," said Shepp, holding up a finger.

"First of all, everyone who lives here simply wants a peaceful Florida vacation for life. There are no new witness protection people moving in. No one from the general public can move in. All residents here have anonymity. That's a big factor in your safety. They all know that I'm not like the last Federal agent who lived here. I won't put up with obvious criminal activity, like the last guy did. I know some crime still goes on here, but it's all hidden from me, and that's ok. They also know that if any one of them gets out of hand, I will shut this entire place down forever in a minute. At that point, they'd all be kicked out into a dangerous world of bigger criminals just waiting to get revenge on them. They won't get a new place to live, at government expense. They won't get their stipends. They'll only have their new identities and nothing else, I'll make sure of that. This is good news for you because all they really want is to live in peace."

"Okay so what do I need to do?"

"I'm glad you're listening. Downy DiCarlo brought you inside this secret world. Once you're inside Hidden Paradise, you're all the way in, all the way committed. That's the way it is whether you like it or not. I know Marie tried to convince your father not to send you here. Your father wouldn't listen. But, that doesn't matter now, because now you need to be responsible for your own survival. There's only one way to do it. First, drop out of everyone's life you ever knew. Erase all the phone numbers from your phone and block them. Drop yourself off the face of the earth. You can keep your parent's email and phone. Erase and block all other emails. Got that Marco, you still with me?" Marco stared in blank disbelief. Shepp continued in his matter of fact tone.

"The reason you need to do this is that someday, somebody here is going to break into your apartment, copy your hard drive and phone contents even if you have a password. You won't know it happened. There are people here who are that good and that sinister, and they'll do it, just for fun."

Shepp continued. "To protect yourself from these hidden criminals, you need to create a self-imposed version of your own witness protection. Using your real name, of course. You need to create and live a new, secret life, just like the criminals here do. You'll need to make yourself safe to them."

"How do I do that?"

"Another good question. Your goal must be to convince everyone here that you're an ok guy, that you're no threat to them, their secrets are your secrets. It's going to take time, months, maybe years. You have to stay here until they believe in you. Then later on, after you're fully accepted, if you want to leave, for whatever reason, they won't track you down."

Marco nodded.

"You need to meet every person here, socially or otherwise, and they need to meet you. You won't be safe until they know you and trust you. You must meet them as an equal–that's very important. If you call them 'sir' or kiss their asses, they'll hate you. They'll sense your fear. They'll turn you into their bitch and believe me Marco, they're experts at it."

Marco cringed as he remembered calling Downy DiCarlo "Sir" several times, and how contemptuous Downy was.

"The tenants here are not all mobsters. We have plenty of white collar criminals too. Most of these residents fall into a few basic types of criminals. There are the monkeys, charmers, and tricksters group. A lot of these people seem ok at first glance, but most of them can't be trusted. And there's the Hyenas. These are the hard core violent types, the predators. Strangely enough, a few of them are actually pretty good people. You need to meet them all. However, one thing you should never do Marco, never ask about their past, or their crimes. That's bad manners, just like in prison. If they talk about their past, don't press for more. Most of what they say will be bullshit. They'll be testing you."

Shepp looked at Carol and Rei.

"What's your advice for Marco?"

"Shepp's right," Carol added. "You need to meet them on equal terms. Over time, you need to go to all the shops in the mall. Talk to people, any place you can meet them. Go to the restaurant. Don't hide."

"I have another idea. What kind of skills do you have?" asked Shepp. "Maybe you can be useful around here."

"Aha. I like this idea," said Carol. Rei nodded.

Marco thought about it for a time.

"I have been enjoying fixing up my place with Rei. I don't

know much about plumbing, carpentry and electricity, but I think I could learn. I like working with you, Rei."

"And I like working with you Marco." Rei agreed with a smile.

Shepp clapped his hands together.

"Perfect. You two are a handyman team from now on. I'll spread the word. You'll get plenty of work. Let me make a suggestion. Don't take on any big remodeling projects for anybody. These knuckleheads will waste your time, they'll play games with you. They'll complain about your work and then after all that, they won't pay you. Do little jobs only and charge full commercial rate. I think $120/hour for a two man team is the commercial rate for Florida handymen. If they don't like paying full price, tell them to hire a regular outside contractor. They won't do it because all of these people hate outsiders coming onto the property. It's an obsession. Also, the Tenants' Grand Council has voted against it. So, only do little jobs and stand your ground as an equal. Don't let them play games and for sure, don't call them 'sir'."

"What else do you know how to do?" Asked Carol.

"I was a golf pro and a tennis pro."

"Ok," said Shepp. "We have nice tennis courts. Put up some signs and hold classes. Maybe one day or two days a week. Rei, can you make up some signs for Marco?"

Rei nodded.

"I'd like some tennis lessons," said Carol.

"Your first customer," said Shepp.

"When you walk out of here today and from now on, act like nothing bad happened. Hold your head up high. Be strong, even if you feel like pissing your pants when you see Downy, even when you remember the gun he pointed at you. Act like it was no big deal."

"I'll try," said Marco, suddenly hating his father for setting up this fiasco and hating Marie for not making him leave the second he arrived. Then he remembered: *She tried to get me to leave.*

"One last thing," Shepp looked serious. "You're a good

looking guy Marco. Someone looking like you giving tennis lessons in this paranoid place is gonna attract the wives of some very dangerous people. Lots of the women will want to take your lessons. Listen. Don't ever be caught alone, even in innocent circumstances, with any of the wives, for any reason, or you'll be a dead man. Capeesh?"

Carol was standing in the doorway to the kitchen. She now smiled and leaned against the door in an exaggerated seductive pose, putting her hand on her hip and in a singsong voice said "What about me-ee?"

Shepp blew a burst of air out of his mouth, and shook his head while looking at Marco.

"Sheesh. See what I have to put up with?"

Feeling wiped out and blurry, Marco headed back to his room. Locking his door and putting a heavy chair in front of it as an extra security measure, he sat on his bed with the booklet on his lap, his mind churned with anxiety. Now cursing Marie; *Why didn't she just warn me directly? She could have said something so I would read the stupid book?* He kept thinking in circles, but always returning to *it's my own damn fault.* He was consumed with self-pity and afraid for his life. Now, his family was in danger. *I guess I have to read the damn thing*, he said to himself. He lay back on his bed, staring into the horizon, Marco opened the thin booklet, about 30 pages long. It was time to learn the full story, and this is what he read:

The Fountain of Scams: Greed, Folly, Murder and the History of Hidden Paradise subdivision, 1991.

Unpublished manuscript by Caspar Melton,
former resident of Hidden Paradise 1988 to 1992.

PREFACE

Call me Caspar Melton, which is a ridiculous name if there ever was one. It is so bad that if my parents had given me a name that stupid, why, at age 10, I might have slit their throats in the night in revenge, and then slit mine afterwards, all just to get away from the name. But fortunately, Caspar Melton is not my real name, which I am not disclosing to you or anyone else. I'm 77 years old and these days I don't care about names, so it's as good a name as the next one, far as I'm concerned. It's 1991 and I'm hiding in witness protection here in Hidden Paradise among the scum de la scum of criminals, in the middle of a swamp, bored out of my gourd. But, enough about me. A couple of months ago, I gave myself a choice: either chronicle the completely unknown but colorful history of Hidden Paradise, or drink myself quickly to death.

So, here is the story of how Florida's Hidden Paradise Subdivision came to be. When you finish reading this, you will know one of Florida's dirty little secrets. It all started way back in the raging Florida land speculation bubble of the 1920's. In 1923, Hidden Paradise was purchased by a speculator during the hysteria of the 1920s, who rode the Florida boom all the way to the land bubble bust in 1927. After this, nothing happened for decades. The property remained the swamp land it was always best suited for, until the second big boom to bust development cycle began again four decades later.

This is a story of how the unexpected twists and turns in life can lead one down a perilous road that won't be seen until it's too late. It's also the story of four ambitious and ingenious men, who thought they were smarter than they really were. They crossed paths in what would be a fateful coincidence that would allow them to be seduced by the thrill of success and the heady aroma of power. The riches they earned were theirs, but so were the problems that came with their great wealth. Most of all, it's a story of how Hidden Paradise would eventually become what I call, 'Club Rat,' the home and refuge of a population of criminals, who no longer have a place in the outside world, thanks to their need for witness protection.

The Hidden Paradise Subdivision has one of the most

infamous histories in Florida, especially since most of the history was kept unknown by design and won't appear in the public records. When all is said and done it's an all-American tale of capitalism run amok. It's the story of how unchecked avarice overwhelmed the better judgment of those involved. It's a good tale, I promise. My source of the tale told me all of it while I was hiding in the confines of Hidden Paradise. He had stewed over this story for a full three decades before the two of us spoke. He was a bit obsessed to be certain, but lucid enough to tell the tale.

The first time that Hidden Paradise even appeared in the Hernando County records, it was listed as a bare parcel of useless swampland. Looking at the place, as I've heard, you would have wondered why anyone would have advertised such a godforsaken mud pit like this, as there wasn't a square inch of it that was suitable for human habitation.

One was liable to sink up to their knees if they took a step in the wrong direction, but it was perfect for something. Apart from getting rid of a body (who knows how many bones have sunk into this mire), it was also useful as a hidey hole during the prohibition era, when smugglers would use just about any plot of land they could to hide away from the law.

It wasn't a spot where people would congregate in great numbers. It was simply a place where a criminal could come and hide if they wanted, provided they didn't get eaten alive by bugs or alligators.

After prohibition was done and over with, and illegal liquor was worth as much as the legal stuff one could find on the shelf, it took another 40 years for this plot of land to become a financial success. Don't ask me why, but some drippy-eyed bugger (my source for this story) had the idea to turn this fetid area into a residential subdivision in the 1950's.

He started the ball rolling, then immediately sold the whole thing to a greedy corporation in the 1950's, that later ended up filing for bankruptcy in the 1980s after Hurricane Elena wiped out the houses. Turns out this land was good for building on apparently, but the effort and the kind of scratch it took to turn this place into a livable community broke the corporation that took on that humongous responsibility. But, don't feel sorry for them. They sucked every dollar out of this place for their investors for 30 years. Oh, and they left a nice place for those of us in witness protection that came later, but I get the feeling it wasn't something my source would be happy to hear since the US government bought it for pennies on the dollar and a song to boot.

You see, this story is one of those that has all the bells and whistles that any historian might raise an eyebrow at since it sounds too outlandish to be true. But, those book-thumping professors that like to cluck their tongues and look down their noses at those of us who know that history isn't always what's written on paper and bound in leather, would likely soil themselves if they knew the truth of this place. From the days of excess, hysteria, fraud, environmental degradation, and financial chicanery between the 20s and 60s to the day the US government stepped in and made this place a landing spot for the worst squealers in history, Hidden Paradise has the type of history you normally hear about in the movies, but don't ever believe is real.

Don't get me wrong, I'm not here to point or wag my finger at anything or anyone for the legal or illegal nature of what they did—far from it. There's a special place in my heart for scoundrels, always has been, since I'm being honest (don't laugh). I was once a scoundrel and a whole lot worse. But, the scoundrel life is over now, or at least it's no longer as obvious. My time in the game involved stuff like fixing the odds in horse races, running numbers, long-con fraud, and fencing stolen merchandise. I wasn't exactly the 'blood on my hands,' mad-dog killer type, but I'd been known to keep a bit of protection on myself now and then. Since witness protection took care of that for me, living in Hidden Paradise surrounded by my fellow lowlifes and criminals has given me the way-point that will serve as my home until that last ride to the neverlands.

If you're not getting the gist yet, my last ride will be in a cardboard box, and the final stop will be a landfill where my ashes will sit for who knows how long. But hey, I'm still above ground and breathing for now, rather than residing at the bottom of a swamp wearing a pair of cement shoes or being listed as a John Doe on some coroner's slab, so I'm not bitter.

To tell the honest to goodness Christ truth, I've had a great run in life and I ran better than quite a few. I don't have regrets. No matter that everyone says we have 'em because we're human. To hell with that, but I have a fantasy that I like to live with, even though it'll never come true. If I had my own honest to goodness time machine, I would've liked to take myself back to being born in 1899 so that I could've gotten in on the Florida of the 1920's. If I had been born in my fantasy year by the 1920s I would have been a young man, unfettered and ready to take on the world in every possible venture I could find.

Of course, my fantasy would require that I turn out as I did now, with the knowledge of how to thrive in every legal or illegal endeavor common in that era. Think about it, a guy with my brains and knowledge of what was coming, back then. I would have been a king, and Hidden Paradise might have been my own little personal kingdom.

I might have been a real estate developer, and a corrupt politician that would triple-dip every finger into whatever business I could, and obviously, I would have been a humble and revered pillar of my community. I could have been a rum runner, a real man of society, and even more, I could have taken the Hidden Paradise Estates and, with Cole Bertram Sr. as the face of it, I could have erased the mistakes he ended up making.

Now, that was a guy that blew his chance on the best thing he had going for him, and this story is to show the how and why of it. Sometimes, I'd like to think that I would gladly rub Bertram's failures in his face if I could, if he were still around. But then I think about it a little more and realize that Bertram Sr. was just a sheltered, pampered bank manager who came from a good family and wouldn't know an ounce of real hardship if it came up and socked him in the nose.

Well, one could say he got a good dose of real hardship at one point, and I'll lay ten to one odds that it smarted for the rest of his days.

This is the type of guy that came to Florida in 1923 on vacation and was openly skeptical of any possible financial success that might have been suggested at the time. Granted, back then there wasn't much to look at in this part of Florida, and there still isn't in the swamp outside of this community. But one thing Cole was good at doing was watching other people that were far less capable than he was. And wouldn't you know it, he saw those types of people hitting it rich in Florida and seeing this he caught a big case of the get rich fever not long after arriving. The poor sucker never had a chance to even second-guess himself since he went all-in and was swept up in the euphoric trance that came from his own success and the power that it came with. Sad to say, young master Bertram Sr. was way out of his league, and he was definitely a poor judge of character despite his powers of observation.

The first business partner he chose was undoubtedly why the wheels started to come off, since Bertram brought on an attention-seeking con man and blackmailer, someone that, strangely enough, went on to become not just a Hollywood screenwriter, but also a drinking buddy and good friend of the one and only W.C. Fields. Go figure, a person that writes and speaks fiction wouldn't be trustworthy, hm?

Well, when that partnership ended in financial failure, big surprise, Cole at least managed to recoup his losses and ended up making a fortune with his second partner, the patriarch of a local gang of Florida crackers. Unfortunately, for this second partner, he would eventually end up getting himself, his wife, and his three sons a lethal dose of lead poisoning that was doled out by the local sheriff, no doubt on contract to the mob.

My source for this sordid, but entertaining tale was Cole Bertram Jr., the original owner's son. Cole Jr had been thinking about Hidden Paradise for decades before our discussion, but he'd never talked much about it until my ears were wide open to hear everything he had to say. This place is a big part of Cole Jr's life story, before he even knew it existed. That sounds funny, right? How in the world can someone be involved with something they've never known about, yeah? But, once he did find out the truth of what happened during his infancy, he started to think about it more and more, until he became a bit obsessed for a while. Once the fever of the history of Hidden Paradise broke in his cortex, he became convinced, just as his old man had at one point, that the Florida-born tale of unchecked exploitation and fortune-hunting was no longer for him.

You see, after a while he wanted nothing to do with the dark, shameful, tattered web that started out in a distant past. But, he was willing to talk about it—hoo boy was he ever. So, I'll go ahead and tell you the story just as he relayed it to me, with plenty of color here and there to make it pop. Kind of like his old man, Cole Jr started out by telling me all about the original Florida tale of greedy men, going way back to the 1500's, who lit the spark of exploitation that has never gone out of style since, and makes Florida so attractive to certain types of people, like myself.

To read the remainder of:
The Fountain of Scams: Greed, Folly, Murder and the History of Hidden Paradise subdivision, 1991
by Caspar Melton.

See the CODA at the end of this book.

Chapter 16

Listening patiently to Marco's debriefing of his fear and regret over and over, Rei tried to lift his spirits. "You should really stop beating yourself up, you know."

"I know, but really, I did pull a Haney at the pool. How stupid could I be, they're right."

It had been two days since his encounter with Downy, and Marco hadn't left his apartment or the roof. Marco was still unloading about his Downy DiCarlo encounter, now for the third or fourth time, until Rei made an excuse to leave, partly because Marco was being tedious repeating himself, and also to buy groceries so Marco wouldn't starve.

After reading the pamphlet, Marco understood the significance of the individual characters mentioned in the history.

'Haney,' one of the historical figures whose story is told in the pamphlet, poked a stick in the eye of Al Capone and paid for it with his life and his family's life. *Now I understand why I'm a Haney. When I announced to everyone around the pool that I was never going to read the booklet, I walked right into their primal fear. These people are terrified for their lives. They're living with the real possibility that one stupid idiot running his mouth could bring their mortal enemies here. To them, I was that idiot, that Haney, boasting my ignorance. Of course I triggered their worst response."*

"Don't beat yourself up," said Rei for the third or fourth or fifth time. "It's done. You survived."

"But for how long?"

Marco's cell phone beeped. It was a text from Shepp: 'Light fixture installation for Maury and Beatrice Caldo, apt 224, this a.m. Confirm time."

Marco showed the text to Rei.

"Tell him yes, I'll go down to my place and get the tools," Rei responded, already walking towards the door. "You bring the step ladder."

Marco texted Shepp, got dressed in work boots, jeans and a blue long sleeve work shirt, and at 9:55 am went downstairs carrying the ladder.

Waiting for Rei at the elevator on the second floor, he heard Rei clomping up the stairs, breathing heavily, carrying a toolbox and wearing a tool belt. Once more, Marco was bitter that Rei was forbidden by the residents to use the elevator.

Marco knocked on apartment 224, which was answered by a heavyset, middle aged man with a fleshy, tanned face, thick salt and pepper hair, and bushy eyebrows.

"Hi. I'm Marco."

"Yes. Yes. Maury Caldo. This here's my wife Beatrice. I know who you are," shaking Marco's hand.

Maury looked past Marco at Rei. "Hey, Quasimodo! My man!" He held up his hand for a high five. "How you doing, Monster?"

Marco was suddenly furious.

"What did you say?"

Maury didn't reply. Rei didn't move.

Marco turned to Rei, and nodded down the hall to the elevators.

"Let's go, Rei." He turned and left. Rei followed.

"Wait! Wait!"

They kept walking.

"I'm sorry. Come on, fellows. I apologize, come on, I meant nothing by it."

Marco turned to Rei. They stopped. Rei nodded slightly. They turned back.

When they got back to Maury, Beatrice had joined her husband. She was holding a small, panting, squirming schipperke dog. She shook her head and directed a look of dismay towards her husband.

"I'm sorry, Reimundo, really," said Maury. "I was never the one that started calling you those names. That was your boss, right? It was him, remember? He encouraged it. Old habits die hard, eh? It won't happen again with me. Scout's honor." Beatrice shook hands with both of them, and led the way into the kitchen.

There was no light in the kitchen except through the window.

Maury pointed at a long box on the counter. "The old fluorescents gave up the ghost. I bought these new LED lights. Can you install them?"

"Sure," said Rei. "Take us about 45 minutes."

Marco did a quick calculation in his head.

"That will be $100, flat rate, half paid now, the rest when we finish." Marco took an invoice pad from his pocket and began filling it out.

"What?" Exclaimed Maury, now feigning outrage, his bushy eyebrows shooting up towards his hairline. "No licensed contractor would ever want to get paid up front. Who do you think you are?"

Marco tore the invoice sheet off the pad and placed it on top of the box. "You're right. We're just handymen. Go ahead and hire a licensed electrician. That's a better idea for you folks. Let's go, Rei."

At this, Beatrice exploded.

"Oh for Christ's sake, Maury, just cut the crap, stop playing games and pay them! I'm tired of opening the fridge just to get enough light to make a cup of coffee or boil an egg. Just pay them!"

Maury stood still for a long moment, weighing the costs and benefits of defending his pride, versus a certain fight with his angry wife. He pulled a roll of cash out of his pocket and handed Marco a $50 bill.

They removed the old fixture and put up the new one within a half hour. There were no problems and the new LED fixture was like having the sun in the kitchen. Beatrice walked to every corner of the kitchen, enjoying the bright new light.

"This light is wonderful guys. I've been trying to get Maury to fix this for years. I can't believe we've been living in this dark cave of a kitchen for so long."

The dog went up to Marco. It stood on its hind legs and begged Marco for petting. Marco bent down and the dog leaped up into his arms, giving Marco a big wet doggie kiss.

"Uma likes you," said Beatrice, smiling broadly.

"Oh come on, Uma likes everyone," said Maury.

Marco put the dog down and Uma immediately moved her attention to Rei who bent down and scratched the dog near its curly tail. The dog's body curled and its happy face twisted into a lopsided look of pleasure.

Maury handed over another $50, and Marco handed him the paid in full invoice in exchange.

"How about if I hire you guys to paint the kitchen for us?" asked Maury.

Marco shook his head, remembering Shepp's warning.

"Sorry, small handyman jobs only. No remodeling. No painting."

Maury shrugged. "Well, how about you coming to this friendly poker game we have a couple of times a month? Just a little game, just for fun."

Marco looked quickly at Rei whose eyes suddenly carried a slight worried look. Marco's memory flashed to Downy DiCarlo's nickel plated 45 pointed at him and he felt a jolt of his paralyzing fear again.

"Uh, no," Marco replied confidently, "I never got into poker. It's not my game." This was a complete lie. Marco had enjoyed thousands of hands of low stakes poker in country club caddy shacks and college dormitories since he was twelve.

"Suit yourself."

They packed the tools and left. When they were out of earshot, Rei whispered: "Very bad man. Very, very bad. He was a Kansas City loan shark. I'm so glad you didn't agree to play."

Chapter 17

As the dawn's light came through the window, Marco woke up. He lay still and felt the breeze off the water. It was like silk against his skin. It might rain today, he thought. Before he considered any tasks of the day, he allowed a feeling of gratitude to fill him. The New York City streets were far away, the car noises were gone. He heard only the wind as it carried the coolness of the ocean onto the shore.

Marco strode to the window and looked out at the overcast day. It was likely the sun would come out and the day would become unbearably bright and searing with heat. But, on this part of the coast, the heat would never stay strong for long. In that moment Marco was soothed by the wind off the water and embraced Hidden Paradise as a paradise even with its undercurrent of woe and shadiness.

Staring at the water's edge miles away from his window, Marco could barely see the boat camp people toiling. Remembering his ugly encounter on the boat, his earlier gratitude faded and he suddenly felt faint, and headed back to his bed. *I'm trapped, and the truth is I can never leave.*

He thought about all he would miss. He would never see his cousin Anthony again, the cousin he used to get into trouble with most of his life. He knew he had to shed his hopes and leave them behind. His dream of becoming a wealthy businessman had already been tainted by his experiences in real estate with his father. He knew he didn't want any part of that. But, what about all the possibilities of work and the pursuit of any curiosity and fervent wishes that might come up? *I'm too young to be in prison for life. I can't break out of this haven of the lower world.*

The silence and the sound of gulls washed over him. His fervent thoughts seemed to endlessly come and go. Disappointments and frustrations, eagerness and restrictions, all his thwarted efforts and ambitions came and went as he surrendered to the sound of the wind, and the mocking of the gulls. *I'm no longer that guy*, he thought, frozen in the moment.

Over the past few days Marco had examined many ways to escape, and failed to find one that could work. The only aspect of life that lent comfort was his work and camaraderie with Rei which held his attention away from the taint of his absolute imprisonment here.

He decided to go see Aunt Marie. After a quick shower, Marco sauntered across the mall to visit her. It'd been over a week since he'd seen her. *I'll pick up my salary, have a cup of coffee, visit and see what she's heard*, thought Marco. The walk to Marie's was always an adventure. Gulls were devouring old bread in the mall. The light fog held low to the ground. Marco could see his aunt moving around making rolls. Maybe he could get a hot one, straight from the oven.

As he approached he could see another figure, very close to her as she worked. *Who's that*, Marco murmured to himself? *He's standing very close to Marie. What's going on here*? Marco stepped through the open floor and wiped his feet on the damp mat.

He saw his aunt in the low light working on the rolls, forming them and setting them in even equal balls on a pan to rise. Behind her stood a wizened man in an apron over a fancy apricot colored jumpsuit. His face and mouth were too close to aunt Marie's neck to be unintentional.

The man was shorter than Marie by an inch or two which made him no more than five feet tall. His curly grey hair was badly cut. He had a long nose and thin pursed lips. His eyes were in a perpetual glazed squint. His smile was a grimace of sorts. His mouth turned neither up nor down, it went straight across as if he was acting like he was smiling, but was angry underneath.

He seemed to be sniffing Marie in the area where her neck and shoulder met. While he was doing so, he whispered something indistinguishable to her. Marco thought he saw the man's pink tongue tip emerge and retract. Marie was smiling as Marco approached.

"Ah Marco, so early. I didn't think you'd be here so early. I have rolls. Please sit down. Have some coffee." She continued rolling the dough as she spoke.

The wiry man behind her looked up and smiled at Marco. He moved away from Marie slightly.

"Romeo," he reached out his hand introducing himself.

"Let me get you some coffee. And the rolls are just out of the oven. How about a hot roll with butter, huh?"

Before Marco could respond, Romeo had set a roll on a plate with a knife and a ramekin of butter.

"Please sit down. How do you take your coffee?"

"That's okay, I'll fix it. So, you two know each other for a while now?" Marco asked.

"Yeah, a long time, but last week I came by to get some treats and there she was, the biggest treat of my life." Romeo went back behind aunt Marie and put his hand squarely on her shoulders and smiled. Marie looked up at Marco and smiled.

"Romeo works with me now. He makes very good pizza. He's from Queens. He won't tell me anything about his past. Isn't that right Romeo?"

"Things change. It's time to move away from the past. I got into a jam, with only one way out to stay alive. And like everyone else here, we're in the middle of nowhere. And guess what? I found the love of my life."

"Well that's great to hear. I'd like to hear more about it some time." Marco sat at the window and stirred his coffee. The smell of the hot roll wafted up from the plate. *Who is this creep?* Marco thought depressingly, trying to convince himself to accept his own circumstances. He glanced out the window letting his eyes pass over the remodeled shop. He admired his work, it was a perfect place to sit in the early hours. He watched Romeo return to his position behind Marie and saw the smile on her face. He was glad she'd found someone who cared about her, even if he looked like a low life weirdo.

I'll probably never have a girlfriend again. I may never even have another date. This place is unreal. What kind of karma is this? Marco felt sad, and disconnected from everything he'd ever known and loved.

Marie continued to roll the dough balls and put tray after tray into the proofing oven. Romeo stood behind her, gently massaging her shoulders as she worked. At one point he stopped, snapped open a four inch stiletto and cleaned his nails. Marco turned away briefly to watch the fog lifting outside. He took another sip and turned back. The stiletto was gone.

Romeo reached his left hand into his shirt and pulled out a heart shaped locket that hung around his neck. As he held Marie's shoulder with his right hand, he flipped open the locket and stared at a picture inside. Marie continued to smile mutely and make rolls. Romeo sighed, returned the locket to his chest, grabbed a napkin and dried tears he had shed. He walked farther back into the bakery, seemingly to settle his emotions. His walk was a short shuffle punctuated by his fancy pointed shoes... shoes no one would ever wear in a bakery as they'd be destroyed. Marco shook his head in disbelief.

I guess Marie is willing to settle for anything, he thought. With Romeo out of earshot for a moment, he saw his opportunity.

"So auntie, you like this guy?" Marco spoke quietly.

"Yeah, sure. And he can make pizza better than most places in New York. He makes me happy, Marco. What can I say? And he's not bad looking." She came out from behind the counter with a plate of assorted day-old pastries.

"Please. Have some of these. They're gonna get hard if you don't eat 'em. Take some to your friend Rei."

"Thank you." Marco smiled at Marie.

"C'mon, Marco. We're having fun. What am I gonna do out here anyhow, he's my boyfriend. Huh?"

"I know aunt Marie, it's just that he seems a little strange. What's with the locket? He was looking at it and crying."

"Oh the locket. Yeah. He's a little unusual about the locket, but he really likes me, you know? Marco, he shows his love for me in so many ways. He's very expressive and so romantic. You know he plays the guitar and sings to me at night over a glass of wine. It makes my heart blush." She looked up in a reverie when she spoke of his charm.

Marco thought it might be best to leave before Romeo returned.

"Inside the locket is his twin sister, Juliet. You know, like from the play. He told me the whole story. It's not pretty. His family was strange, they encouraged this behavior between them. His sister, he really loved her, then she died."

"I don't get it. You mean he loved her like that? Not like a sister? He was looking at the picture when he was near you, touching your shoulder."

"Yeah, he does that all the time. At first, I felt cheated. Like he loves someone else and I was just, you know, filling in. But, he's here for me. He helps me. He doesn't ask for money. And who am I gonna get to stay with me, an old lady. So what if he's got some problems, it's not hurting me any. So what?" She gestured with her hands as she tried to explain away Romeo's troubling dysfunction.

"So, she told you about my Juliet." Romeo emerged from the semi-darkness wiping his hands. "You don't always get what you want in life. You know? You try, but it don't happen sometimes, eh?"

Romeo tilted his head and his mouth was turned down. A sadness overcame him. He told the story of his abnormal parents. They thought they could keep him at home working at the family business if he had the love of his life Juliette always beside him at home. They wanted him to never leave. And he didn't, until Juliet met her unfortunate demise in a mysterious, somewhat suspicious subway accident.

Romeo didn't describe the incident, but as he referred to it, his eyes filled with tears. He pulled out the locket to show Marco.

"I was devoted to her. She was my very own." He sobbed.

Marco looked at the old sepia photo, hand colored, rouged cheeks, a pretty smile on the young girl's face.

Romeo sobbed and reached out to Marco. His arms went around his waist and he drew him close like a lover would. His pointed marionette chin pressed into Marco's shoulder and Romeo's runny nose dripped onto the collar of Marco's shirt. Marco felt compassionate at first, but his initial feeling faded as the enormity of Romeo's incestuous past emerged. This was a man co-habitating with his own aunt, who ratted out a crime figure and was sent to Hidden Paradise. He was a man with perverse propensities, now being intimate with his aunt. He was a man who was now embracing him in a strange and unseemly way. Romeo was a man brought up in a sleazy anomalous lifestyle. Marco knew there was no way this slime could be trusted.

Marco's repulsion hit him like eight shots of tequila on an empty stomach. It felt like his soul was dry heaving, vomiting up corruption. He was in the arms of a disturbed man who was using him for his own comfort.

"Oh darn, what time is it? I gotta go." Marco disconnected from the awkward embrace and walked to the door.

"Wait, here, take this," Marie approached and handed him an envelope of money, "we'll talk later in the week. Have a lovely day Marco," she smiled.

Marco turned to see Romeo sitting in the chair he had just left, eating what was left of his buttered roll quickly, like a mouse scurrying for crumbs.

Chapter 18

When Marco got back to his apartment he checked the time to discover the battery in his Citizen Satellite Wave GPS watch had died. His titanium yachting watch was his most prized possession. It was a gift from his father presented to him at age 13. As a junior crew member in a sailboat race, Marco sailed in a 1,200 mile Newport to Bahamas race. The race was a fiasco and an ordeal from start to finish. Even though the sailboat finished dead last, it was lucky they made it home at all. Finishing this race was a singular major achievement for Marco.

The near disaster began with four fabulously wealthy male crew members, totally unprepared for a grueling race, trading bluster and sea stories over single malt scotch in the yacht club bar. It would have been a better choice for them to stay home drinking than sailing as wanna be sailors. However, bluster and bravado won out, and to the unforgiving ocean they risked their lives, and the lives of Marco, and Todd Freitag, the 14 year old son of the owner of the sailboat.

The 'Fiona' was a 25 year old, 46 foot Beneteau sailboat. A sleek beauty designed for racing around the world. It had been purchased, fully equipped, a month before the race by a hedge fund manager named Egon Freitag. Before that, the Fiona had sat growing barnacles and seaweed in Newport harbor for five years. After buying it, Egon never checked the condition of the old sails, ropes, sheets, cables, engine, batteries, radios or emergency equipment. He did purchase new life preservers for everyone and he installed an ice maker in the galley so the crew would not have to drink warm whiskey.

Fifteen sailboats started the race to the Bahamas. For the first two days of the seven day race, The Fiona maintained a respectable pace among the racers. Marco and Todd learned how to handle all aspects of sailing and the crew got along like good old shipmates, even drinking scotch and telling stories. Not a care on the sea.

On day three, things started getting weird. The ice maker drew too much power from the old batteries causing them to die while creating a cascade of failures of everything powered by batteries, including radios and the lights. When they tried to recharge the batteries with the generator, a power surge fried the circuits and wiring on the ice machine, and nobody had the slightest idea how to fix it.

Egon called a meeting of the crew. Fred, the eldest, having been seasick continually, was ready to turn back. He'd had enough sailing to last a lifetime. Alan, the know it all, wanted to take down the sails and run the diesel motor for 6 hours to recharge the batteries giving Fred a break from racing. Egon and his co-worker Vin were naturally aggressive in all aspects of life and sports. They were *in it to win it*. Collectively they voted to continue without electrical power. The boys were not included in the vote.

On the fourth day, 400 miles from Nassau, with winds at 25 knots, the 20 year old mainsail ripped apart during the night and the replacement sail soon also ripped apart. As the other racers surged past them, The Fiona was reduced to sailing with just the jib and a jury-rigged spinnaker. On day 11, the Fiona limped into Nassau harbor. Nobody greeted them. The race had ended days ago.

"No point in sailing further mates if winning is no longer part of the game, we're out. Booking our way back home from here." With that comment Fred and Vin were on the next flight leaving Nassau, leaving the boys, the captain and one adult crew member to carry on.

A second crew meeting was called, and this time Todd and Marco were included in voting. Marco could have flown home, but instead he voted with the three others to continue their adventure. They made plans to sail back to Newport. Egon had learned his lesson. He bought new sails, new batteries and updated the electronic equipment. He rented some scuba gear and Todd and

Marco dove under the boat to scrape the barnacles and seaweed off the hull.

Four days of frantic activity later, this renewed, tight-knit, sea-tested, four man crew sailed out of Nassau, heading back home to Newport. The seas were rough and the weather was foul, but they made no big mistakes. Santo was waiting on the dock when the Fiona sailed into Newport. He watched 13 year old tanned and muscular Marco standing tall, working as an equal next to his shipmates. On the dock, Santo hugged his son and presented him with the Citizen Satellite Wave GPS watch. Marco had never felt so proud.

Now, 10 years later, looking at his prized watch, Marco decided it was time for the battery to be replaced. Marco's first thought was to call around to professional jewelers on route 19 to get a new one.

This is the one thing my father gave to me that I treasure. I miss him. I'll wear it to keep him with me. With that thought, Shepp's suggestion immediately popped in his mind: *Become acquainted with all the residents of Hidden Paradise, get to know them, do business with them, get them to like you.* The words echoed in his mind.

Slotzky Jewelers was three stores away from Marie's bakery. Marco called from his apartment.

"Slotzky's Jewelry. Irving speaking."

"Hi Irving, this is Marco Cavallo."

"Uh huh."

"Can you put a battery in a watch?"

"Sure. Bring it over."

"See you in five minutes."

The front door of the tiny Slotzky's Jewelry store was thick, heavy, and bulletproof. Marco pushed through, triggering a buzzer. Behind the counter sat a morose man in his early fifties with sad eyes, thin lips, and tortoise shell glasses. His dark, sparse hair was plastered-down in a sad attempt at a comb-over. It was arranged so it looked like a full head of hair, but only when you looked at his face straight on. He was a former mob money launderer turned snitch, turned jeweler while in witness protection.

"Hi. I'm Marco. I just called."

"Nice to meet you." Slotzky rose to shake his hand. After shaking, Marco noticed that Slotzky backed straight up, purposely keeping his face pointed directly towards Marco for the *full head of hair look*.

"Let's see the watch," said Slotzky.

Marco took off his watch and laid it on the black velvet cushion. Slotzky picked it up.

"Hmmm. A Citizen Satellite Wave GPS. You don't see many of these. Lots of fakes. Is it real?" Slotzky picked up a loupe. He bent over the watch, keeping his face square on to Marco, examining thoroughly. He put the loupe down.

"This is a beautiful watch, a real treat to see one."

"Can you put in a new battery?"

"Sure. Leave it overnight. Call me tomorrow late morning."

Marco again remembered Shepp's advice. He decided to make some conversation. He pointed at the jewelry case.

"Nice diamonds. Do you sell everything from this store?"

"No, not at all. 95% of my business is over the internet. I love Ebay. I simply love it. Here, let me show you something."

Slotzky used a key to open a drawer. He took out a small box and opened it. Inside was a medium sized sparkling gem. Carefully, Slotzky took the gem out and put it into the palm of his hand. He held it out for Marco to examine.

"Now this is a diamond!"

Marco knew nothing of diamonds. It just looked like a diamond.

Slotzky smiled for the first time. His smile was forced into being, by raising his upper lip and exposing too much front upper teeth. It was like a horse about to eat an apple.

"This diamond, my friend, is special. Why don't you hold it?" He put the diamond into Marco's hand.

Slotzky leaned towards Marco. He whispered, "This

diamond, if I put it in my pocket, I get a hard on." He nodded his head up and down in a suggestive way, and the smile turned into a leer.

"Go ahead," said Slotzky.

"What?"

"Go ahead."

"What do you mean?"

Slotzky leaned closer. His eyes went from Marco's head to his crotch.

"Go ahead, put it in your pocket. Am I right?"

Marco quickly dropped the diamond, now unbearably unclean, back on the black velvet cushion near his watch. The leer stayed on Slotzky's face. Marco needed to change the subject. Anything to get rid of the leer. He pointed at a display of rings in the glass case.

"This is a beautiful ring," pointing at the most ornate diamond ring.

Slotzky looked down. He took out the display of rings, picked up the large diamond ring and held it up for Marco to examine.

"Ahhh... yes. This ring....this ring. This ring is the exact duplicate of the ring I gave my ex-wife. I made two of them at the same time. Oh, she loved that ring." Slotzky looked up and away dreamily. "Oh, she was so proud of that ring... she looked so good in that ring... so good in that ring…"

His dreamy look disappeared, replaced by an outburst of anger. "She looked so good in that ring while she was ripping my god damned nuts off with her three-inch sharpened, pink nails!"

Marco took a step back. Slotzky was glaring. He took the diamond ring and shook it under Marco's nose.

"They say diamonds are forever? Bullshit. I'll tell you what's forever, my ex-wife's goddamned alimony. That's forever. Every single month, $1,500 a month, year after year. She's collecting my money, smiling, and that sound you are hearing Mark, Marco I mean, is her Rrrrrrripping my balls off."

Slotzky was getting quite worked up. His voice rose to an

even louder pitch. "12 years of marriage and I make one single mistake, just one, and she takes me to the cleaners. And you know what's worse? She won't even marry the lazy schmuck she's been boning all these years, even though he lives with her, in my goddamn house! They even have a dog together–no, I take that back–this is their second goddamned dog. The first dog died of old age and they got some mutt as a puppy."

Slotzky gathered his small hands into two impotent fists of rage in front of his chest.

"Her fangs will drain every last god damned dollar I have until I'm just a dried husk! How do you feel about that, kid?"

He was spitting mad. He glared at Marco with pure hatred over the top of his glasses, as if it were Marco who had been boning Slotzky's vengeful wife all these years.

Marco realized that this attempt at making a Hidden Paradise connection was a hellish exercise in dysfunction. Retreat was now his only defense.

"So. Will my watch be ready tomorrow?"

Still glaring, Slotzky said, "Yeah. Call me at 11am."

Chapter 19

The next morning, at 11am sharp, Marco called Slotzky's Jewelry. Slotzky picked up on the first ring.

"Hi, this is Marco. Are you open?"

"Sure. Come on by."

Marco arrived at the jewelry store within five minutes, it was dark and locked, he peered through the window. The display cases were empty and the lights were off. He called the store and the phone rang through to voicemail. He left a message and waited 10 minutes before going back upstairs.

He came down an hour later, then two hours later, and one last time at 4pm. The store was closed. There was no answer on the phone.

Marco decided that some sort of emergency must have arisen.

The next day at 11am, he called again. Slotzky answered.

"Hi. This is Marco. I was there yesterday to pick up my watch. Where were you?"

"Oh. I am so sorry. Something came up suddenly. I had to leave."

"Can I come down now?"

"Absolutely."

Two minutes later Marco was at the jewelry store. Again, it was dark and locked. He tried 3 more times during the day–same story.

Two days in a row of the same game was inexcusable. Marco was irate. All he could think of now was getting his precious watch back. Marco spent the afternoon repeatedly obsessing over the disrespect Slotzky was showing him.

The next morning at 11am, he didn't call, he just showed up, and walked in the open store. Slotzky saw him through the glass door. For a second it looked like he might race Marco to the door and lock it, but Marco was too fast. As soon as Marco entered the store, Slotzky started going through boxes, opening drawers, and making a big show of looking for something lost.

"Where's my watch?"

Slotzky tried to look as harried and innocent as possible.

"I should ask you the same thing!"

"What?"

"Your watch. Somebody stole it!"

"They stole my watch? What about the jewels and rings? Did they steal those?"

"No. Just your watch."

"Who would do such a thing?" asked Marco, incredulously.

"I think you did it. You stole your watch, to pin the theft on me."

"Why on earth would I steal my own watch? That doesn't make any sense."

"How should I know why? You're the one who stole it. You tell me."

"I didn't steal it."

"That's your opinion. I have mine. Get out of here!" Slotzky shouted and pointed to the door.

After giving Slotzky a murderous look, Marco left, but was ready to tear the store apart. Fortunately, he realized he needed to cool down. Back to his room he went to recalculate his next action. Pacing back and forth in his kitchen he replayed his entire interaction with Slotzky over the past three days.

Then he had a brainstorm. He took his cell phone out and went to Ebay to search: 'Citizen Satellite Wave GPS watch.'

There was his watch. He was certain of it. The scratch on the face was visible, and the address of the seller was Bonny Shores, Florida, just five miles away. There was one day left on the auction, and the price was already up to $950.

"That son of a bitch,' Marco yelled, as he ran down the stairs, and burst into Slotzky's jewelry. Slotzky gave him a snarling look from behind the counter. Marco walked up and showed Slotzky the Ebay site.

"That's my watch, you crook!" Marco was breathing heavily.

His teeth were bared. Nobody was stealing his watch today, or ever.

Like a cornered rat, Slotzky puffed himself up with his own anger, and went on the offensive. "Get out of here!" He pointed at Marco. "Get out of my store!"

"Give me my watch!"

"You little punk. You should know that I'm good friends with Downy DiCarlo. That's right. I'm also special friends with Maury Caldo, Nicolo Barare and Fonseca the chainsaw hit man. Now get out of my store!"

Marco was seeing red. He wouldn't back down. He went all in. He played his last card.

"Listen to me, you pathetic, greasy thief," Marco shouted back. "You give me my watch now or I'm gonna tell Shepp you're swindling the residents, and committing criminal behavior right under his nose. He'll kick your ass out of Hidden Paradise. You won't have a stipend or a place to live anymore. It'll just be you, out on the street, all alone, with your Ebay jewels, and your ugly comb-over. Your ex-wife and all the mobsters you ratted out, will come feast on you. You won't last a week. You'll be history, Slotzky."

Slotzky's chest was heaving with his own fury. They stared at each other with matching hatred not flinching an eyelash.

Finally, Slotzky's shoulders slumped forward, deflated, he sat down heavily on his chair, once more glum, beaten, and deflated.

Marco took a deep breath. His Shepp card had trumped Slotzky's DiCarlo card. Slotzky took out a set of keys, opened a drawer, took out Marco's watch and set it on the counter. Marco picked it up.

"We could have made some real money with that watch. I would have shared profits with you if you'd asked nicely," Slotzky smirked.

Marco paid no attention. He examined the watch.

"After all that, you didn't replace the battery."

"Leave it overnight. I'll have it ready by noon tomorrow."

Marco shook his head. "Unfrigginbelievable," he muttered.

He stuffed the watch in his pocket, and headed for the door.

Later that night, down and disheartened, thinking about his watch, Marco was bewildered as he cleaned the pool and thought about how much he missed his dad.

Skimming the pool was usually very calming and meditative, but not tonight. *This place is so sick and corrupt. Everyone's trying to take advantage of the weak.* Marco was frustrated. His peripheral vision caught sight of something unusual and out of place. As he turned his alarm spiked, as he spotted two alligators about 10 feet away, creeping slowly and silently towards him.

Without thinking, he instinctively leaped backwards, slipped on the edge of the pool and fell into the shallow end. He panicked, remembering from nature shows how gators grab their prey in the water and roll over and over until the victim drowns.

Marco swam for his life. He felt like a cartoon character swimming crazy fast across the top of the water, getting to the deep end and heaving himself out with a sigh of relief.

I made it, he thought, with great relief. Now looking back, he saw they had stopped, right at the edge of the pool.

Marco and the gators stared at each other. Marco, dripping wet, held his hands in front of him as he backed away slowly.

"I get it," he said to the gators. "Everyone here is angry, everyone wants to get me, even nature. You win. Take the pool. It's all yours." He backed up and continued backing his way until he reached the stairs.

Chapter 20

The next evening, just before the sun went down, hyper-vigilant for gators, Marco stood beside the pool with the long net in his hand. He swept through the water languidly. A slight breeze blew causing ripples on the clear water. The bright pool radiated turquoise. Until last night, Marco usually daydreamed while he did his job, not today. He'd slept poorly last night after a day that included fighting for his watch with Slotzky and then escaping two predatory alligators.

Nevertheless, here he was again, performing the last task of the day, trying unsuccessfully to recreate his ritual moment of reflection. He considered how he would move forward with his life, what he'd like to do. Once again realizing, there was no way out.

After deftly sweeping out the minor debris, Marco set about the water testing and pump cleaning when he heard the approach of someone coming up behind him.

"Hey there Marco," the cheery voice rang out under the metal overhang at the edge of the pool. Marco turned to see a light stepping, well dressed, dapper man in his late 40's, ready to converse.

"Have we met?" Marco asked.

"Not yet, my friend, but this is our lucky day." He stuck out his hand. "D'angelo Brown."

Marco was wary. "Nice to meet you, D'angelo, how's it going?" They shook.

"The world is in a groove. The axis is tilted our way, my friend. We can make it what we want as long as we use our innate creative energy. We are always in the moment of transformation, because we are the creation, my friend, creation is our mission. Can you dig this Marco?"

Marco stared at this new arrival to his already bizarre life scene. *What's this guy smokin?* He thought. *What's he talking about, my innate creative energy, creation is our mission?*

"I'm just finishing up with the pool before the sun sets." Marco replied, squinting to get a better look at his new Hidden Paradise acquaintance.

"I have a proposal for you to consider, my friend. I have an incredible opportunity that I want to share with you. It'll only take a few minutes of your time to determine where you are on the spectrum of creation and the levels of energy running through you." D'angelo paused and waited while Marco finished his brief tasks.

"You want a beer, D'angelo?"

"Sure."

Marco sat down with his beer, and stretched out his legs.

"So, what's this new project?" Marco seemed open.

"I'm glad you asked, Marco. Here it is. It's an opportunity of a lifetime. It can change the lifestyle of millions of people all over the world. Let me explain." D'angelo cleared his throat and began.

"If someone told you that your health would rely mainly on chewing your food, how much attention would you pay to it?" Marco looked at D'angelo perplexed and intrigued. D'angelo continued with vigor.

"If I told you all the current advertising was geared toward undermining man's digestive processes by making every bite and swallow increasingly quicker and quicker. If I told you, eating at our current pace is what's actually killing us AND, it's truly not *what we eat* that's the problem, because, if we were able to chew long enough, well enough, every bit of food would digest perfectly. With this slow eating method no one would be able to overeat! It's just that simple!"

Marco looked confused, responded, "interesting information D'angelo, but I'm not seeing how someone chewing their food slowly can make me money. Tell me more, you have my attention."

"You see, chewing slowly is the answer to almost all of our ills as humans. If we eat those crappy burgers that cost less than a dollar, they can't be quality ingredients. If we eat refined flours that have been on the shelf for years, that can't be good for us either, right? But, imagine eating so slowly that you would never eat more than you need, you would never have indigestion, you would never have gut problems. Are you following me here?"

"Well yeah, kind of makes sense, sure, go on, still not seeing the dollars here." Marco asked thoughtfully. He had been following D'angelo's pleasant voice into the balmy beginnings of another beery Florida sundown.

"So, I have this product that synchronizes with the pulse. It naturally meters a rhythm as you chew. Automatically, within minutes the eater begins to follow the pulse. I used it for a couple of weeks and I lost about 7 pounds. It's amazing." D'angelo pulled out a small black box that looked like a cell phone plug.

"This is it, my friend. It doesn't look like much but let me show you. Give me your arm." Marco extended his left arm and rested it on the table. D'angelo attached the box to his arm above the wrist and turned it on.

"You feel that?"

"Yeah, it's pulsing. Feels pleasant,, Marco responded, now a little more engaged to humor the man. "Now what?"

"Well, if you were eating, you'd automatically synchronize your chewing with this rhythm. It's similar to a hypnotic suggestion. It takes over and you automatically eat more slowly. You don't think about it, you don't have to do anything. It's just that easy. Clip it over your arm at every meal and within moments, you're eating slower. No more rushing through meals. No dieting. You can eat questionable products and because of the pulsing, you will eat less, digest better, feel fuller faster, and more satisfied. It works like a charm." D'angelo stood up and showed the roominess of his belt line. He turned and showed Marco a 360 degree view.

"Last week I felt bloated. Now I feel full and satisfied and I've eaten less than half as much food. Think of the money you'll save. It's a miracle. I have old Mrs. Donatelli hooked up to this right now. So far she's lost 14 Lbs in about a month. That's unheard of, my friend. Imagine what it can do to our obese population.

Imagine how much money insurance companies will save. I can walk in right now and talk to the FDA, but I don't want to. This is too valuable, and besides, they won't talk to me. But, if you went in there and had a conversation about the statistics I'm going to prepare, it'd be approved in no time. We can be billionaires within a year... year and a half. I know how to fast track this."

D'angelo sat down. He smiled at Marco. Marco continued sipping his beer and said nothing for a moment.

"Look, I know it's sudden, but, maybe you'd be willing to have a conversation with your father about this product. If he understood the far reaching effects of this product he'd want to fund me, right this second."

Marco said nothing. He understood. D'Angelo was playing an angle. He was another Slotzky type character, wanting his father's money this time, another scheming, scamming criminal on the prowl. D'angelo tried again.

"What if there's not a word about weight loss or improved digestion? What if nothing trespasses the medical device boundaries? It's just a comfort device to help calm folks during a meal. That's not medicine. Right?"

Marco continued to glance alternately at the sun going down and at D'angelo. He hoped his silence sent a message.

Befuddled, D'angelo changed the subject.

"Beautiful weather we've been having, don't you think?"

"It's been great," Marco lied. "Especially at the end of the day. I love the peaceful feeling of sitting by the pool." Another lie. Every minute he found himself checking for alligators."

"Yeah," said D'angelo, understanding that he just got the brush off. He decided not to say another word. He took a deep breath and relaxed. They sat together silently for the next half hour as the night took hold.

Chapter 21

Later, Marco asked Rei about D'angelo Brown.

"So who is this guy Rei? You know him? What's up with him?"

"D'angelo Brown is a hustler. He's smart and he has a kind of energy about him. He's very creative, you could say. He's untrustworthy, and he talks a lot. But, he is friendly and kind of happy in his soul. I like him. He can't sell me anything because I don't have much money. So he leaves me alone, mostly."

Rei continued to describe what D'angelo told him. Apparently, Brown has sold everything from cars to encyclopedias. He's had the worst and the best sales jobs throughout his life. He talked a great game because he was always able to get people to listen to him.

As Rei had heard it, Brown's first breakthrough was when he talked his way into an infomercial and played the "after" person who loved the product and the results he got. He was featured in numerous commercials in that same role, sometimes disguised and speaking with an accent so that the low budget company could keep costs down.

The turning point in his career was when his employer, who was making quite a bit of money, refused to pay him for his work. It motivated him to go out on his own and began to run his own show.

Brown aimed his products to appeal to the worried, bored, obsessive, neurotic, and depressed people who watched and wanted something to stimulate them.

He let his creative juices flow, found struggling inventors, and took their products on for a flat fee. Sometimes, he succeeded wildly at selling oddball home improvement items. Most of the time, he lost money and didn't pay the inventors. Soon he realized he had to pay up or run. So, he reached out for a little help from a loan shark named Charlie Shue thinking it was his best option for handling his looming financial situation.

Unfortunately, Charlie Shue, aka Charlie the Shoe, was a mobbed up guy which meant that D'angelo was now *sleeping with the devil.*

After paying off his inventors with little remorse for the pain he had caused them, he had a greater challenge. He needed to constantly invent new products so he could *feed his new beast,* the loan shark. D'angelo knew if he didn't feed the beast–he'd soon become the beast's food. Creating his own inventions was his only way to earn and put money into the hands of his beast, the mob financier.

After spending many sleepless nights, D'angelo had a vision for a new product. He woke up with the words, "Hairgrow Chapeau" and vision of a cap with cream under it. From this he crafted a waterproof beret that helped make hair grow. It was made from stretchable vinyl/rubber material, the kind typically used to make dominatrix clothing.

On the fly, he mixed up a yeasty cream that permeated the scalp and stimulated circulation. He added hot pepper so the client would feel the burn and think something productive was happening to them. He added some vitamins and Vaseline to soothe the pain of the burning. He was ready to sell it. He called the ointment "Stem Salve," noting that a doctor in Italy said, "it very well could" stimulate stem cells.

The hat sold well for nearly a year before complaints came rolling in. The main complaint was burnt scalp and cheesy smelling scurf that formed on bare skin.

Before any lawsuits could take him down, D'angelo pulled the product off the market and with his shark's financial assistance he created many more failed products. Charlie the Shoe stayed with D'angelo because while using this product, despite a burned scalp, some of his own hair grew back.

He had other questionable products. D'angelo's unique oral hygiene product, 'DentoWite,' was painted onto the teeth to create a nearly permanent color change. The problem was that it never came off because it was tinted epoxy. Flossing became impossible. It was an impermeable covering that prevented normal dental adjustment.

The slogan, too, was a challenge to the ADA. *"You'll never need to clean your teeth again. Yes that's right, one coating of DentoWite and your smile will last forever."* Unfortunately, even if the slogan were correct, any unsubstantiated claims were frowned upon, and the ADA noticed it, and complained to the FDA.

So, when the big dogs at the justice department gave D'angelo a call and told him he was in really hot water, he knew the jig was up. They started asking questions about his other products as well as DentoWite and let him know that they had evidence of a track record of fraud. D'angelo realized this was not going to be a slap on the wrist and a little cease and desist letter. They were talking about fraudulent medical devices and damage suits. It looked like he could be doing time.

After weeks of negotiating with the feds it became apparent that D'angelo had no defense and would soon be charged. He feared imprisonment and suggested that perhaps he could be of service to his beloved government by revealing what he knew about the illegal dealings of his made-man partner.

The feds took him up on his offer and cut a deal with him. As the typical Hidden Paradise tale goes, his 'partner' was imprisoned, D'angelo's businesses disappeared, and D'angelo Brown was sent to cozy perdition in Florida for the remainder of his life.

Chapter 22

Marco loved when the late morning sun was overcast. He was out early, on the roof watering the raised garden beds and feeding aunt Marie's leftover cookies to the gulls, when the call came in.

"Marco, it's Shepp. You have time today to take care of a Paradise resident, looks like he needs a closet door repair?"

"Yeah, sure, what's the problem?"

"#290 is complaining 'bout the door of his closet needs adjusting. He's not one to complain much–like I'd like you to handle it asap."

"Sure, we'll do it. What's his name?"

"His name is Grigori, I can't pronounce his last name. He's on the second floor at the end of the hallway. I know I don't have to tell you this but, please be very polite. He's kind of sensitive and he's from Russia. He understands everything you say but he doesn't speak much, at least not to me. I've never been able to have a real conversation with him. So don't push it, and be as clear as possible."

"I can be over there within the hour." Marco responded.

"Good kid, I'll let him know. You may have to run out to pick up some items from the hardware store, whatever it takes Marco, okay? Thanks. We'll talk later." With that, Shepp hung up and returned to his online game of chess and his hard boiled egg sandwich. Putting his feet up, setting his laptop on his lap, Shepp resumed 'play.'

Marco finished watering the beds of greens and put together a case of tools including his bag of odds and ends he'd kept in the repair closet. Looking up at the sky he was grateful his new home prison in paradise was so beautiful, and that he still had freedom of movement behind these illusory prison walls. He took a deep breath and descended the stairs. *It's not so bad,* he thought.

When the housekeeper opened the door, Marco could hear the sound of orchestral music playing quietly. It was a pensive, studious sound. Marco was not acquainted with classical music. The sounds drew him in.

"It's the Rachmaninoff Concerto Number 4. One of my favorites," said a voice from the next room, as if it had been reading Marco's mind.

The housekeeper turned toward the voice and spoke in a quiet comforting tone.

"That's Mr. Grigori, I'm Celia, I keep house here. If you have any questions you can ask me. Please come in and stand on that floor pad for just a minute."

Curious and compliant, he set down his tools and stood while Celia looked at what appeared to be a cell phone.

"Okay, you can bring your tools now, please follow me."

They entered a dark front room filled with soft classical music. The sound system was deep, superior, and Marco was captivated by the modernity and the yearning feeling that music produced in him. It was as if he craved a missing piece of himself, that had been lost in some unlived lifetime. The feeling was haunting.

From the dark, a heavily accented voice asked him, "Please sit and listen with me." Grigori turned a table lamp up and Marco saw him for the first time. He sat on the couch, a thin man with a short cropped salt and pepper beard and curly short hair. He had a small pot belly. His skin was snowy white. His face was bigger than most faces. It was disproportionately big in fact. His jaw was huge like that of a hormonal giant. His arms were thin under his white dress shirt.

"Celia, please bring tea for the young man, dear."

"With pleasure. On its way." Celia was turning the corner with a teapot, cups, and cookies before his sentence ended.

"And Celia, please…" he didn't finish his sentence. Celia had set down the tea and drew back the heavy curtains to allow the bright overcast light into the enormous front room.

"These are lime sugar cookies, a Cuban tradition," Celia offered, as Marco was just about to ask.

"I have never met you Marco, yet, I feel you are someone I can trust. Can I trust you?" Grigori asked.

"Sure." Marco responded, sipping tea, biting into a cookie.

"I rarely allow access into my living space. I'm a private man. You understand the circumstances of this community, I'm sure. My need for privacy is greater than most."

Marco nodded and wondered about Grigori and his secret past.

"I can tell you that I was part of the great Russian tradition of mystic sciences. I was part of a group that developed sensitivities for spying. Have you heard of distant viewing Marco?"

"I thought that was just…"

"Science fiction? No. I worked for many years with the government and spy organizations. I organized the official group and trained many people."

"So what…." again Marco's question was interrupted by the answer to it.

"So what did we do? I can only say we were able to undermine many of the US plans to dominate mother Russia. We foiled them at every turn. It was their mission. But, it wasn't mine. I sought only to activate the mental sensitivities, in the army of young men under my command."

Grigori was able to anticipate every one of Marco's questions. He intercepted them mid ask and responded as if the questions had been spoken out loud. But, they weren't.

"At some point, there was a power struggle in Moscow. The Russian military let go of me and a criminal element entered my life. They wanted to use my skills to benefit their profits. I worked for them to predict and assure the outcomes of their investments, so to speak. As time moved on, I was afforded every creature comfort a man could want while sitting and living in the nether world of distant viewing. I was ninety percent accurate in my work for them and was paid very well. I was spoiled like a lap dog, stroked like a house cat. I had everything... but my family. This, they would not allow. It was the coercive aspect of their treatment of me that eventually turned me against them." Grigori lifted the cup to his lips and paused.

Marco hung on his every word. As he glanced around the room he noted the subtle classical artwork on the walls. Romantic portraits of Kings and court paintings; lovely vases and ornate sculptures dotted the room.

"My family was taken from me by these monsters. I've been tortured by this event. I didn't see my son grow up. He was held against his will in another part of the country. It was something I couldn't deal with in my heart, you know, I was deeply sad. But, this story is too long to tell right now Marco. Suffice it to say, with my mental abilities I was able to send a message out and get help."

Marco began to ask a question and was once again immediately preempted by Grigori's response.

"Yes, I turned on my Kremlin-connected bosses when they arrived in the United States to pursue further monetary gains. I talked them into taking me to the United States with them. I devised the ultimate plan to avenge them for all the loss they forced on my life. I had been their slave because of my psychic abilities. They used and abused me, and I hated them for that, so I got even."

Grigori stopped to bite a cookie. The lime flavor filled his mouth with a smile. It was one of the small pleasures that now made his life worth living. The loss of his family was the tragic background noise he had to contend with always. Yet somehow, he managed to resolve his pain with great, wise tenderness and sensitivity to himself.

"Have you heard of the Chechan Nucleotide Argument, Marco? I would think not. It was like the Piltdown Man. You know of this? I know you do not. This Piltdown Man was a hoax. A false archaeological find. So too, was this 'argument' that I posited for this group of hoodlums. I got them to invest in the success of a new way of creating energy. Thus, I made them lose everything. It was my way of revenge. But two weeks before that, one night I escaped from my hotel in Chicago. I reached out to the FBI."

Grigori was about to reach for the tea when Celia entered and poured more into each cup then silently exited.

"Celia and I have a rare connection. We are tuned in, as you may have noticed. I have trained her in these ways. It is because she already has a gift. And because of her son, Efrain. He too is gifted and very helpful to me."

"So, now I am here, in exile, because I brought down the Russian mob, and you know, I'm proud of my accomplishment. I beat them at their own game. They are without everything now, including their God, money. Now their life is timeless, in prison. They don't know where I am. I have no connection to the world outside. I have no computer. I ask questions and get news only through Efrain. He is my eyes and ears. I have disappeared from the world and so I am free. No computers, no internet. I keep track of my family at a distance with the help of Efrain. He's always home, always in his wheelchair. He is like a burning ember. His intelligence is beyond measurement. I am forever thankful to Celia and her son, for this reason I feel life didn't forget about me."

At this point, Marco noticed Grigori's voice quavering. He was near tears. Celia arrived instantly with a handkerchief, removing the tea and cookies. Her intent was to change the subject and move the conversation forward.

"Grigori will show you the repairs he wants you to do Marco." Celia remotely lowered the sound of the concerto to a whisper and turned on several lights.

Grigori stood and reached out his hand to Marco.

"I trust you. There are very few here who can be trusted. You are one of them. I know this to be true because I see you, beyond your surface persona, Marco. Please come with me."

In the next room, Grigori moved a small table aside and pushed against the wall panel. The wall bounced outward toward them: a secret closet, he motioned to Marco and they stepped into the room. It was full of memorabilia from a bygone era. Russian books and medal decorated uniforms hung alongside tuxedos, festooned hats and regalia.

"You see all these bygones Marco? They're all a part of my life history. I need you to destroy everything, I want every trace of my past life gone. Can you do this for me, Marco?"

"Sure. I can burn them. Or dump them in the ocean?"

"That's it, dump them in the ocean. A fire would bring attention. I know you want to know why I'm making this dramatic move. It's because I must let go of all of this stuff to release myself from the agony of my past. It's a gulag of my own making, memories that serve only to torture me. I know it's time to let go now, I've mourned my misery long enough." Grigori stood beside Marco. He was taller than expected. He seemed willowy and weak, but underneath, Marco felt a sinewy willful strength exuding from Grigori's every pore.

Grigori went to his desk and pulled out an 8x11 loose leaf notebook from the bottom drawer. He presented it to Marco, as if it were a great gift.

"This booklet was given to me by my friend Caspar Melton."

"You knew Caspar Melton?"

"Yes. We came to Hidden Paradise the same year. He was a good friend. I knew he was trustworthy. We spent many afternoons in this room before he got too sick. Before he died, he gave me this book. It contains all of his secrets for making millions from fixing the odds in horse racing. I don't know why I have kept it. I need you to decide what to do with it. Use these secrets for yourself, sell them, or destroy the book. The choice is yours."

Marco pulled out a roll of super heavy construction bags and immediately began to fill them. In all, he had six huge bags full. The closet was empty. He put Caspar Melton's book of race fixing secrets on top of the last bag.

"So there is no repair?"

"I am the one who is being repaired here, Marco. You have been of great service. Would you mind if I invite you for a visit from time to time? Maybe we can have tea and cookies in the future and you can share your stories."

"I look forward to spending more time with you Grigori," Marco responded.

The extreme peace and calm that filled Grigori's apartment was like a drug to Marco. He couldn't wait to return and inundate himself with its profound serenity.

Chapter 23

Three trips later, Marco hauled the last of Grigori's six overstuffed bags to his apartment. He took out the book of Caspar Melton's secrets, *How to Make Millions Fixing the Probabilities in Horse Racing.* He thought about opening the plain covered booklet. He hesitated. *This would make me as corrupt and criminal as the residents here.* It was late morning, the glaring white Florida sun was beginning to dominate the day. Rei was tying young tomato plants to trestles in one of his raised beds when Marco arrived on the roof. They greeted each other with a nod.

"Do you know anyone who has a boat I can borrow?"

Rei thought for a minute while he continued to tie tomatoes.

"I think so, but I'll definitely have to go with you. Why do you need a boat Marco?"

Marco told him about meeting with Grigori and the task he was assigned of sinking 6 bags of dark memories from his mob driven, distant viewing, psychic life among the Russians.

"That's his story, Marco? I think you might be the only one here who has met Grigori, you and Shepp. Grigori was here long before I arrived eleven years ago. I've met his housekeeper many times. She's very interesting and now I understand why."

"Grigori's very unusual Rei. He said he chose me to visit him because of his psychic powers. He said he could read my energy field long before we even met. After this visit, I know it is true. The man is definitely an anomaly in life."

Rei pulled out his cell phone and dialed. Marco walked over to the storage hut, grabbed water and found a seat in the shade of the new wooden trellis, Rei had finished building it yesterday.

"Nice trellis structure, has just enough shade to take the edge off the bright sun, I' like-eee, Rei!." They both chuckled.

Rei came closer, cell phone up to his ear speaking in a whisper.

"I've got us a boat. Shall we go, now?"

"You mean now? Sure. Okay. Like right now Rei? Okay, yes, I guess, Let's do this...we'll need six cinder blocks or something like it to weigh the bags down."

"No problem." Rei responded to Marco.

Rei spoke into the phone, "I really appreciate this, I owe you one brother. You know I'm always here for you right? Thanks, bye!" With that, Rei turned to Marco, "We're good to go. Let's get these bags downstairs onto the golf cart." In a few minutes they were beyond the chain link fence, heading along the pothole bumpy road towards Boat Camp.

Along the roadside Marco saw crumbling houses and abandoned cars all disappearing into the swamp jungle. The abandoned homes were from the victims of the 1985 Hurricane Elena that flooded Hidden Paradise, who were never able to return because of the loophole scams of the insurance companies, who refused to cover storm surge damage to otherwise insured houses.

Finally, they reached Boat Camp which included at least 10 acres of scabbed together buildings, storage sheds, and ramshackle docks. Boats, boat parts and boat junk scattered everywhere and a thick stench was in the air. Marco figured out the God-awful smell came from the open sewer drainage ditch running behind a row of houses closest to the road. The place seemed barren of people. The only sound came from a couple of small generators purring somewhere out in the dismal neighborhood.

Near the end of the road was a rough building displaying a hand painted sign above a heavy door, reading: "Bayou Bill's Boat Club." The front wall was festooned with alligator skulls. The windows were boarded up. Someone had hung a bikini bathing suit in the teeth of the largest gator skull mounted above the door. Christmas lights hung on the gutters. To Marco, this resembled a post-apocalyptic last-stand bunker, or a dangerous third world roadhouse. There was no parking lot, but there was a dock in front for boats to tie up. It was empty now. Even while empty in daylight with no carousing boat customers, the place was disturbing and sordid looking.

"A tragic place, it's God-awful here," Rei commented quietly, shaking his head.

At the end of the road was an orderly complex of heavy docks and metal buildings. These appeared to be here for servicing professional fishing boats, and processing the catch. But, there were no boats, so maybe things aren't always as they appear?

Off to the side of the docks stood a lanky, super skinny teenager methodically stripping down an outboard engine mounted on a stand. When he saw Rei, he put down his tools and climbed down into a battered ski boat that looked like it had been painted by children. He started filling a trash bag with the cans, bottles and garbage littering the bottom of the boat. Rei parked the golf cart. They grabbed Grigori's bags, the cinder blocks, and walked to the dock.

"Hey Robo," said Rei. "This is Marco."

"Hi Robo," said Marco.

Robo waved as he continued cleaning junk from a boat covered with stickers of all kinds, and cigarette burns everywhere. The throttle was a metal rod with an eight ball attached to the end. For all intents and purposes, this appeared to be the teenage party boat. Robo finished cleaning and waved the guys over. They brought over Grigori's bags.

Robo said, "Can you take this garbage away for me? Throw it in the condo's dumpster?"

"Sure," said Rei.

Robo put the bag on the golf cart. Then he went to a metal building, and gathered up several more overflowing garbage bags. He tossed them all onto the cart.

Rei and Marco climbed on board. Underneath the seat was a single slalom water ski and a tow rope. Robo passed Grigori's bags and the cinder blocks to them.

"How much for an hour or two?" asked Rei.

"Forty bucks. There's a full tank and I just rebuilt the motor.

It runs like it looks... mean and lean." Marco traded money for the keys.

Rei started the outboard, took a red bandanna out of his pocket and tied it around his damaged partially bald head. He looked like a battle scarred buccaneer, and away they flew.

Once they were far enough away from the shoreline mangroves, Rei opened the throttle and glided swiftly over the smooth, glassy water. Twenty minutes later, Rei stopped, "I think the water's deep enough here."

Marco opened the garbage bag containing Caspar Melton's allegedly *foolproof method of fixing the odds in horse racing*. He opened it. Inside the manuscript was a mass of incomprehensible math, written formulas, barely legible and mixed with page after page of equally tiny writing, taking up every millimeter of space on the page. There were no paragraphs, just an endless run-on screed. Marco knew, to protect his direction in a clean life, he must sink this *foolproof method to crime* of Caspar Melton. He dismissed the opportunities it presented, tossing it back in the bag. He added a cinder block and sealed it.

Together they sealed the bags, and poked holes in each to allow the air out to help them sink. Marco sat quietly and watched as each bag disappeared into the water forever. He felt good being able to help this strange tortured man Grigori, to let go and move on from his mobster interrupted life.

Glancing up at Rei with a smile, "We got this man. Grigori's mission is complete. You think you could drive while I ski, Rei? I like that sound, Ski Rei, pretty cool, Ski Rei."

Rei started to laugh, "Funny guy, you're good medicine for me Marco, think I'll keep you around for a while. Go for it, grab the ski, let's see what you got." Rei started the engine.

Marco laughed while he put on the life jacket, jumped in the water, ski and tow rope in hand, big smiles exchanged. *This is what life is all about.* Marco was smiling to himself, thinking: *freedom to fly freely on your feet across the waters.* Rei moved slowly forward taking slack out of the rope.

Marco gave Rei a 'thumbs up!' And up, out of the water he shot. "This boat's got some power," Marco shouted, even though Rei was looking forward. "Don't be afraid to use it Rei!" Within seconds they were at full speed. Marco felt exhilarated crossing the wake of the boat, gathering speed with each whiplash turn. He felt timeless. For just these few moments he was free, without any boundaries in life. He was his own boss now. His face sprayed with water and the sunshine of Florida. For a few moments, Marco felt great. But then, his mood darkened. His new home was an open air prison. He was living in fear amongst dangerous criminals. Even here, with the ocean breeze on his face, he was trapped.

It isn't fair. And with that one thought, his mood hardened. *I don't deserve this isolation and exile. I committed no crime, nor did I rat anyone out.* Thinking deeply to himself, a solution emerged: *What if I just let go, slip out of the life jacket, take a great big breath of seawater, and sink to the bottom? Why not just end it all right now, I have nothing here to live for. Release myself. I'd rather be anywhere but paradise now.*

But, he knew he wouldn't do that, and as he slalomed back and forth, he began yelling as loud as he could in frustration and fury. It turned into a long primal scream. Aggressively, he leaped over the wake, catching air with each pass behind the boat. When his throat felt raw and he had no scream left, he started bawling, feeling infinite self-pity. *Why me?*

When he was all cried out, he felt numb and exhausted. As they got close to land Rei stopped the boat, and Marco pulled himself aboard. His legs felt like rubber. His arms were aching with exhaustion.

Rei turned to Marco. His face full of sympathy, "You feel better?"

Marco realized that Rei had heard him screaming.

"Actually I do."

"Good."

Marco was more than a bit surprised when he heard himself chuckling at Rei's question. He wasn't embarrassed, he felt blessed to have a friend–a friend like Rei.

As the canal turned a corner into the mangrove swamp, they came upon a group of sandhill cranes, curve-billed ibises and great blue herons standing on a sandy bank. The boat passed within 30 feet of the birds, who watched Marco as he watched them.

With the blue sky filtering through mangrove, cypress and Spanish moss, the sun mirroring off the still water, it was a picture fit for a National Geographic photograph. Open and vulnerable after screaming and crying, Marco allowed himself to be drawn into the splendid beauty of the natural world. Despite his distress, sadness and anger, he felt part of everything. It was a brief, unexpected moment of profound clarity, wonder, and even gladness.

Chapter 24

Marco arrived early at the tennis courts for the first group lesson he'd be teaching. It had been two weeks since his run-in with DiCarlo. He brought with him several new cans of tennis balls. The court was dry after yesterday's rain. He opened up a can of balls and started a volley with himself against the fence while he waited. He hoped at least a couple of people would respond to the flyers he had posted around the condo and stores. He put a sign-up sheet on a clipboard that hung on a fence near the entrance. With it he left envelopes for the $10 lesson fee.

Five minutes later, a man in a wheelchair pushed himself onto the courts. To Marco, he appeared to be of Indian or Pakistani descent, with pudgy apple cheeks and a small black mustache. But, his most distinctive feature was a well-coiffed helmet of tight black curly hair and an overly wide forehead making the top half of his skull appear much larger than the round, chubby bottom half, like a space alien cartoon character.

Marco stopped volleying and went over, holding out his hand

"Hi. I'm Marco, You're here for a tennis lesson?"

"I'm Arn Pekohr," said the man, with a New Jersey accent and very strong handshake.

"Yes, I'm here to play tennis."

"Where's your racket? The flyer said to bring your racket and tennis balls if you have them." Marco spoke politely, though it may have come off sounding a bit demanding.

"What? Don't you have a racket for me?"

"No."

Pekohr shook his head and winced with irritation. "I have one in my apartment."

"Good."

"Can you get it for me?" asked Pekohr.

"No, I need to be here when the others arrive."

"If you run fast, it shouldn't take you more than five minutes."

"Tell you what, Arn. Why don't you watch this lesson from outside, and next week you can bring your racket and join us?"

Pekohr turned his wheelchair and left without a word.

A couple minutes before 10am, more people started arriving. Shepp's wife Carol greeted Marco with a wave. She was closely followed by a group, all carrying rackets and tennis balls. Marco walked over to greet them.

The first person forward to say hello was D'Angelo Brown, who winked conspiratorially while squeezing his hand. Next, Marco greeted Mysti Barare, the beautiful, sensuous swimmer from that day at the pool, now etched in his memory by the Downy DiCarlo trauma that followed it. Mysti greeted Marco with a coquettish smile, and when she shook hands, she pulled him close to her with way too much familiarity. Marco was certain he had not spoken to her at the pool that day. "Hi sweetie," she whispered, inches from his face.

Just then, a very tan, trim balding man in his 50's was quickly approaching. He was of medium height and a fringe of red hair surrounding his tanned dome. He introduced himself as Don Nealey. Another attendee was an older, nonathletic woman named Kathy Fortuna, who said she was Aunt Marie's best friend. This was followed by a friendly man in his 30's with dark wavy hair and a Tony Bennett nose that fit his chiseled face perfectly, his name was Kyle Ross. He arrived with a very attractive woman in her late 20's, her sandy hair pulled back in a ponytail. She gave her name as Hannah LaVerre.

There were six students in all, pretty good for a first class, Marco thought. And with his most enthusiastic voice, he shouted, "Alright, all you tennis pro's let's hit some balls."

Marco had them line up in doubles, explaining he was going to watch and correct their forehand and backhand swings, while each volleyed with the person directly across the net.

"No overhand serving for this lesson," he called out.

Arn Pekohr returned to the courts with a tennis racket on his lap. He scowled as he opened the gate to the courts, deliberately wheeling himself through the middle of everyone, while they were finding their places on the court. Pekohr took the last slot, with nobody opposite him. Marco handed out balls to the people who didn't have them, and told Pekohr he'd be over to volley with him once he got the rest of the group going. Pekohr didn't acknowledge him, he just sat frowning and unresponsive in his chair with his racket and balls in his lap.

The students started volleying, and Marco noticed their skill level varied from beginner to pretty good. Mysti Barare was a beginner, lined up opposite Don Nealey, who was slightly better. D'Angelo Brown was quite a good tennis player. He was lined up against Carol Shepp, who was doing her best to keep the ball from hitting the net, or sailing out of the court. Hannah LaVerre and Kyle Ross were pretty good at keeping a gentle volley going. Everyone except Arn Pekohr was smiling, laughing and having a good time.

Marco then went to each person giving encouragement and subtle corrections. Remembering Arn Pekohr, he trotted over to the far court where Pekohr remained in the exact position Marco had left him, frowning and unresponsive.

Marco lined up on the other side of the net from scowling Pekohr. He hit a slow lob to Pekohr's forehand. Pekohr swung his racket with all his might and sent the ball flying back at Marco's head. Marco stepped out of the way and returned the ball to Pekohr's backhand. Pekohr ignored it. He picked up another ball from his lap, tossed it up in the air, and served it towards Marco's body. He made no effort to keep the ball within the lines of the court. Marco returned it, and again, Pekohr ignored the invitation to volley, and instead he sent his last two balls in quick succession at Marco.

What an asshole, thought Marco. He turned away from Pekohr and began correcting and encouraging the other students. When he was farthest away from Pekohr, he noticed that Pekohr was wheeling his chair into the midst of the other players. Stopping his chair next to the net, he began swinging his racket at any tennis ball within reach. He managed to hit one ball, and sent it flying out of the tennis courts entirely.

"Pecker!" shouted Don Nealey, angrily. "Get out of here with your chair! Move it Pecker!"

Pekohr didn't move, a scowl imprinted on his face. Nealey shook his head furiously. He ran up to Pekohr, turned the chair roughly around, and gave it a huge shove towards the far corner of the tennis courts.

"Damn you Pecker! Get the heck off the court!" Pekohr's chair went sailing off towards the far corner. Pekohr made no effort to stop it. The chair slowed down by itself and stopped in the corner. Pekohr didn't move. He was facing away from the others like a naughty school kid being shamed and made to sit in the corner. He stayed there, still and sulking.

The rest of the group ignored him and went back to their friendly vollies. *Serves him right*, thought Marco. *He asked for it. I'm gonna let this disruptive jerk sit there awhile*. Pekohr didn't move, sitting in his corner, perfectly ignored.

D'Angelo Brown's phone rang. He took the call, waved goodbye to Marco and the others, and left the courts. After making the rounds with the other players, Marco went back to Pekohr's corner, turned him around, and wheeled him back to the courts. He dropped a few balls in his lap. Carol Shepp, who had been volleying with Kathy Fortuna, lined up opposite Pekohr. She sent an easy volley towards Pekohr, who, to Marco's amazement, returned it softly to Carol. He was not bad at wheelchair tennis. She returned it. Pekohr lobbed a ball softly towards her. A volley was finally happening and Pekohr was smiling.

Soon the hour was over and Marco called an end to the lesson, thanking everyone, and expressing his wish to see them for the next tennis lesson soon. The last ones to leave were Kyle Ross and Hannah LaVerre.

"Good lesson," said Kyle, holding out his hand. Marco shook it.

"I'm playing a music set at Chez Roué next Saturday. Hannah

and I were wondering if you'd like to join us for a drink at 8:30 before I go on? I can give a call beforehand. Interested?"

"I'd love it. Let's do it. I look forward to your call Kyle," Marco replied.

After gathering all the tennis balls, his racket, the sign up sheet and the envelope of money, Marco exited feeling hopeful. He'd forgotten momentarily that this idyllic country club setting was inside a prison.

Chapter 25

A couple days later, when Shepp asked Marco if he would take a repair call at Arn Pekohr's apartment to install some new LED light bulbs, Marco's first instinct was to refuse, remembering how Pekohr had tried to ruin his first group tennis lesson, a lesson that included the ugly scene of Don Nealey angrily shoving Pekohr's wheelchair across the tennis courts. Marco wondered if the two had some bad history.

"I'm not so sure," Marco replied. "He was a real jerk at my first tennis lesson."

"Yeah. Carol told me. But come on, the guy's in a wheelchair. We all pitch in to help him out from time to time."

"Alright, ok, I'll do it."

Marco called. Pekohr was delighted and asked Marco to be at his door at 4pm sharp.

Don Nealey and Arn Pekohr had an unpleasant history dating back to Nealey's arrival at Hidden Paradise 13 years ago. Nealey, whose pre-witness protection name was Steven Young, had been the County Auditor for Walla Walla County in Washington State. A devout Mormon, and a direct descendant of Brigham Young, he had schemed with various city, county, prison and state officials for ten years. He was 'the skimmer, a skim man' who stole money from taxpayers. His share had been in the millions. Finally, the sheer size of the greed and graft caught someone's attention and as a result, he was charged with a dozen federal racketeering and RICO charges.

Facing decades in prison, he turned on his co-conspirators in exchange for a fresh start. He abandoned his family and his four children. The Feds sent him to Florida, a place he had never been. This suited him fine. The farther away the better.

He knew no one at Hidden Paradise. The first person to befriend him was wheelchair bound Arn Pekohr, who seemed friendly enough. Pekohr lived two apartments away on the second floor. They spent some pleasant time together during his first few weeks, until one day Nealey came back to his apartment and found Pekohr inside snooping around. Pekohr had gained access using a master key.

He didn't steal anything. He rifled through financial reports and medical records getting to know whatever intimate details he could find on Nealey. There wasn't much to find, but when Nealy saw Pekohr in his home he erupted in anger ordering him out. That was the last they spoke. Nealey never forgave Pekohr. As a result of the invasion, he immediately changed the locks.

Furthermore, after a few more confrontations, Nealey decided to never trust anyone at Hidden Paradise again. He didn't like the rough people he encountered. They were criminals and their histories were frightening. Nealey turned to the community outside of Hidden Paradise for socializing, never again going to the Hidden Paradise shops near the lake, and never again, letting anyone get to know him.

Before long, Nealey became active in the local Mormon Church, and joined the exclusive Sandy Pines Country Club for golf where he became the club treasurer. He was saving his witness protection stipend to buy a small home near the country club. Nealey's goal was to escape Hidden Paradise forever. At the same time, he was wooing a wealthy widow from his church, 14 years his elder.

Pekohr had been at Hidden Paradise for 14 years. His pre-witness protection name was Arjun Kapoor. He was from New Jersey. He and his partners had sold fraudulent vacation timeshare properties located in the Virgin Islands, Mexico and the Bahamas. Over a career of 11 years, Ruby Bay Timeshares fleeced thousands of victims in New Jersey and New York.

 A typical fleecing began with an introductory high pressure luncheon during which vacation timeshares were touted as a fantastic investment, with easy mortgage terms. The salesmen were trained to blatantly lie about the contracts, which bound each unsuspecting buyer to ever increasing fees of up to $19,000 yearly. Even worse, the buyer had to assume complete financial responsibility in the case of ordinary maintenance, or losses due to hurricane damage. The contracts were so one-sided that the unsophisticated victims were legally obligated to a bottomless pit of financial enslavement.

Not only that, but the Timeshares could not be easily sold or transferred and if someone stopped paying, Ruby Bay's lawyers and debt collectors went to work on them. Thousands of people went bankrupt. Thousands had their credit ruined and were evicted from their timeshares. Afterwards, Ruby Bay claimed that *the evicted owners still owed all the fees*. After evicting an owner, Ruby Bay would re-sell their timeshare to a new victim. The process was repeated continuously.

When Federal charges were brought, Arjun/Arn was the first to squeal. He turned on everyone. He got witness protection and his partners got prison. On the same day he gave his court testimony, a van with no license plates ran him down, right in front of the courthouse. No one was ever caught. The police were never sure if the driver was a dissatisfied customer, or someone hired by his partners. Arjun/Arn spent 4 months in the hospital where doctors saved his legs. However, Arn was destined to live in some degree of pain for the rest of his life.

When he arrived at Hidden Paradise, tricky Arn Pekohr decided to never tell anyone he could walk. For 14 years, he appeared to be a paraplegic. In his apartment, with the curtains drawn tight, he walked and even exercised. His pain was minimal these days. He needed no painkillers. Arn thrived on the benefits and privileges that went with disability. He could get people to do all kinds of things for him. This pleased him. He thrived on attention.

Chapter 26

At 3:45, before Marco's arrival to change the light bulbs in Arn Pekohr's apartment, Arn was downstairs, waiting for the pizza delivery man. Thursday's was 25% off Marie's Pizza with Free delivery for Hidden Paradise residents from DiCarlo Bakery. Pizza was a new item at the bakery, and Romeo was in charge. DiCarlo's delivery service was instantly popular for the residents who didn't want to socialize with the same criminals they had to live next to and see, year in and year out. Romeo demanded prepayment and he delivered at 5pm only. No one complained. Romeo had a bad temper, and a worse reputation, and besides, this was the best pizza they'd ever get.

Romeo usually carried a stack of boxes up to the second and third floors and delivered them himself, but this week Arn met him on the ground floor and offered to deliver the second floor pizzas. They rode the elevator together up to the third floor. Romeo loaded six pizza boxes on Arn's lap and stepped out to deliver to the third floor residents. Arn closed the elevator door and immediately killed the power.

The emergency bell in the elevator had been disabled years ago. Locked in, Arn put on rubber gloves, removed a syringe filled with peanut oil from his wheelchair pocket and found Don Nealey's pizza. He carefully injected tiny amounts of peanut oil in many places under the cheese layer. This took about 15 seconds. Arn turned the power back on, took off the gloves, and went to the second floor. *If this works*, he thought, *that son of a bitch Romeo will get blamed.*

Eight years ago, one of the pieces of information Arn found when he snooped into Don Nealey's personal information, was that Nealey had allergic reactions to penicillin and peanuts. Now, two days later, Pekohr was still seething with humiliation over the tennis court incident.

As soon as Pekohr emerged from the elevator on the second floor, he saw Marco waiting in front of Arn's apartment.

"Hey Marco! Sorry I'm late. Could you help me here?"

Marco came over.

"Thursday is half price pizza night from DiCarlo Bakery," said Arn. "Could you knock on the doors of these five people, and deliver their pizzas? The apartment numbers are on the sides of the boxes."

"Sure, why not." Marco said, thinking it would be a good opportunity to have some normal social interaction with people on the second floor. He hustled to the five apartments and had a brief exchange with the residents. Arn, meanwhile, had taken his own pizza, went into his apartment and closed the door.

Don Nealey's pizza was the last one Marco had to deliver. He was pleased when he saw Marco.

"What a pleasant surprise, Marco." He took his pizza. "I'll see you at the next tennis lesson. Maybe we could play a round of golf at my club sometime?"

"You bet, Don, I'd love that. Golf is my game. Enjoy your pizza."

Marco went to Arn's apartment. Inside, Arn offered him a slice. It was excellent pizza. Arn offered him a soda and invited him to sit while they ate. Arn was friendly. He asked questions about Marco's family and their education. He seemed to take real interest in Marco's life.

As Marco was finishing, Arn said, "Wouldn't Hidden Paradise be great, if only people would treat each other with kindness?" As he said this, Arn's smile was replaced by a dark, almost fearful look. Marco thought Arn was on the verge of sharing something very personal and possibly disturbing. But, he didn't say anything, and the practiced smile came back onto his chubby face.

"That's a lovely thought," Marco replied. "If everyone could just be kinder to each other the whole world could be repaired, in one day." Then Marco went to work installing the bulbs. He thought that maybe Arn wasn't so bad after all. He was probably just having a bad day at the tennis lesson. Marco couldn't imagine what it would be like to be trapped in a wheelchair. *I should give him a second chance.*

When he finished, Arn paid for the house call, friendly and smiling. Marco left, totally unaware that his fingerprints were the only ones on Don Nealey's pizza box.

Four days later, the smell of something dead drew the attention of the residents. Somebody called Shepp. They quickly determined that the smell came from Don Nealey's apartment. Shepp called the paramedics and a locksmith. It was an ordeal to get through the locks and the security chain. Inside the apartment, Nealey's bloated, putrefying corpse was on the couch. The pizza box was on the table, beside him. One slice was missing.

Since the door was locked and Nealey had avoided socializing with any of the residents, the death got scant attention at Hidden Paradise, or with the police for that matter. Afterwards, nobody expressed sympathy about losing the standoffish Nealey. Nobody felt like raising the thorny and probably dangerous issue that Romeo's pizza could be at fault. As the paramedics were wheeling Nealey away, Romeo himself suggested that a bee sting was the likely culprit.

"The wasps have been terrible this year," Romeo suggested. The other residents nodded in agreement.

The next day, Shepp hired professional cleaners to sanitize the place, shred Nealey's personal records, and take away the couch. The memorial service was held at the Mormon church where it was attended by many of Don Nealey's country club friends. No one from Hidden Paradise showed their face.

After a few days, things went back to normal, and Arn Pekohr's fear was replaced by elation. It had been the most satisfying enterprise for him since his old days of foreclosing timeshares and chasing poor people around with pit bull lawyers and debt collectors.

Marco never found out that he could have become the fall guy in Nealy's murder.

Chapter 27

A few days after the first group tennis lesson, Kyle Ross called Marco and invited him to meet Hannah and him for drinks before Kyle's music set. He was playing at the main Paradise restaurant, Chez Roué. Marco readily agreed knowing he needed to break out of his mental funk. Little did he know what the night would bring.

Chez Roué was a favorite spot for residents to socialize in the evening. The tenant's association, called pretentiously The Grand Council, met there from time to time.

The restaurant had been in existence for 12 years, opened by a 62 year old, dark skinned Haitian man, Maurice Boite–a former smuggler and human trafficker–and his wife, Cassandra Maurice. He was known to everyone at Hidden Paradise by his nickname Gommeux, meaning "gummy," and pronounced as "Gomu" by English speakers. He earned this odd name from a childhood incident in Haiti at age 3. He'd somehow gotten himself into a can of rubber cement at his father's tire repair shop, covering himself from head to toe, then covering everything around him, before they noticed.

Gommeux was born, Henri DuPont, one of eight children from a Port Au Prince slum. Naturally curious and intelligent, he was an excellent student at school. But, the crushing poverty of Haiti, and one of the devastating hurricanes, drew him to seek escape by sea. He left home at age 11 to work on fishing boats, dropping his childhood nickname in favor of his birth name Henri.

By the age of 14 he could sail, repair or rebuild anything that floated. He obtained his first boat by scuba diving into 50 feet of shark infested waters to re-float a sunken fishing boat near The Turks and Caicos Islands. That was his first boat. Through a series of sales and trades, he acquired one boat after another, all of which could sail in any and all waters.

Gommeux became an expert captain and smuggler, running drugs and people for the cartels throughout the Caribbean and the Americas for over 40 years. He was caught twice in US waters. Fortunately, he was able to ditch the drugs just in time. So, without hard evidence, he was merely deported. He was on every law enforcement's radar screen, until finally his luck ran out. He got caught red handed with 1,900 pounds of cocaine and heroin off the Miami coast.

Facing a lifetime in the pen, he cut a deal, turning in everyone he'd ever worked for, in every country where he'd run drugs. His information and court testimony led to the eventual arrest of over 200 people in 5 different countries. He exposed the secrets of 4 cartels and became one of the most hated and wanted men in The Americas. The cartels put a multi-million dollar price on his head, more than enough to inspire the darkest of shadows to hunt him down.

Fortunately for Gommeux, he and Cassandra were both universally well liked at Hidden Paradise. They were trustworthy, funny, resourceful and companionable. It was unlikely anyone would ever turn them in to the cartels for the reward. Especially since Shepp regularly proclaimed that if anyone were ever assassinated on his watch, he would shut down Hidden Paradise. Not only that, he would revoke everyone's stipend and turn them loose to fend for themselves in the hostile world outside. A world that wanted each of them dead.

Gommeux's deal with witness protection forbade him to ever set foot on any boat, on any water, forever. If so, he would be facing the drug charges that had been temporarily dropped.

When he and Cassandra moved to Hidden Paradise, he took back his old childhood nickname, and began a new creative passion, cooking. At Chez Roué, the food was excellent. The menu changed nearly every night and they served only one or two main courses, whatever Cassandra and he decided they wanted to cook.

Chapter 28

Marco dressed for the evening at Chez Roué in a muted print Hawaiian shirt and clean pressed blue jeans.

Located at the very end of the strip mall on the boardwalk, Chez Roué overhung the lake. The kitchen and bar areas were compact and closest to the lake, while the rest of the seating area extended outwards under a large thatched roof covering the entire sidewalk.

Stopping at the grand entrance, Marco observed the interior of the restaurant. It was Caribbean themed, of course, with seafaring knick knacks and fishing nets hanging from everywhere. Light came in from the colored glass fishing floats, made into fixtures, suspended from the thatched roof. An old diving helmet and a stuffed sailfish perched high above the bar next to a large flat screen TV, currently showing the news. *Looks like a swinging place,* he laughed to himself.

Scanning the room Marco noticed a well dressed, elegant woman, with light brown skin in her late 50's standing next to a cage of colorful songbirds. She was fussing over them, making kissing noises and talking to them.

Marco spotted Kyle across the mahogany tables seated in a wicker chair. He was wearing a print shirt and brown slacks. He was a handsome bloke. His thick, curly black hair and bushy eyebrows went well with his large nose and strong chin. He waved Marco over, and set aside a stack of sheet music.

"Thanks for coming out." They shook hands. Kyle had a rich baritone voice, one that would have sounded great on the radio.

Hannah arrived a few minutes later.

"Sorry, I had to close up shop," directing her apology to Marco, with a slightly lopsided smile that Marco immediately found adorable.

Hannah was wearing a dark blue cocktail dress, muted

makeup and lipstick. Marco wondered why she was so nicely dressed just to have a drink after work. Her straight, longer than shoulder length reddish brown hair had subtle golden highlights. It was held back with a ponytail scrunchie. She was about 5'8", more than cute, and slightly less than stunningly beautiful. Her cheekbones and jawline were perfect, but her intelligent brown eyes were set a bit far apart on her face, with a worry line underneath each. Her strong nose was just a bit long for perfection and had a slight bump in the middle. Marco wondered if it had once been broken.

"What shop are you talking about?" asked Marco as Hannah sat down.

"We own The Paradise hair salon and barber shop next door. I'm the hairdresser, and I do nails."

"I'm a massage therapist," added Kyle. "For years I operated out of my apartment, but I moved to The Paradise when Hannah opened it a year ago."

The woman who had been messing with the songbirds came over with a pad and pen.

"Coucou mes amis," she said. She bent forward towards Hannah. She and Hannah made little kissing noises as they touched right and left cheeks in greeting, followed by Kyle with the same greeting.

The woman turned to Marco. "I'm Cassandra. My husband," she said, indicating the man working in the open kitchen, "his name is Gommeux. Bienvenue à Chez Roué." She held out her hand to Marco, which was a relief, since he was not familiar with performing a French double kiss greeting.

"We're just going to have a drink before my set," said Kyle. "I'll have an iced tea." Hannah ordered red wine, and Marco asked what they had for beer.

"Aha," said Cassandra. "We have ordinary commercial beer." She made a bad face. "But you should know, we brew our own beer. Our latest is a chocolate porter. I think you'll like it." Marco ordered the chocolate porter and Cassandra bustled back to the bar.

Somebody sitting at the bar turned up the volume on the flat screen TV. The lead story was another gun massacre, 11 dead in Alabama, this time in a nursery school. The dead included eight preschool children, two teachers and the gunman who killed himself. The announcer said the killer's name was Duane Earl Wayne, a 25 year old man with a history of failure and hostility, but no criminal record. He had purchased the AR-15 the day before the rampage.

The anchorwoman began an interview with the Republican US Senator from Alabama. "My thoughts and prayers are with the victims," he said, "but the only thing that will stop bad guys with guns, are more good guys with guns. More guns are the answer, not liberal, communist gun control. It's the price we pay for living in a free society."

The drinks arrived. Marco's frothy chocolate porter was excellent.

Kyle shook his head. "Can you believe he is getting away with saying that about a school shooting? What's happening to us? Daniel Patrick Moynihan was correct, when he said that our society is continually downgrading the definition of deviancy. 50 years ago, nobody from either political party could have uttered such a callous, cruel statement about child murder without being stained, stigmatized and universally condemned. It would've crossed a line. Now, such talk from an ass-hat like him is completely acceptable. Deviance has been quietly defined downward over the years, so that "normal" behavior now includes conduct and beliefs that would have been abnormal and abhorrent by earlier standards."

"Just like the cesspool that is social media," said Hannah. "Meanness and trolling behavior are perfectly acceptable conduct."

Cassandra turned the sound down on the TV, and the three of them breathed a sigh of relief.

"It's relentless," said Kyle. "It reaches in and poisons our lives."

Marco decided he liked both of them. He wondered what horrible crimes Kyle had committed to get into witness protection.

He had such an open and honest face, such a gentle demeanor. Hannah was harder to read, more guarded and there was a slight air of sadness behind her pleasant social chit chat.

They sat quietly for a minute, sipping their drinks, trying to find a way back into conversation.

"Did you finish that book?" Kyle asked Hannah.

"Almost." She turned to Marco. "Kyle turned me on to *'The Sum of Us*, by Heather McGhee, which shows how racial discrimination hurts everyone, not just African Americans. It's an important book, persuasively argued, and eye opening. You can read it next, if you like."

"I'd like that," said Marco.

"What are you reading Marco?" Kyle asked as Hannah looked at Marco with a bit of curiosity.

"The only thing I have read recently was that little booklet about Hidden Paradise."

"Oh, you mean *The Fountain of Scams: Greed, Folly, Murder and the History of Hidden Paradise subdivision*, by Caspar Melton?"

"Yeah. You've read it?" He looked at Hannah.

She nodded. "Of course. Everyone's read it."

Gummeux approached the piano and grabbed the microphone.

"Ladies and gentleman, tonight reading a recent poem is our poet in residence, the one and only, our very own, the esteemed and charming D'Angelo Brown."

D'Angelo Brown, with his wavy, game show host hair and a car salesman's smile, dressed in a cream colored suit bounced to the stage with a page of paper in hand and nodded to the audience. He cleared his throat and began to read:

Come close, stay away.
The more modest and covered up you were
the more every crease and freckle,
every hair strand stood out to my searching you.
You may not know my hunger is profound

my brooding depths will drown you
and I will keep you under with my teeth
like a crocodile
and you will be my sad feast:
this ritual murder that is love.

When he stopped reading, the audience clapped vigorously.

"Thank you, thank you very much." D'Angelo nodded.

Kyle looked at his watch. He stood up. "Time to go to work."

Marco turned to Hannah. "So, you two opened the shop a year ago?"

"We did. I moved here about 13 months ago with my ex. He ran off a month later. I was broke and stuck here. Then Kyle and I opened the shop."

"So things went wrong with you and your ex?" Marco asked. He instantly regretted asking.

Hannah sat back in her chair. Her frown was both wary and weary, a clear warning to Marco not to proceed further. She wasn't about to discuss details of her personal life with a stranger at Hidden Paradise, this snake pit of treacherous informers and criminals.

Marco winced to himself: *Oh no, what a klutz. Smooth move, pal. Nice way to forget where you are and embarrass yourself.*

Hannah turned away towards the stage, sparing him a second awkward moment, certain to occur if he were to stammer an apology and thereby dig a deeper hole.

Marco noticed that all the tables were now filled. People were standing in the back talking and socializing with each other. Kyle walked over to an electric piano in front of the bar, turned on the PA system, did a quick sound check, and started playing.

Beginning with an upbeat Latin tune by Antonio Carlos Jobim called 'Wave,' which showcased the extended range of Kyle's rich singing voice and his ability to sing low notes with power. His piano playing was bold and confident. His paced solos were smooth and easy, and he moved through chord changes with smooth agility. He was an excellent musician and entertainer, and he knew it. Kyle was in his element.

From an instrumental version of 'Night in Tunisia' to Thelonius Monk's 'Straight No Chaser,' Kyle played on, song after song, without interruption. He finished with a medley of show tunes, ending with 'Life is a Cabaret,' then pushing his microphone away, he stood smiling and proud at the piano. The place roared with appreciation.

"MesDames et Messieurs, Herr und Herren, Ladies and Gentlemen, and Signore e Signori, it is my true pleasure to now invite one of my dearest and most favorite friends up here to sing the final song of the evening. Please give a warm welcome to the lovely Hannah LaVerre."

The crowd clapped as Hannah stepped onto the stage. She smiled sweetly to the audience and stood next to the electric piano. Taking the microphone she said softly, "Thank you. This is for all of us."

Now the cocktail dress and makeup make sense, Marco thought. Kyle started playing. He recognized the slow melancholy ballad, 'Alone Together' from an old Chet Baker record his college roommate owned. Hannah had a good voice, smoky, a bit like Sade or Nora Jones, but without a lot of natural volume. She held the mic in both hands, looking at Kyle while he played the lush intro. Kyle, focusing on his keyboard, offered beautiful, cascading notes with his right hand as he transitioned through the minor chords with his left. Then she started to sing.

"Alone together, beyond the crowd,
above the world, we're not too proud.
To cling together, we're strong,
as long as we're together."

When Kyle played his solo, Hannah closed her eyes and moved gently with the music. Marco was entranced by her sensuous beauty as she swayed. Listening to Hannah sing this sad song reminded Marco once more of his life. It seemed there was a bright line separating his current trapped existence and his former carefree life, before he wandered into Hidden Paradise. His past life seemed so long ago, almost like it never happened. Once more, he despaired, believing he would never be able to leave this hidden home for felons.

Now Kyle, looking up at Hannah, added his voice to hers. They sang like they were two experts in loneliness who knew their rescue ship had sailed, watching it disappear over the horizon, knowing that the ship wasn't ever coming back. Their vulnerability and honesty added new dimensions to the words and their performance touched Marco deeply. The crowd was rapt and stone silent. Gommeux and Cassandra danced slowly in each other's arms by the bar.

Marco felt a connection to Kyle and Hannah. *I could watch her sing forever.* He desperately hoped the three of them might become friends, a friendship as true and deep and genuine as their portrayal of the song. *I'll take this moment, even if that's all there is.* He was just glad he met them, and glad he had experienced this deep, shared moment with the audience. *Maybe I'll hear Hannah sing again one day.* Marco felt profound relief at finally having a positive and intimate social interaction at Hidden Paradise. *Maybe there is a ray of sunshine here at devil's cove.*

When Kyle and Hannah got back to their seats, the crowd started going home, but not before many of them came over to the table to congratulate the two musicians. While several people were still around the table, Marco saw 60-ish Nicolo Barare come up to Hannah to add his praise. He put a hairy hand on her right shoulder and leaned down to talk to her up close. Marco sensed a person standing very close next to him and looked up. It was Mysti Barare, the woman in the pool, stunning in shorts and a tight top that left nothing to the imagination. Marco guessed she was 30 years younger than the dangerous old goat she was married to.

Mysti smiled beckoningly, leaving no doubt about her intentions, and whispered, "How about a private lesson sometime, or a game? I bet I could really make you sweat." She licked her top lip once.

Alarm bells went off for Marco, remembering Shepp's warning not to socialize with wives of criminals.

"Uh. No. I'm just going to be doing the group lesson. No private lessons or games. Come next week to the group lesson. I look forward to it."

Mysti surreptitiously rubbed her foot once down Marco's calf under the table. She put on a fake, exaggerated, sad and pouty look that probably got her what she wanted from men only about 98% of the time.

Marco was worried. No question about it, Mysti was trouble.

Chapter 29

As time moved on, all days became the same with little variation in his routine, and often Marco forgot what day it was. He faded in and out of a mild depression over his confinement at Hidden Paradise. He lamented to Rei at times and listened to Rei's words of encouragement. But, nothing helped him come to terms with his incarcerated state. Marco was in a place with no light at the end of his tunnel.

His inner voice tried to convince himself how beautiful and well-kept the condominium area was, how magnificent the nature preserve was, and how lucky he was to have a situation that was so easy for him to live without punching a time clock. That rationalizing inner voice told him that this was the best thing he could be doing right now, that nothing in life is really permanent, and anything was possible. He imagined himself being content with his situation. *It is as it is, right now, nothing is forever,* he told himself. *Enjoy the pleasures of the breeze, the garden rooftop and his friendship with Rei. That's better than being in New York with the goons and thieves.* He portrayed his life as being a rich and wondrous circumstance that worked well... until reality crashed in on him.

His blissful imagining came with the stark loneliness that stood like a stone on the beach, solitary and defined. Gone was the complex fabric of the city and the culture that grew along the matrix of its structure. There was no escape from himself here in this Hidden Paradise. Marco often sat staring, sinking deeper into his own despair, thinking, *I have no distractions to immerse myself in, no possibilities to engage in a hopeful future, nothing to look forward to. It's like I'm brilliantly alive, in the land of nothingness.*

All he had here was sporadic repair work and a series of little tasks to complete daily. His options were miserably slim. He could ride the bike he found around the small peripheral road, go into town with Rei, take a walk up to the swamp and observe nature. He could have conversations with aging criminals and eccentric sociopaths, he could try to create a gig that would earn him money, but to what end? He couldn't spend money except to buy stuff on the internet. He was in a loop, an endless opportunity to fill his life with objects of little value, and baubles to calm him for a few moments.

Marco found himself fluctuating between the listlessness that encourages the urge to drink, drug, sex or spend money; the daily addictions that never feed the soul. But, Marco knew there was more to life and he did not want to be a degenerate or a criminal. His stubborn goal was finding something worthwhile to do, in life. Something that would lift him and the world, from the doldrums of his own exhausted spirit. He was tired and he missed his friends, he missed his life.

Bright and early one morning, four months after arriving at Hidden Paradise, Marco headed to Marie's just in time to miss the morning rush. He needed to be alone with Marie. Romeo was there briefly, standing behind her, sniffing her neck as was his habit. Marco greeted them both and was happy to see Romeo leave within a minute.

"Don't you miss the city, aunt Marie?"

"I'm tired today Marco." It was a rare moment of stopping work. "Romeo kept me awake last night. I just want to go home. I need to lay down all alone, or sit by the pool for a while before the lunch crowd comes." She let out a sigh, then turned her attention back to her tea, and blew some air over the tea cup to cool it.

"Enough about me. How are you doing, sonny?" She patted Marco's hand, an unusual gesture of affection that had not occurred for a long while.

"I miss the freedom of movement. I need to go somewhere and have some fun. You know what I mean Aunt Marie. It's incredibly confining in this lousy place." Marco made himself laugh, which seemed to be enough for him.

"Shush your mouth Marco, don't talk about those things.

People don't talk about the obvious here. It hurts too much. It's better to pretend nothing's really wrong, and everything is just how it appears on the surface."

Marie paused and said kindly, "You play it close sonny, you keep your eyes open, your heart open and nothing else. Keep your distance, listen to your gut always. That's all I gotta say. You hear me?"

"I do aunt Marie, I hear you. Thank You. Who knew we'd be in a place like this." Marco paused. "I'm afraid I might go crazy if I can't get out."

Marie nodded with understanding. "It was the same for me at first. I'm much older now, I don't care about wandering around. I have a simple life now. A good night's sleep, mostly, a few TV shows, a movie, always good food, a job, a boyfriend. I have all I could want. I don't care about restaurants or museums. And people? They're overrated. Most people don't really care about you. I gave up that idea a long time ago." She shook her head and let out another sigh.

"How are you doing with Romeo? He left almost as soon as I got here. He nodded at me, no conversation, nothing. Is he okay?" Marco sipped his first coffee of the day. The hot bitter drip at the back of his throat went a long way to wake him up.

"He's not what you think, Marco. You know how it is. Everyone was someone different before they are who they are now. I still don't know who he once was. He won't tell me. But, he fools around." She put her tea down and looked directly into Marco's eyes. He sat back in his chair, shocked and worried.

"I'm upset. I thought it was perfect. I was at peace with him, but now I feel upset. I thought I was his one and only. I know, I know, it's a romantic thing or maybe a true love thing. I want someone just for myself. Then I find out he's in this group from town. They mess around, wives and husbands, girlfriends, boyfriends. It's not for me Marco, I'm old school." She looked down, disappointed.

"I'm sorry, aunt Marie, I had no idea he did that kind of stuff."

"And the way he's always behind me and all night long with the sniffing and the locket. It's getting to me Marco. But, I don't know if I can just let him go. He's so good to me and he makes me happy in so many ways." She looked out the window wistfully as she finished her sentence.

"I'm sorry, I wish there was something I could do. I guess I can just listen." Marco reached across the table and put his hand on top of hers.

"There's nothing to do Marco. He wants me to go with him to this group thing. I just don't want to. I want true love. A man that wants me for me. I don't want to be a *trading piece* in a club to be shared with other men, or women. That's just not for me." Her mouth was down-turned and Marco saw tears on her cheek.

"It's gonna be alright auntie Marie." He held both her hands and squeezed them. He felt like a parent comforting a child. He wanted to hug her like he did when he was young.

"I can't look into his eyes anymore. But, I don't want him to go away from me." Her face twisted with pain and she sobbed.

Marco got up and went to her side. "This hurts, I know. It's none of my business, but I think you have to end it." She stood and allowed him to give her a hug. She sobbed in his arms and in a moment her tears subsided.

"I should start getting ready for the lunch crowd, or maybe I'll just put up the closed sign and go home for the rest of the day. I don't know. But, you gotta try this new pastry Marco," she said, switching subjects. "I'll get it for you sonny. I'm so happy you stopped by to see me, your timing was perfect."

Perfect for both of us, Marco thought. He needed his aunt's familial closeness.

With new energy she went to her case and brought out a cinnamon bun with cardamom, lightly sweetened and crisp. It was a cross between brioche and croissant dough. Marco never tasted anything like it.

"This is great Marie," he said, stuffing his mouth.

"Hey, if you really want to get away from here and go into

town sometime, go talk to the butcher. He goes everywhere. He gets around. He lives in town. Big family. He's one of the few who has real freedom. If you go with him maybe you won't feel so stuck, maybe you'll appreciate being here a little better." Aunt Marie smiled at him in the most loving way. All the tension from their past disagreements dissipated as they were there for each other now in challenging times. Once again, they were *familia*.

Chapter 30

Marco left the bakery and passed the butcher shop his aunt had talked about. Through the window he saw a man wielding a cleaver. His rhythmic hacking could be heard beyond the quiet mall.

This could be my ticket out of Paradise, Marco thought. *And I'm ready for some real paradise, freedom. In fact, I'm ready for anything other than here.*

As Marco stood there thinking, Leeray Bruce strolled outside his shop to sit on a bench. He was burly and powerful looking, about 6'4," with massive arms he grew from lifting sides of beef his whole life. Leeray was one of the only townies who worked in Hidden Paradise. He was not a part of the witness protection program, and he had no criminal record. He was clean as a whistle.

Leeray Bruce seemed to be the exception to the Hidden Paradise rule of no outsiders allowed in without intense scrutiny. Even the maids, specialty companions, and health care personnel, went through informal, but thorough scrutiny. But not the butcher. He had a special deal.

Leeray charged high prices for his unique specialty meats and sausage. They were the rage of the sequestered populace. He charged high prices and got away with it, because he could, and because of who his boss was. He'd go to the local supermarket in town, buy the meat and double the price. Leeray was a hamburger craftsman. He'd get the cheap meat, add cuts of better quality meat and increase the fat content using smoked fatback. This created a highly addictive combination, and a combo the condo crowd seemed to love.

When asked what was in the burger meat, Leeray would decline the question and answer, "A special mixture. All good but I can't tell a soul, if I did, I'd have to kill ya. HA HA, enjoy it," he'd laugh.

Marco didn't know any of the above before walking over

to Leeray's bench. With all the charm he could conjure, Marco approached Leeray.

"Hello, I'm Marco. My aunt is Marie from the bakery. You must be Leeray, Leeray Bruce?

Leeray nodded, half smiling.

"Mind if I sit with you?" said Marco.

"Not at all, if you don't mind the cigar."

Marco recognized the twig-like cigar Leeray held. It was the traditional cigar of the old timers. The aroma was harsh and it tended to turn the lips brown. It was a Parodi cigar.

"Your cigar reminds me of my childhood, that rich smell," he started the conversation, "my grandfather smoked them. He used to send me to the store up the street to get a box of his Parodi's. That and a pint of whiskey. We'd sit in the backyard by the tomatoes, hiding from my grandmother who wanted desperately for him to stop smoking. He always tried to keep it a secret, but she knew it, you can't hide that smell, except to the smoker, they can't smell their own smoke. Weird right?"

"I know what you mean. My wife, she doesn't care. After ten kids, what does she care about? Nothing at this point? Maybe money, I don't know. I don't know my wife anymore. Sometimes, I sleep in the back of the shop so I don't have to go home. My youngest is seven, a real hell raiser. My wife wants me to come home, but it's just too much, you know?" Marco nodded as he listened.

"I can't do anything to this kid. He's so smart. Even in school. He gets good grades for a seven year old. My other kids are all working. Nobody wants to be a butcher these days. It's all about the fake meat and the gluten free and the algae. The world's coming to an end. That's all you hear on the news."

"Yeah, I know. I can't listen to the news anymore," Marco responded. "I don't know what to believe and what not to believe. I don't know who to believe." He paused.

Leeray waited for Marco to continue. "All the biased, corporate messages being created and narrated to confuse and manipulate the people. And on the surface, everything looks so normal."

Marco wondered if he was chattering too much. *The hell with it*. He took a deep breath and continued.

"It's a strange world everywhere these days. I'm hoping somewhere, out there, there's some logic to all this madness. But I'm not buying it anymore." Marco paused. "I know, it's toxic. But hey, maybe the world is coming to an end. The government just declassified all the UFO reports. The outer space people could be real."

Leeray looked at Marco like an indulgent parent listening to a two year old chattering baby talk nonsense. He took a puff, shook his head, and chuckled to himself in a lopsided manner out of one side of his mouth, showing a couple of teeth, a combination smirk and deep guttural 'heh, heh, heh.' Then he paused for a minute, looking away. After a while he looked at Marco.

"I like you kid, you got a good head on your shoulders. Sounds like a pretty decent heart too."

"I came down to help my aunt Marie at the bakery but that didn't work out. Now I clean the pool and do odd jobs with Rei."

"Yeah I know. You don't have to tell me. I've heard about you. Marie is a good friend. She sure knows how to bake. I sometimes bring Marie's pastries to my wife and kids, but not too much."

Leeray chuckled in his lopsided manner again, and flicked the dark ash.

"So you like it here?" asked Leeray.

"I think it's pretty and I set up a rooftop garden, up there." He pointed to the condo. "Nobody has access but me and Rei. We work the garden together," Marco confided.

Leeray nodded. "Rei. The main guys here don't like him. They find him hard to look at. It hurts their vanity. Assholes!"

Marco was beginning to like this guy. The more he spoke the more their sentiments flowed together.

"Well to tell you the truth, Leeray, I'm not used to being here,

I can't seem to settle in. I get anxious. I just want to get out and check out the area, ride into town, go out on a boat, be free. I got major ants in my pants."

"Have a cigar," Leeray flipped the pack open and one came out farther than all the others. Marco took it. He hadn't smoked since his teen years and then only cigarettes for a short few months. It made him nauseous and it made his clothes smell terrible. But cigars, that was grandpa territory. He loved the lingering smell on his grandfather. It brought back rich, sweet memories.

Marco grabbed the cigar and lit up. Immediately, he felt relaxed.

"This is alright. I just went from major jitterbug to chill. And I didn't even inhale."

Leeray cleared his throat, "Don't get hooked on 'em. I started early. It helped me settle down, but now I gotta have one every two, three hours at least."

"I'll take your word for it," Marco said.

"Come hang out here some time if you don't feel like going home."

Marco, feeling safe with Leeray, reached out. "Maybe you can come up to the rooftop sometime, it's a great place to hang out. The garden's up there, growing greens. We have cool lights, a grill, and a super sweet view." Marco painted the picture.

"Sounds great, Marco, maybe I will sometime. How 'bout you come with me to town, tomorrow? I have errands, you know? I'll show you around, have some lunch, you can help me load up the truck. What'd ya think? It'll be good for you to leave paradise and have a little fun."

Marco laughed. "Leave paradise to have a little fun. I'm ready for some of that."

Leeray chuckled once more. "Maybe you can meet the kids and wife?"

"That would be great."

Leeray looked at his watch.

"Time to put up the smoker. I'll see you tomorrow, let's say around eleven?"

"I'll be here. Thanks Leeray." Marco walked away with the cigar smoldering between his lips. The smell of his grandfather comforted his agitated nervous system. He turned to wave to Leeray and saw him throwing what looked like meat over the chain link fence. *How curious*, Marco thought.

By the time he got to the pool to do his chores, the cigar had made him dizzy and the thick tarry substance on his lips was bitter and caustic. He spit repeatedly and drank copious cups of water before he began to capture the day's debris with his net from the pool.

As he swung the net through the aqua pool he thought how exciting it would be to get out of Paradise, even for a few hours.

Chapter 31

"We're officially out of Hidden Paradise" Leeray announced as they crossed the old railroad tie bridge. "We should have lunch first, you know? There's this great place. You're gonna love it."

"I'm all in, Marco replied, feeling a bit distracted by the sounds of the empty meat hooks banging and rattling as they bounced off the insides of the freezer van. *Leeray doesn't seem to notice the loud clanging sounds coming from his van.* Marco thought.

"I'm glad we could get away," Leeray said, interrupting Marco's flow of thoughts. "I need to play hookie from time to time. It's good for us, right?" The steering wheel looked like a child's toy in his massive hands.

"Sure. Thanks for inviting me," Marco responded as he was seeing the outside world for only the fourth time since he had arrived.

Five miles later, they were driving through a run down, mixed neighborhood of light industrial warehouses and ramshackle homes on the outskirts of Bonny Shores. It was 90 degrees, and the blazing Florida sun had driven everyone indoors. The van had no air conditioning. Even with the windows wide open, the smell of old meat and blood was unbearable.

"You like Korean food?" asked Leeray.

"Sure."

"Oh boy, do I have a treat for you, Marco. They have bulgogi that will melt in your mouth. The mandoo dumplings and the chap chae noodles are…"

Stopping in the middle of his sentence, Leeray looked out the window, still driving. Marco became a little concerned.

"No, It couldn't be…." Leeray poked his head out the window and looked back down the street. There was a tall, muscular Hispanic looking man carrying a shoulder bag. He was on the opposite side of the street walking next to a deserted warehouse.

The man was unaware he had been seen.

"Oh yeah. Oh Damn. It's him alright. It's him."

At that moment, Leeray became someone else altogether. He took the next left, sped up like a madman, took another quick left, then accelerated and jolted down an unpaved alley with deep potholes full of last night's rain.

"Oh no," said Leeray, shaking his head, looking extremely agitated. "He's not getting away this time."

He took another left and parked. Jumping out of the car, Leeray ran to the end of the street, flattened himself against the building, and waited to ambush the man.

When the man came into view, Leeray darted out and sucker punched him on the side of his head. It was a punch so hard it would have knocked out a steer. As the man started falling, Leeray grabbed his shirt collar, calmly and efficiently smashed a second sledgehammer blow to the other side of the man's head. The man crumpled to the ground and lay dead still.

Oh my God, thought Marco. He watched Leeray take the shoulder bag, calmly empty the man's pockets into his own pockets, and walk casually back to the car. *Oh no, I'm an accessory to aggravated assault and robbery. Or maybe murder. Oh God, no. Please, why me?*

Leeray got into the car without looking at Marco and started driving away, staring straight ahead.

"Yes!" he said to nobody. "It's payday! Oh man, it's payday! Yes! Yes, Yes!"

He was breathing heavily, staring straight ahead.

Marco couldn't move. He looked at Leeray only out of the corner of his eyes. He had no idea what would happen next. Leeray was agitated, and drove in a complicated pattern through back streets. Finally slowing on a deserted road next to a row of long abandoned houses where the sound of insects was overwhelmingly loud.

Leeray parked the van under a massive oak tree. He continued breathing heavily. His heavy brow and frown gave him a frightening look.

He was not looking at Marco when he said. "I didn't mean for you to see that. That wasn't the plan for today."

They sat for a few minutes, each breathing heavily.

"I'm a good man. I'm a good man," Leeray said after a long silence. His words seemed not to be directed to Marco. It felt like an attempt to convince himself. All the time he continued looking straight ahead.

"I'm a good man. I'm good. Oh no, oh no, I am a good man."

They sat there for minutes as Leeray mumbled to himself, each of them staring ahead. The cooling engine tick ticked away, the sound of insects droned their static. The sweat began to pour off Marco from the stress of the moment and the intense heat of the day. The added smell of meat scraps and blood from the back of the truck was unbearable.

Leeray turned towards Marco. "I'm a good man." He looked anguished.

Marco nodded slightly.

"I'm sorry you saw that. I had no choice. I had no choice."

Marco nodded again.

They sat there for a while longer, then Leeray turned towards Marco, put a massive arm on the back of Marco's seat and said, "You can't ever tell anyone what you saw."

"I won't ever tell anyone." Marco spoke sincerely, he knew his life depended on it.

"I'm serious. You have to keep your mouth shut. If you ever tell anyone what you saw–I swear to God–the man I work for back at Hidden Paradise will make me feed your balls to the gators –while you watch. And if I refuse, he will do it to both of us." He nodded. "I swear to God, that's the honest to God truth."

"I won't ever tell anyone."

Leeray took his arm off Marco's seat, and sat back heavily. He kept quiet for a minute. Marco wasn't sure if his answer was sufficient. Leeray seemed lost in his own thoughts.

"I had no choice. No choice whatsoever. I have 11 other

mouths to feed in my family. Do you know how much a butcher makes in Florida? Before I came to Hidden Paradise, I made 10 bucks an hour, maybe 12. That's it! You think I could support a family on that?"

Leeray pointed a finger at Marco. "You think I'm making a living selling meat from a tiny shop to the old people at Hidden Paradise?"

He looked at Marco as if Marco was a blathering idiot.

"They don't eat that much meat, those old people. They would each have to eat 20 pounds of meat a week for me to get by. Even though I overcharge 'em. They still don't want to pay, but they have no choice, do they?"

He lowered his voice to a near whisper.

"Do you think anyone operating any shop at Hidden Paradise is making an honest living from what they sell?" He shook his head. "No way. They're all subsidized criminal enterprises. Mine, your aunt's bakery, all of 'em."

He shook his massive head.

"I do what I have to do. Before I came to Hidden Paradise, my wife was about to leave me, the rent was always overdue. I had no credit, open hungry mouths to feed. I had no choice. I was given an opportunity by a bad man. I was desperate. I took it. I had to. Now my family eats. We have a house. I can pay the mortgage."

"I get it," said Marco, trying to get on Leeray's good side. It had the opposite effect. Leeray put his arm back on Marco's seat.

"You get it? You? You? I've worked hard for low wages my entire life. Heavy work. Hard work. Always, since I was 13 years old. I never went to high school. And you?" He paused. "College Boy."

Leeray was becoming unglued, going off on a savage tangent. Marco was afraid.

Leeray started breathing heavily again. "What do you know about work, college boy? What do you know about anything? What do you do for a living? Tennis teacher?" Spitting the words, as if being a tennis teacher was synonymous with being a child molester. "Tennis teacher." He shook his head in disgust, and sat back in his own seat.

In his growing terror, Marco flashed on an absurd and macabre thought, one that forced him to stifle an erupting nervous giggle: *I might get beaten to death today by a crazy redneck, simply because I pose the risk that one day, I might give that redneck's beloved children tennis lessons.* He bit his bottom lip and kept it together.

They sat there in silence for several minutes. Leeray seemed unfocused, lost in his thoughts. Marco knew he couldn't open the door and run. He could only hope that Leeray's emotional crisis would run its course.

"Do you believe in God, Marco?"

Oh no, thought Marco, realizing things could get worse, if Leeray were to add an existential religious crisis on top of his disintegrating mental state. Not helpful.

"Do you believe in God?" he repeated.

What is the safe answer? Leeray probably believes in God.

"Yeah. I suppose I do."

"Good."

Whew.

"Do you believe in God, Leeray?"

"Absolutely I believe in God." Leeray paused, as if considering whether to continue talking, but then he said, "At one time, before I came to Hidden Paradise, I knew in my heart that Jesus Christ was truly my Lord and Saviour. I went to church with my family every Sunday. I believed in Jesus. He was my salvation. I was convinced and gladdened. Not any more though. The family still goes to church. I don't." He looked very sad.

"I'm sorry," said Marco. "That sounds awful."

Leeray sat still, looking straight ahead. He sighed a long, heavy despairing sigh. "Do you believe in hell, Marco?"

Uh oh. Not good. Marco hesitated "I never really thought about it."

"I do. I believe in hell. I really do. I believe in hell because I cannot believe in a God that would give me salvation for what I've done. That would not be justice. I have done terrible things since I came to Hidden Paradise, all to serve my family. Worse than what you just saw."

Leeray lowered his voice to a whisper.

"Marco, I'm going to hell. I know it. I'm going to hell."

Leeray started crying. His enormous face contorted with sorrow.

"I'm going to hell. I won't see my beautiful children."

He recovered his composure after a couple of long minutes. He wiped his eyes with his hands, and calmly said, "I will be in hell, and you know who will be there with me for eternity? My God damned boss. Him and me, in hell."

More time passed. Marco wondered when it was going to be over.

"We're pals, right Marco?"

"Yes, we're pals."

"Pals stick together, right?"

"Pals stick together, absolutely. I'm your pal."

"I watch your back, you watch mine."

"I'll watch your back, Leeray. You can count on it."

Leeray sighed. He seemed relieved. He took out his Parodi cigars.

"Smoke?"

Marco really didn't want to, but he didn't want to jeopardize his new status as a pal, not when he was so close to surviving.

"Sure." They lit up. When Marco took his first puff, he knew he would never associate cigar smoke with the smell of his gentle old grandfather. It would always take him back to this day, watching Leeray calmly plant two devastating punches, dropping his boss's enemy into a heap on the ground.

"I need to get back to Hidden Paradise," Leeray announced, starting the van, "I have some things to deliver, and I have to collect a very large sum of money."

As they neared Hidden Paradise, Leeray continued, "You'll

have to come out to my house for Sunday dinner sometime, meet my wife. My kids are great. Well, some of them are at least." He chuckled to himself, and smiled broadly, remembering an event from his parenthood.

"Kids are great. I love 'em. I really love 'em. They're so innocent and smart. They're the best thing that's ever happened to me."

Chapter 32

Replays of the day were crackling through his mind like massive lightning storms. It was after 10pm as Marco paced back and forth the length of the pool, skimming the top, lost in the disturbing memories of his trip to town with Leeray Bruce. Leeray's disintegrating mental state, and him driving like a crazy man careening through the potholed alley had been terrifying. Seeing him commit mayhem, and coming so close to getting beaten to death himself, was too much to process.

Somehow he had survived another insane day here.

Marco turned his focus to completing his pool chores as quickly as possible so he could finally escape the day by lying down and going far away in his head. Just as his pool chores were complete, a skinny old man, wearing baggy shorts, orthopedic shoes and a plain blue tee slowly pushed his walker over to Marco. He was having trouble breathing, and gasped with every slow step.

"Hello Marco," he gasped.

Marco was certain he had never seen this man before. Everyone seemed to know Marco, but Marco didn't really want to know most of them. He stopped skimming the pool, and acknowledged his new paradise visitor. *What now?* he thought. *What next?*

"I'm Johnny O'Meara," the old man said, holding out his hand. The handshake was dry, bony and weak. Marco detected a very strong Boston accent.

"Pleased to meet you Johnny. I'm Marco. You okay?"

Breathing rapidly and shallow, like a fish out of water, Johnny took a handkerchief out of his back pocket and wiped his forehead. He looked unwell, but his eyes were bright, crafty, cruel and intelligent as he carefully examined Marco.

"Jesus. I can't do anything anymore," said O'Meara. "Coming down the elevator to find you felt like running a marathon to the top of Mt. Everest. Don't ever get old, kid."

After all of his uncomfortable encounters, Marco believed it unlikely that he would ever get to middle age, let alone old. *So what's this guy's angle?* By now he knew most everyone had an agenda, no one here did anything out of the goodness of their heart -- most didn't seem to have a heart, or a conscience.

"I need a favor, Marco."

"Of course," *you do*, Marco nodded non-committedly saying only the first part out loud.

"A very important person around here needs some emergency help. I understand you have a certain skill that could help him out."

Gasp…. alarm bells sounded immediately for Marco.

"This is a big favor, Marco. It's the type of favor, that if you do it, you will be owed a very big favor in return. Very big. I'm talking about getting an Aladdin's lamp type of wish. I promise you, this is the truth. This guy is big. You might even say he runs this place."

The thought of asking for freedom to leave Hidden Paradise was the first and only thought, in Marco's mind.

"Why me?"

"It's the skill you have. Marie told me that you know how to scuba dive. Is that correct?"

Marco groaned inwardly. *What was Marie getting me involved in now? Doesn't she have the slightest interest in protecting me from these criminals? First, she sends me to hang out with a butcher, aka, the reluctant hit man Leeray Bruce, who beat a man half to death in front of me. Now what? Is she signing me up to rescue some guido with cement in his shoes at the bottom of the bay?* Nevertheless, it was true. Marco had his scuba certification and enjoyed the sport as a hobby, but he was hardly an expert.

"I'm a diver, but just for fun, and not too deep."

O'Meara looked directly into Marco's eyes, "How about 45 feet?"

"That's not too deep." Marco confirmed

"Good. What's happening is that someone made a big mistake, and we need a second diver. We need someone we can trust to keep his mouth shut for a two man salvage operation. It shouldn't take too long. I think you could be back here in 2-3 hours tops."

This had to be something highly illegal, but at least it didn't seem like he'd be retrieving a dead body. *What am I getting into now?* Marco thought.

"I have no equipment," Marco blurted, hoping that would remove him from consideration.

"No problem. The other diver will be the leader for this operation. He knows what to do. He's a pro. He'll bring your equipment. All you have to do is follow his instructions."

Marco felt trapped, once again by the imminent possibility of prison or death. *This is the final blow*, he said to himself, feeling both dread and depressed resignation.

Yet, the possibility of a favor was tantalizing. He needed a break. *What the hell, I'm probably going to die here anyway, so why not? What the heck, life is a cabaret and this could be my final performance, diving deep for the mob!*

"Okay Johnny, I'll do it. I'll dive if the big boss really needs me."

O'Meara checked his watch, "Be down at the marina at 1:30am."

"A night dive?" Marco had completed only a handful of night dives, and only on shallow coral reefs with trusted friends. *I'm gonna die.* He was certain he was being involved in big league crime in which most people were expendable, upon completion of their 'job'.

"That's right," said O'Meara. "Don't worry. You'll be fine. Remember, a very important person will not forget that you did this. I promise."

What's a promise worth to a geezer who looks like he's about to keel over any second? Marco thought, as O'Meara slowly hobbled away.

Chapter 33

It was 1:30am, no lights, no moon. Standing alone on the dock, Marco heard a boat quietly moving up the canal. It pulled up and Marco climbed aboard. He could barely see.

"Hi. I'm Tran."

"Hey. I'm Marco."

"This is my sister, Minh," pointing at the young woman wearing a hoodie, driving the boat. She turned briefly towards Marco, without smiling, and continued steering the boat towards the Gulf.

Tran opened the large locker under a bench seat and started pulling out equipment.

"Let's suit up."

Marco's wet suit fit tightly. He checked over the face mask, air regulator and scuba tank. *Seems to be in good working order. But who knows,* Marco considered dreadfully.

"At 45 feet we'll need 20 minutes to safely decompress on our way up. I am setting my timer for 50 possible minutes of searching followed by 20 minutes of slow time coming up so we don't get the bends."

The decompression time sounded correct to Marco.

"If we don't find what we are looking for tonight, we come back tomorrow." Tran pulled two telescoping metal poles out. "These poles reach about 10 feet. The search area will be lit up by a big light from the other boat. We'll stay 20 feet apart and sweep with the poles."

"What are we looking for?"

"A big metal case, about 6x3x3. It is brown colored. It could be hidden in the silt. That's what the poles are for. We'll search the area they light up. When we finish one area, they'll move the lights."

In the pitch black, with no running lights, the three motored slowly up the coast. After about 30 minutes, Minh took a powerful flashlight out and gave a signal of three short flashes of light, followed by two long flashes. From the far distance came an answering signal of three long flashes followed by two short. When the lights stopped, it was black night once more.

"There they are," Tran announced, putting on his face mask. *Who are they?* Trying not to alarm himself by thinking of the horrible possibilities that could await him underwater, Marco put on tanks and flippers, and adjusted his weight belt. Sitting on edge, he was ready to dive or die.

As the other boat pulled alongside, words were spoken, but not in English. Marco had no clue. The other boat turned on lights and Marco saw a boat of Vietnamese men. Two were carrying automatic rifles. Their fishing boat was much larger than the one Marco was in. Minh tossed over an anchor. The men on the other boat hung a powerful light in the water, dimly illuminating the sandy bottom.

The men seemed to be angry at one man, yelling at him as he kept repeating the same words, which Marco couldn't understand.

"It's down below. I'm certain," one man on the other boat kept repeating. A man standing over him, gave him a shove. *For his sake, I hope he's right. These men are not playing around.* They were angry and intense. Marco knew not to ask for details.

Just before Marco and Tran went into the water, Marco's terror peaked: *what if we attract sharks with that damned light, we're dead. WTF, I'm a dead man regardless.* Marco was sure his life was over, and down into the deep blackness he went.

Tran carefully watched Marco as they sank down, looking for signs of panic. When they reached the bottom, they immediately began searching, sweeping their poles out front and side to side, trying to find the missing metal case. They reached the end of the lit area and waited while the fishing boat moved the search light.

After only 10 minutes of searching, Marco found the case. His metal pole touched it and he gestured to Tran who swam over to confirm it. Tran pulled on the signal rope, and a heavy cable appeared to hook onto. Another tug and the case rose quickly to the surface. The underwater lights went out. All they had now was their head lamps in the blackness. The fishing boat started its motors and quickly drove away into deep Gulf waters.

After a minute, it was quiet. *Don't freak out* Marco thought. *That's how divers die. Freaking out is not an option, it really messes with the breathing.* Now Marco was trying not to think of sharks.

Reaching the dive boat's anchor rope, they both held still at the first decompression stop, checking the ascent timer and depth gauge. Stopping three more times on the way up, they reached the dive boat in about 20 minutes.

"Hurry. Get out of your suits," Minh said. As the boat headed home, this time with running lights, Marco was chilled by the wind on his wet skin. Tran and Minh said nothing to him. Once back to the canal of Hidden Paradise, Minh turned off the outboard and the running lights, and switched on a tiny electric motor. They ghosted quietly up to the marina. At the dock, Marco hopped out quickly, grateful to be alive. The boat turned and headed back into the black night towards Boat Camp.

The night was still and quiet except for the humming symphonies of insects. Marco glanced at his watch, it was 3:30am. *Another freaking bizarre day in paradise...and I survived it. Better get some sleep*, he thought, *my group tennis lesson is later today.* Marco headed for his apartment.

Chapter 34

The next day, Marco sat outside the Bakery eating a muffin and sipping tea. It had been a harrowing couple of days. The sunny bench was a great place to get the benefits of the wind off the water. He was surfing the web on his cell phone when he heard the familiar voice of D'angelo Brown.

"Say, is this seat taken?" He spoke in his usual charming tone like a song sung acapella to a child.

"I hope you are doing well this fine day, Marco." D'angelo's lilt continued.

Marco smiled thinly. *Yeah right*, he thought, *I'm just fine. Yesterday I barely escaped getting beaten to death by a hit man suffering from religious delusions. Then, a few hours later, I was coerced to make a terrifying night dive to retrieve something obscure and important lying at the bottom of the ocean. Sure, I'm just fine. Off the frickin' charts, great, in fact.*

"What new project do you have to sell me today?" Marco asked.

"Oh, I'm not here to sell you anything, my friend. I just want to tell you about something I came across in my research that might be of interest to you."

Marco's soul shook its head. *Oh no, no and NO!* His head was speaking to him now, *not another product, not from this snake oil salesman.*

"What if there was a way you could work while you slept? Would that be an amazing ability?" D'angelo continued.

"You mean, for example, like sleepwalking while baking bread for my aunt? That would be a feat." Marco had a wary smile on his face.

"You know the best work is done when one is able to visualize success and efficiency, prior to actually doing the job. If you want to be a better tennis player, you would imagine hitting the ball perfectly over the net, every time. Next thing you know, you're better at whatever you're focused on. It's the practice of visualizing. It's nothing new, my friend, visualization has been practiced for eons, even by artists like me." D'angelo snickered."

"How does it work?" Marco inquired reluctantly.

"I have this device that guides your visions during the night. It's a timed speaker that infiltrates your dreams, to bring you great success."

"So... it's like an earbud that guides you, at night?"

"That's it! It's simple. It's programmable menu has a number of options: General success orientation is the main one. After that you can customize your tracks however you want. Let's say you want a new car. Well, this can be used to help you find a car you want. It sharpens your ability to manifest in the world. Do you follow me?"

"D'angelo, seriously, what are you smoking? This is Silicon Valley stuff. It's like the latest LSD thinking. Have you experienced this?"

"I've been programming my desires to achieve greater wealth, by creating inventions. If it can help me, Marco, maybe it can help all of us manifest our deepest desires in the world."

"I must say D'angelo, this is surprising, and kind of strange to see you interested in such a humanitarian goal. You actually care about the world? Hmm, okay, I've bitten your bait. How can I try it out?"

"Soon my friend, soon. I'm finishing the prototype with a bit more refinement. Like the earbud, it keeps coming out of my ear while I sleep. Maybe you can give me your feedback? I'll bring it to you. You give it a try then give me feedback."

"No lawsuits on this one?"

"No, it's all harmless."

"Okay, let me know when you can drop it by."

"I have a little bit of work yet to do, so it won't be right away."

"You don't actually have it, do you?"

"Well not quite. I'm in the visualizing stage at the moment.

I still need to buy a few more parts and well, they're a little costly so…"

"So you're looking for an investor, right?"

"Well yes, something like that. Know anybody who might find this ear-resistible? Haha."

Marco stood and smiled. It was hard to dislike the friendly, relentless huckster. "Haha. Thanks for sharing your 'earful concept'. I'd love to 'ear' more when you've built the prototype."

"So… I suppose you won't be investing in this one right now?" D'angelo asked.

"Not this time, my friend." With that, Marco smiled, turned and walked away.

Chapter 35

Back home, Marco stood staring into the mirror. I need to get out of these doldrums and I desperately need a shave. The last blade was too dull to use without me becoming a bloody mess. The only store on the mall that might have razor blades was a little hole in the wall. Everyone called it the Sundry store, a term likely from the 1940's.

The store was a collection of everything, from cigarettes to gift boxes of chocolate, to fingernail clippers, to foxy magazines and crossword puzzle books. It was a narrow store, only wide enough to hold two or three people at once, each being required to turn sideways as they passed on the one way isles. This store was awash with cultural jetsam from forgotten neighborhood candy stores.

On the right side, behind a glass case filled with random watches, outmoded electronic devices, transistor radios, chargers, and tiny cassette recorders, sat a 60ish man, Guy Marsh, whose pre-witness protection name was Edgar Tomin. Whenever anyone entered, he stood, extended to his full height of 6'8," and greeted the incoming shopper. This was Marsh's way of making contact with his customers and watching over his stock to make sure there was no pilferage. Marsh took great pleasure, guiding people around the store and gently intimidating them.

His aggressiveness was made emphatic by the shape of his face. It was as if it had been chiseled into a hatchet shape by time or a vise applied in infancy. He was like a hawk with his beady eyes. And, although he smiled constantly, underneath his twisted friendly demeanor was anger and socially adept manipulation.

Guy Marsh was a talker. He spoke all the time. There was no respite. It was never a conversation, solely a verbal patter. His probing banter was his way to find out what you might want him to do, to fix, to obtain for you. It was his way toward profit.

"Do you have a razor blade to fit this handle?" Marco held up the handle and Guy snatched it from his hand like a crow grabbing a peanut.

"This is not the best razor, you know that? It might be newer than most we have here, but it's not the best. Come with me." Nothing on the wall resembled what Marco needed.

"This is what you want." Marsh pulled a pack from the wall. It was a handle with ten blades with a price tag of thirty bucks. Marco thought he would spend six dollars for some blades and call it good.

"Your blade may be different from the one I have here, kid, but believe me it's the real deal. It's the best you can get and you won't be back here in a week looking for more blades, these blades last. I shave everyday, look at this," he turned his head and slid his hand along his cheek, "nice and smooth. Here, feel it, don't be shy, go ahead, kid."

"That's alright. It looks good. I'll take the one you have." Marco reluctantly agreed thinking *What choice do I have?*

"You're new here, right?" Marsh peered over Marco like a hawk viewing prey in a meadow. Their height difference was substantial. Marsh cocked his head to look at Marco out of one eye at a time, switching from one to the other every eight seconds or so. It was a nervous tic that he repeated throughout the visit. Guy Marsh was disconcerting, and alarming.

"Yeah. My aunt Marie runs the bakery. I came down to help her out, but that didn't work out. So, now I do odd jobs and clean the pool." Marco reached into his pocket and counted out more money than he wanted to spend.

"Well, I might need some help one of these days. Inventory day is coming up." Marco glanced around at this closet of a store, an eyesore for any shopper.

"Maybe you need other jobs done. I don't think inventory is my cup of tea but thanks for your kind offer." Marco felt claustrophobic and headed for the door.

"There's always plenty of errands to be done." Marsh cocked his head to the left and then to the right, alternately viewing Marco with each eyeball.

"You let me know." They shook hands.

"You know sometimes, young guys like you miss great opportunities, being in a hurry. Know what I mean kid?" His voice took an angry turn, "Keep your eyes open Marco. Don't dismiss doing inventory, it could take you up to the next level, to the next area of expertise."

Marsh's face became red as he spoke, "I don't like being brushed off, pal, you understand? I thought we could be friends, you know, one hand washes the other? But, you seem to be saying 'No' to that. Well, I got news for you, sonny, I had big plans for you. I could tell by the way you looked when you walked in." His twitchy side-eyed glances continued more rapidly now.

"I just want to get some blades and take a shave, Guy. Maybe we can meet up and have a cup of coffee at my aunt's place. We can talk about possibilities and options over Marie's delicious cake." Marco wanted out of the shop. It was closing in on him.

Marco nodded and backed out of the shop, smiling to placate Marsh.

"In a hurry pal? Busy day? What's the rush?" Marsh walked toward him as if he had a surprise knife behind his back.

"You're not working, you're just running off aren't you? That's the way of youth today, kid. You can only run so far and then it's time to come back. You'll be back, I can smell it on you. You'll be begging me for work before long." Marsh closed the distance between them speaking insistently, spitting out his words and ridiculous accusations.

"See you soon, Guy." Marco nodded, waved and turned, all in one swift gesture. His simple response was intended to neutralize Marsh's abrasive outpouring. He could feel Marsh's beady glare on his shoulders as he crossed the mall. He dared not turn to look.

Sure, I'll be back, I think we'll become best friends, Marco joked to himself shaking his head in disbelief, wondering what miserable events led him to Paradise.

Chapter 36

By the time he went to high school, Edgar Tomin, aka Guy Marsh, was 6'5". His father, a beer distributor in upstate New York urged him to join the basketball team with the hopes that his son Edgar, would get a scholarship for college.

Edgar was awkward, shy, and anxious. He could dunk the ball with ease which made two aggressive teammates very jealous of him. During team tryouts they deliberately played rough, running into him, stepping on his feet, and repeatedly elbowing him in the gut.

On one notable drive, the aggressive guard charged at him and at the last millisecond Edgar stepped aside allowing the youngster to throw himself with full force into the bleachers. A fractured wrist took him out of the running to make the team. He swore revenge on Edgar.

The other culprit, a taller boy with a strong physique, shoved and prodded Edgar with his shoulders and elbows continually. At one point, he knocked the breath out of Edgar who had to lean over for a minute to catch his breath. Once recovered and back into the flow of the game, Edgar moved away from the ball and the attention of the referee, and tripped the kid in such a way that it looked like an accident. The boy broke his elbow and was out of the team tryouts.

This event changed Edgar's life. He learned the power of his anger and would never be bullied again. The following day he found the two boys and held a sharpened butter knife to the throat of the larger boy, taunted him, and stabbed him in the throat.

"If you ever say anything about this, I'll kill your pet, then your parents. It's your call. I'll deny we met here today and I'll get away with it." Edgar threatened.

The terrified boys left without a word. Edgar never had a conversation with either of them again.

From that point forward, Edgar became a full time bully. He never paid for lunch throughout high school days. In college, he threatened the lives of his professors and their families for money. If the professors dismissed his threats, they found their car tires flattened and their flower beds torn apart. Not one had the courage to stop him.

Edgar extorted monthly payments from a closeted homosexual professor to keep quiet about the man's sexual orientation. In another incident he coerced his senior advisor to pay-up by killing the man's dog and threatening to abuse his wife and daughter.

Edgar had become a monster of a human and his dad had a great deal of influence in creating him that way.

Chapter 37

Edgar's aging dad had lugged beer for years. His distributorship was doing well and he wanted to sell it and retire. Edgar had worked for his dad every summer and spare weekend, since childhood. He spent no time away at college, instead he went to the local state college of New York nearby. He was a slave to a cruel and demanding father.

His mom had passed ten years earlier and his dad's ferocious brutality had continued to increase over the years. Every morning his father would take him aside, insult him, slap him hard across the face. This was his dad's way of making his son tough. Edgar knew it was ruthless sadism and anger that drove his father to continually strike and abuse him throughout his adulthood. Edgar's older brother lived in Manhattan·trading stocks, smart enough to keep away from their vile father.

When Edgar learned from their family doctor that his dad had been suffering from a form of progressive dementia for many years, it served as a partial explanation for his father's barbaric inhumane behavior. Before Edgar understood the depth of impact the diagnosis had, his father sold the business well below its value out from under Edgar, who would have inherited the business. Edgar had been a slave to the business most of his adult years.

His father's enfeebled mind miscalculated its value. This put Edgar over the edge. From that point on, Edgar used his anger as a bludgeon and punished his demented father every day.

Each day his father's condition worsened.

"Dad, see my hand?" His father numbly nodded, docile and unsuspecting. Edgar slapped him hard across the face repeatedly.

"You feel that? You piece of shit." Edgar slapped him hard repeatedly. His passive, helpless father sat feeling his red cheek, not remembering what he'd done and why he was being slapped.

Edgar was distant and angry. He never learned morals from

his father, so he had none. He took from the world and brutalized everyone. Inside he was seething. His father's dementia reached the point at which he would need full time help. One night in the wee dawn hours, Edgar smothered his father with a pillow.

With no prospects, Edgar created a lucrative business buying tax-free cigarettes in bulk from the local Native American tribe. He'd purchase and repackage them in counterfeit boxes using forged tax stamps. The profit was staggering.

His business went on for years before a local criminal syndicate wanted to "wet its beak" in the profits. Edgar had no choice but to play ball and do nothing as his profits were cut instantly.

One night, Edgar followed the syndicate lieutenant as he left his regular card game. As the man sat in his car, Edgar moved in and quickly slit his throat. Over the course of the next year, four members of the syndicate crew died mysteriously: an electrical home fire, a tragic auto accident, a toxic meal, an unexplained fall from a great height.

As the crew dwindled, Edgar was offered an insulting raise from fifteen to twenty percent of the take. It was too risky to murder the head of the syndicate, so Edgar made a call to the FBI. Within two weeks he gathered enough evidence for the agency to convict and put the remaining syndicate members away forever. Edgar made a deal and retired to Hidden Paradise with his new identity, Guy Marsh. However, Edgar's vicious anger and aggressive behavior remained intact.

Chapter 38

A few weeks had passed since Kyle Ross and Hannah LaVerre performed at Chez Roué. Marco decided it might be a good time to get his hair trimmed. In truth, he was intrigued by and attracted to lovely Hannah. He decided he'd try to get to know her. He picked up a bag of pastries for them from the bakery and headed over to the salon so he'd be the first hair appointment of the day. Kyle was washing a window, and Hannah was straightening things up around the single chair salon.

"Good morning my two favorite people of paradise," Marco said with as much perkiness as he could muster. "Got time for a quick haircut?"

Hannah looked at the clock.

"It'll have to be quick. I have a 10:30 perm and dye."

"I brought some pastries."

"Sorry. I don't eat those. I'd weigh 300 pounds if I ate those bombs."

"Kyle?" Marco motioned, holding out the bag.

"No thanks" Kyle said. "They're all white flour and sugar. Terribly unhealthy. There's nothing real in them. The older residents here love them. Can't blame Marie. She tried making healthier pastries, but I was the only one who would buy 'em, so she stopped."

"How about if I get us coffee?"

"We have an espresso machine here," Hannah motioned, "I'll make you one. I used to get coffee exclusively at Marie's. I won't go back there since she hired Romeo. He undresses me with his eyes whenever he sees me, openly, right in front of Marie's face. She does nothing. He licks his lips and fondles his locket. He thinks he's such a clever wit, but he's a disgusting old lecher. I can't stand being around him."

"The old people who go to the bakery seem to love him,"

Marco commented, trying to show another point of view.

"Yeah. But he doesn't act like a predator on the hunt with them."

"And don't forget... he's dangerous," Kyle chimed in.

"Super dangerous, if you believe what people say," Hannah continued.

"He does make a good pizza," said Kyle.

"Marie is lonely," Marco consoled.

"Ugh. If Romeo is the best she thinks she deserves, she has self esteem issues."

He sat in the salon chair, telling Hannah what he was looking for and she went right to work. The feel of her hands on his head, and the feel of her body when she leaned against him, made him realize that nobody had touched him tenderly since he'd become a resident at Hidden Paradise. He and Rei always gave each other a companionable hug, but it wasn't like this. This felt wonderful. He wanted to know more about her and about Kyle too.

"You have great hair. Kyle, look how naturally wavy and thick Marco's hair is." She ran her fingers slowly and sensually through Marco's hair and a shiver of pleasure rolled over him.

"Movie star hair, wouldn't you say?"

Kyle smiled, nodded, and went back to cleaning windows.

"So, tell me about yourself," Marco asked Hannah.

"I have a better idea. Kyle, why don't you tell Marco about yourself first. I'm using sharp scissors. I don't want to get distracted and cut off Marco's ear."

"Yes, let's avoid the ear cut," Marco smiled, always ready to play with words.

"I get it. I'm dying of laughter," said Hannah. "Now be quiet."

Kyle stopped cleaning the window. "First of all, of course I wasn't born Kyle Ross, I was born Paul Ketchum. Raised in Laguna Beach California. My father was a psychologist, and my mother was a dance teacher. I grew up surfing, partying and playing piano. I knew I was bisexual or gay from a young age, but hid it and chose my partners carefully."

Marco listened intently. Kyle had a couple of semesters at UC Irvine, but quit when he stupidly decided to go after big money, and wound up dealing massive amounts of cocaine and other drugs in partnership with some heavy hitting musician acquaintances. He himself had never gotten into it.

Their venture in drug dealing was unlucky from the start. He got busted in a sting operation and faced 20 years in Federal prison. He turned witness for the prosecution, and now lives full time at Hidden Paradise.

He was thankful not to be in prison. He knew he never would have survived it. And he was ashamed he had squandered his opportunities with his poor life choices. It hurt that some of the people he had turned in were friends.

His arrest and disappearance cut him off from his parents, whom he missed, especially his mother. He was 36 years old and had spent 12 long, lonely and depressed years in Florida witness protection. In the last year, Kyle finally pulled himself out of his long funk. He dedicated himself to eating healthy, keeping his body fit, and trying to live a good and decent life.

"And that's it," he said. "Before I met Hannah, who arrived a little more than a year ago, the only people I trusted were Shepp and Carol. My only comforts were music and reading. Now, with Hannah here, she became my one true friend and confidant."

Hannah finished the haircut right on cue. Marco got up and she told her story while she swept up his fallen hair.

Hannah LaVerre was 24 years old. She was not in witness protection. She grew up as an Air Force brat, living in one place just long enough to make a few friends before moving to the next military deployment. Both her parents served in the military until they divorced, when Hannah was eight and her brother was ten. After their divorce, both parents quit the military and her father disappeared. The rest of her childhood was spent living with her Mother and brother in the same rural area her mother was raised, outside of Moorhead, Minnesota.

They lived with Hannah's aunt and her family on 20 acres.

Hannah had a horse and a dog. She knew how to operate a tractor and farm machinery. She sang in the church choir, and dreamed of going to college to become an elementary school teacher. She worked her way all the way through her junior year of college at the University of Minnesota, living cheaply, and avoiding big student loans. In the summer, she worked at a resort in Hilton Head, South Carolina.

It was at the resort two summers ago that Hannah had the bad luck to run into Albert Fonseca, a guest who was staying at the resort. He was handsome, charming, and seemed to have unlimited money. He took an interest in Hannah who fell hard for him. He was her first real boyfriend. At his urging, she quit her steady job, and followed him to Hidden Paradise.

Two days after they arrived, things went bad. He became moody and possessive. His temper was volcanic. They fought. He hit her. In a chilling encounter on the day he left, a day she replayed over and over again in her mind, he calmly promised he would kill her slowly if he ever saw her again. She responded by calling him a coward, a liar and an insecure, weak man.

He got in his car and left with half his clothes. When Shepp found out, he told her the true stories about Albert "Sicko" Fonseca, the chainsaw torturer and hit man from Chicago. Shepp informed her that Hidden Paradise was actually a haven for witness protection criminals.

Hannah was devastated. She had taken a youthful detour, on a whim, away from her careful life plan and had gotten stuck in a dangerous place. She was stuck in Florida. Her options were bleak. She had no money, no family to help her, no job, and on top of that the semester of her final year at University of Minnesota, had already begun.

Shepp generously offered her free rent in Fonseca's old apartment. He promised that he would warn her if Fonseca came back. After talking to Carol, she opened the salon with the last of her money, met Kyle, and accepted his offer of a loan to complete the salon renovation. For the last year and a half, she had been trying to save enough to go back to college.

Over time, she gradually heard every bloody story and rumor about Sicko Fonseca, and once she knew the truth, she was absolutely terrified of him and his legendary psychopathic temper. Fortunately, there was no one at Hidden Paradise who wanted to see Sicko Fonseca return.

Hannah sat next to Kyle in the chairs for customers while she told the rest of her story. Looking at her lovely face, Marco felt an attraction like none he had ever felt before. He flashed a fantasy of Hannah and him. He saw Hannah and him here, there, everywhere, always. He admired her country girl toughness, her unselfconscious beauty, and her resilience.

"Why teaching?" he asked.

"Besides liking kids and being disappointed with most adults in general, I grew up poor." Hannah smiled. "The idea of a reliable job, with summers off, and a decent pension when I retire, has always been mighty attractive to me."

"Yeah, I get what you're saying. I've always enjoyed teaching but most teaching I've done has been sports related like, golf, tennis, swimming."

"I just want to do my small part in making the world a little bit better." Hannah continued. "I feel hope when I'm around unspoiled things, like children. They're like nature. I had that feeling with my horse when I was a kid. Animals are honest. You know, from the little I've seen I think you'd be a decent teacher, Marco."

Marco's heart skipped a beat. "Thanks. I've been thinking a lot about how important it is to make positive choices. Truth is, I've been drifting through life so far and this is where I washed up. Is this place what I deserve? God, I hope not. I think I'm done with drifting. I truly believe, more than ever now, that we're all responsible for creating our own happiness, and maybe creating a little happiness for others. Right now, I'm living a bittersweet life, mostly bitter, you know?" Looking down sadly, Marco got up to leave.

"I know what you're saying, I've had bitter experiences too,"

Hannah consoled. "A disorienting love fantasy landed me here. Sometimes, it seems that there may be no way out."

Kyle nodded his head in agreement. "Well I followed my nose and my greed into a foiled drug deal and here I am. Then I spent years reliving my mistakes over and over, until I wore myself out. I can't do it anymore. I say to hell with it. Dwelling on regrets is pointless. Life goes on. How about if we go out tonight to the restaurant and have some laughs?"

Hannah quickly agreed. "Good idea. Marco, why don't you come back here around 5?" she said, touching his arm lightly. An electric buzz of pleasure hit Marco. "The three of us can grab dinner at Chez Roué."

Marco could feel his heart beat escalating, he was falling for her hard.

Chapter 39

Arriving back at the salon a little before 5pm, Marco waited while Hannah and Kyle closed up shop. At that moment the phone rang and Hannah moved off to the side. Marco watched, as her face in a few seconds, went from happy to worried to panic. When she hung up, she looked ready to cry.

"Oh no. That was Shepp." She looked terrified. "He's coming back."

"Oh no!," said Kyle.

"He'll be here in an hour. What should I do?"

"Who?" asked Marco.

Hannah didn't answer. She looked like a deer cornered by a mountain lion.

"Fonseca's back, Hannah's ex," said Kyle. "We were hoping he'd stay away forever."

"It's his apartment," said Hannah. "Shepp says I have to move all my stuff out now, and I have to get to someplace safe."

Marco reacted to the desperation in her voice.

"My place. You can move to my place. I have an extra bedroom. Fonseca doesn't know me. He doesn't know I'm here. Nobody else is on the fifth floor. If that's not safe enough, we can go up on the roof. Rei put in a solid steel door. It's a fortress. Let's clean out your apartment and bring your stuff to my place. I'll call Rei. He can help. We'll help you disappear to the top."

Off they ran to Hannah's apartment on the third floor. Rei arrived shortly. They began throwing things into bags and boxes. Rei, Kyle and Marco ran up the stairs multiple times with their arms filled with Hannah's possessions. They left her dishes and appliances. Before she closed the door, she tossed her apartment keys on the kitchen table.

Up in Marco's apartment, they all caught their breath. Marco said, "You can have the master bedroom, and I'll take the guest bedroom."

"No," said Hannah firmly. "I'm definitely not putting you out of your bedroom. The guest bedroom is fine."

Hannah's phone rang again. She listened, then hung up.

"That was Shepp. They are going to direct Fonseca to Chez Roué. As soon as he gets there, they'll assess his state of mind."

They sat in the living room. Quiet.

"What do you think we should do, Rei?" Marco asked

Thinking for a moment, Rei responded slowly and clearly. "I think you and Hannah should go to the roof, lock yourselves in, and barricade the door. I'll get the lift ready in case you need to make an emergency exit to the ground floor. I'll go to the ground floor area and hide in a place where I can see the elevator and stairs. If I see Sicko coming up, I'll call you. Kyle, you keep watch from your apartment where you can see Hannah's door and the stairs to the fifth floor. If Fonseca goes higher than the third floor, call Hannah."

"Ok. Sounds good. Once again, Rei comes through," said Marco. They immediately left to execute the plan.

Kyle and Rei left Marco's apartment and went downstairs. On their way out Marco grabbed blankets, while Hannah filled a bag with food in preparation for what might be one long night or a rooftop siege.

Chapter 40

Back at Shepp's place, Shepp got dressed for the occasion, tan slacks and a Hawaiian shirt. He took his Glock from the wall safe, loaded the 10 round magazine, placed it in the pocket of his baggy linen jacket and added handcuffs to his other pocket.

"Be careful, dear," said Carol.

"Always." Shepp gave his wife a quick kiss and walked out the door.

In the DiCarlo apartment, Downey took his nickel plated 45 out of the bedside table, stuck it into the back of his pants, put on a jacket and was ready to play.

"You need to get yourself a smaller gun," said his wife Victoria, who loved to mess with him. "You'll give yourself a slipped disc hauling around that stupid cannon."

"I like it."

"You're an idiot."

Nicolo Barare put a 38 special in one pant's pocket, and brass knuckles in the other.

"Stay here, Kitten," Nicolo told Mysti.

"You never let me do any of the fun stuff," she complained.

"You got my love Kitten, what more could you want?" Nicolo laughed as he trailed away down the hall.

Carmine Senzio, who owned the butcher shop, put a 250,000 volt stun gun in his pocket, added a can of pepper spray, and left for the meeting of the minds.

Behind the bar of Chez Roué, Gommeux loaded a skin diver's spear gun and put it within easy reach. His wife Cassandra mixed a tiny vial of puffer-fish toxin, in case a spiked drink was called for.

Marie put a tiny 25 automatic pistol in her purse. She, like everyone, knew that Hannah was upstairs with Marco. Her kin was in danger and she was going to do her part to protect him. Romeo carried his stiletto and a lead-weighted beaver tail sap.

In the butcher shop, Leeray Bruce sat glumly sharpening his cleavers, knives and bone saws. He wished he had a different life. He didn't want any part of what he feared may happen. Leeray knew this meeting could get really ugly. He opened the back window and made some kissy noises, his signal for the gators. Within a minute, they came silently gliding up to the window. He tossed some hamburger and chicken parts into the lake, and the gators thrashed while they chomped it all down. He went back to sharpening his bone saw, waiting for his cue to spring into action. He'd be responsible for carving the body, if it came to that.

Gino Caprese, a former New Jersey crime boss, carried only a wicked piano wire garotte.

Fat Tony Olivio came unarmed, figuring there was plenty of firepower without another gun.

Maury Caldo was the last to arrive at Chez Roué. He carried a Beretta 9mm pistol.

Shepp took charge. "Looks like we're all here. Take your seats. Cassandra, please bring out some food and drinks. The government is buying tonight. Let's act like it's just a normal night at the restaurant. Keep the table nearest the parking lot open for Fonseca. That should give most of us a clear field of fire."

They all took their places. Gommeux and Cassandra poured drinks and served some of their amazing Italian appetizers.

A car pulled into the parking lot. Fonseca got out, followed by a tall young brunette, looking like a supermodel ready for the runway with her stunning expensive red dress, and silver five inch heels. She was a perfect 10, except for one thing... she was chewing gum. She had just turned 19 years of age. She popped a huge bubble.

"It's showtime," said Shepp.

Chapter 41

Everyone in Chez Roué acted calmly. Most kept to quiet conversations and didn't look up at Fonseca.

Shepp got up to meet Fonseca. Fonseca moved towards Shepp while keeping his arm around his girl and gazing at her. He interrupted his gazing and entwinement for a moment to greet Shepp.

"Hey. Look who's here!" said Shepp. Everyone turned to look

"Hey, welcome back," someone spoke up.

"Fonseca. You son of a gun. How's it going?" said another.

"Good to see you, man. Glad you're back."

More greetings continued while Fonseca waved with his free hand, the other wrapped tightly around his girlfriend's waist.

Gommeux put two glasses of water on the table and invited them to sit. "What'll you have to drink?"

They sat. Fonseca pulled his chair closer to his girlfriend so they could continue their exaggerated affection. "I'll have a jack and coke, Gommeux". Then, out of the blue, he stood and announced.

"I'm a changed man everyone, this is my fiance Jessica, she's the love of my life."

He sat back down, whispering to his '10.'

"Do you want anything to drink, honey?"

"No, sweetie, my one and only," touching him lightly on the neck, "let's go to your apartment. I'm tired. I'm hot. This place looks like a dump."

She looks awfully young, Shepp observed to himself as he addressed Fonseca.

"Welcome back, your apartment is ready. But, there is one thing you need to know, Hannah still lives in the condo. Is that going to be a problem?"

Everyone in the room froze. This was the moment when

things could turn ugly, and Fonseca's legendary bad temper might explode. Hands gripped weapons.

"What's she doing here?" he snarled. "She has no right to be here. What's going on?"

Jessica sat back in her chair and frowned, "I thought you said that bitch was gone?"

"Well, she does live here," Shepp calmly interjected. "She doesn't have to leave. Do you have a problem with that?"

Fonseca thought. His handsome face turned dark and mean.

"Does she want anything from me?"

"No." Shepp responded.

"She better stay away from Fonseca," Jessica lashed back with her vinegar attitude.

"Don't worry. She's not interested in Fonseca. That's over." Shepp responded.

"I'll cut her. I swear," warned Jessica.

"Whoa, whoa honey. No need for that. It's ok. You're my everything." Fonseca gave her another kiss. "If Shepp says she'll stay away, then let's give it a chance."

They sat there for a minute. Finally Jessica put both arms around Fonseca's neck and said, "Let's go to your place. I want to see it."

Shepp cleared his throat, "So, are we good, Fonseca? Everything cool here? No problems?" Shepp pushed to get Fonseca's agreement.

Fonseca nodded. "I'm a changed man. We're getting married soon. You're all invited to the wedding. I don't care if Hannah lives here. So what, Que sera sera, live and let live."

Everyone in the room relaxed as Fonseca and Jessica left for their love nest condo in paradise.

As soon as they were out of sight, the room cleared and Chez Roué closed for the night.

Up in his apartment, Downy DiCarlo groaned as he took his gun out from behind the small of his back. Victoria was reading a magazine in bed, "No drama tonight, Vic. Everything's fine. But, maybe I will get a smaller gun."

Victoria looked up from her magazine and shook her head. "No you won't. I've been saying that for ages. You're a knucklehead."

Back at the butcher shop, Leeray answered the long awaited phone call from his boss, Carmine Senzio. He listened and nodded. Relieved, he put away his knives and saws and made kissing sounds at the window overlooking the lake. He heard the alligators swimming up and tossed them leftover chicken pieces.

"Sorry, my pets. All I have is chicken," he said softly. "You won't be eating Italian tonight."

Chapter 42

Marco and Hannah had been hiding out on the roof, while Fonseca and Jessica were at the restaurant. Hannah was on a chair, shivering with fear even though it was a warm night. Marco put a blanket around her and pulled a chair next to her. He put his arm around her. She didn't flinch. He drew her close. This feels so right, he thought. I could do this forever.

Right then, Marco's phone rang, it was Rei.

"I'm keeping an eye on the elevator from a dark spot on the ground floor. Fonseca and Jessica are carrying a suitcase each and heading to the elevator." He hung up.

30 seconds later, Kyle called.

"They just went into Sicko's apartment. It doesn't look like they're coming out. He's not angry. He appears to be in love."

"Let me talk to Kyle," said Hannah. They talked. She was satisfied. "I guess that's it." She shrugged her shoulders with great relief.

"Shall we get off the roof?" he asked.

"Sure."

They went down and Hannah busied herself unpacking in the guest room. Marco watched. It was so nice having her here.

"Good night," she said, closing the door. He went to bed.

A couple hours later, he woke to the sound of his door opening. She was standing in the doorway wearing pajamas.

"I'm still scared. I keep imagining him busting down the door."

"Come on in," said Marco. She slid into his bed, he put his arm around her and held her tight. She nuzzled into his chest and they stayed that way until they both fell asleep.

In the early morning, as they woke he kissed her lightly on the lips. She smiled and kissed him back passionately. They made slow gentle love, twice, and fell asleep again in each other's arms.

Chapter 43

Two nights after the big meeting with Fonseca and Jessica at Chez Roué, Maury Caldo was walking his schipperke around 3 am, as he usually did most nights. Maury suffered from chronic insomnia. He didn't like the effects of sleeping drugs so he dealt with his condition as naturally as he could. He considered himself lucky, if he got three or four good hours of sleep a night. Over the years, he had learned to enjoy the emptiness and quiet of the night when Hidden Paradise was all his. But, he kept his eyes wide open just in case, especially for gators.

Coming back from the marina area, he spotted a woman running to the parking lot carrying two bags. When she passed under a street light, it looked like Fonseca's girlfriend, the #10 chickie, Jessica. She got in Fonseca's car, and drove off.

This was strange. Maury wondered why Jessica would leave in the middle of the night, and with her suitcases? Maury continued down the sidewalk in front of Hidden Paradise. Then he saw something in the hedge next to the condo. He walked over. It was Fonseca laying in a heap, his head at an impossible angle to his body. The side of his skull was bashed in. *She really let him have it,* he thought. He looked around in the dark and still night. He sighed. *What a mess. What are we going to do with you Sicko?*

Maury had seen plenty of death, first during his hitch as a Marine in Vietnam. Then later, in his career working for mobsters, before he turned on them, sending them to prison. That was 15 years ago.

I gotta call Fat Tony, he thought and dialed. "Hey Tony. Sorry to bother you so late. It looks like Sicko did a Peter Pan off his balcony with a little help from his chickie. He's dead. We need to clean this up, and dump him in the Gulf. Call five guys. Bring plastic, rubber gloves, and cinder blocks, the usual. And we need your boat. We can't let Shepp find out. Hurry!"

Five minutes later, DiCarlo, Fat Tony, Gommeux, Cassandra, Gino Caprese and Angelo Caputo arrived. In near silence, they tarped and hauled Fonseca onto Fat Tony Olivio's sleek cigarette boat, "Party Doll," named after his ex-girlfriend Peg.

"I'll need some help to get him into the water," Fat Tony called out. Gommeux kissed Cassandra and joined Fat Tony. It was his first time on a boat in 16 years.

Fat Tony smiled broadly, "There you go, Mon Capitaine, would you like to drive?"

"Mais oui. Avec plaisir." He started the quiet motor and the boat moved down the canal to the Gulf.

Meanwhile, Maury straightened out the plants where the body had landed and the rest of the crew cleaned Fonseca's apartment. The murder weapon, a cast iron skillet, was found in the dishwasher. They wiped and bagged it for disposal along with Fonseca's clothing and personal belongings, all taken to Caprese's van. Before they left, they tossed the keys on the kitchen table, next to the dirty dishes.

It was a good cleanup. If anyone bothered to look, it would appear that Fonseca and Jessica had escaped paradise in the middle of the night in Fonseca's car. There was no indication they'd ever return.

Chapter 44

"So I'm giving Rebecca a shampoo, and she tells me her daughter says her useless ex-husband will stop paying his alimony unless her daughter lets his parents visit their grandkids."

Hannah was doing dishes at the sink of Marco's apartment. Marco was sitting at the kitchen table with his laptop open. She'd been living in Marco's apartment for only a month, but it seemed like they'd been happily together for years already.

"He can't legally do that, can he?" responded Marco.

"Oh course not. But now, she has to hire an attorney."

"Uh huh."

"God, people can be such jerks to the people they once claimed they loved."

"Uh huh."

Marco flashed back to a shameful memory of three years back. He had broken up with a girl he had dated for a couple of weeks, loudly, in public. He was drunk, and surrounded by his college friends. The girl was humiliated, the hurt look on her face as she ran out of the restaurant still made him wince with regret.

"Hello, Marco," said Hannah, who had turned around from the sink. She caught him staring out into space. "Earth to Marco. Are you there? Did you hear me?"

"I'm sorry. Um, I was just spacing out."

"Oh really? Am I boring you that much?"

Marco got up and walked over to her.

"No. Not at all. I don't take you for granted. I'm sorry. I was listening. It is just that I was thinking of what you said, about people being jerks. It's so common, and so true."

"Are you sure it's not me boring you?"

"Yes. Absolutely not." He reached out and embraced her. They held each other for a minute, swaying together in the morning sunshine through the kitchen window. Their relationship was new and exciting. Marco never wanted it to end.

While they hugged, he wondered if he should share his idea with her. He had been thinking about it for two weeks, wondering if he should risk telling her. He decided to go for it.

"Can I show you something?"

"Sure." He walked over to his laptop and sat down. She stood behind him, with her hands on his shoulders, gently massaging them.

He found the page on the internet, and said, "There. That's what I want to show you."

She leaned over to see the screen. The web page was from the University of Minnesota, Hannah's college. Happy students with books were socializing in a springtime courtyard, outside of the education department building. At the top of the page were the words "Fifth Year Master's Degree in Education Program."

"Hmm," said Hannah. "Fifth year masters. Ok. Good program. Why are you looking at this?"

"If I'm lucky enough to ever get safely out of this place, without criminals chasing me, I think I want to apply."

"Really? You want to be a teacher?"

"I do. Yes. I've been thinking of the reasons you wanted to be a teacher and it makes sense. I've learned so much since I arrived here in Hitman's Paradise, facing the everyday despair of this place, being locked in here. And since I met you I've been looking at where I want to be, what has meaning in my life, all the big questions. I need something real. I've thought about it long enough. I'm going to be a teacher, like you." Marco was sincere.

"Okaaaaay" Hannah spoke very slowly.

"I need to be the real me, not someone following imposed values. I want to do something that makes sense." Marco continued passionately. "After living here, I yearn for real life, natural life, unspoiled things. Believe it or not, I've learned a lot from the garden on the roof. I love being around those plants, taking care of them, connecting with them, thinking about them, even talking to 'em."

"Oh believe me, I can see how they love living with you." She swung her arm and pointed all around the kitchen. There were plants everywhere, on the table, on the windowsill, and big potted plants on the floor.

"Yeah, well actually, Rei and I got carried away one day before you moved in. The point is, I'm never not going to have at least one living plant around me. But, it's not only plants. I crave nature and natural living."

She was still standing behind him. Marco pointed out the window. "We live in a nature preserve. It's delicate. It's balanced. I stopped using my little driving range on the roof. I'm gonna take it apart and make another garden bed. The idea of hitting plastic golf balls that won't deteriorate for 200 years into the wetlands really bothers me now. What was I thinking? Who was that person? I want to be around animals. I want unspoiled things. That's part of who I am. That is what I crave now."

Hannah had stopped massaging his shoulders. She was still and silent. Marco wondered if he had revealed too much, too soon in their relationship. But, it was too late for reconsidering. He pushed on.

"And that's why I'm thinking of teaching, Hannah. Children haven't been ruined by the world, they're innocent. There's hope for them. If I can help. I want to be there."

Hannah stayed standing, frozen in the same spot, so Marco continued.

"I want to be there with you. I adore you Hannah. No, that's not right. I love you. I love you and I want to be with you. That is, uh... if that is what you want also?"

He turned around and faced her for the first time since he began his soliloquy. Her wet eyes and glistening tears gave Marco her answer.

Chapter 45

It was 1am and silence had fallen over Hidden Paradise. A gentle warm breeze blew out of the mangrove swamp and was met by a cooler air current coming in from the ocean. A pleasant time of night, all was at rest except for the couple in apartment 319.

"No Romeo, I don't like that. Please. It hurts me, Romeo. Please don't."

"I'm almost done, dear, you're so sweet Marie. You know how much I care about you. You're my favorite." Romeo pressed more tightly.

"No. I said no, Romeo. Can't you hear me? You're hurting me."

"But Marie, dear, shhhhh." His breath became jagged as he panted in his excitement.

"I said I don't want this. Stop!" Marie's voice rose as she tried to turn and break away from his firm hold.

Romeo murmured in near ecstatic whispers. His grasp weakened for a second and Marie turned with all her strength, slapped him in the chest and jumped off the side of the bed and stood there.

"You don't get to tell me what I can do." Romeo snarled and punched her hard in the gut and rapidly landed another punch just below her cheek bone. She buckled and slipped to the floor. Romeo kicked her hard in the ribs and spit on her.

"You disgusting whore. You're a nobody. A piece of shit. You'll never be my Juliette." He stood over her menacingly, his loud voice could be heard through the open windows in the quiet parking lot and the mall. But... no one was there to listen.

He grabbed his clothes, put them on quickly and left, slamming the door. *He is a despicable lizard of a man, cruel and abrasive*, thought Marie. She lay on the floor sobbing in the fetal position holding her bleeding face and bruised ribs. It was over.

That was her only relief.

Romeo slid into his white Lexus and sped out the gates aiming for his favorite pay for play location. His rage continued as the memories of Marie played in his mind. His savage anger accelerated into the quiet night.

Marie slid onto the bed and cried herself to sleep. In the early morning she went to the bakery and put a sign on the door letting folks know she was taking the next two days off. She slid back into bed to sleep the entire day, icing her bruises every hour or so.

Later that morning, Downy DiCarlo tapped at her door. "Marie, you okay?"

"Yeah, I'm okay."

"Can I get you something? You sick? Need some medicine?"

"Give me another day, I'm getting better already."

"You don't sound so good Marie? Let me come in for a minute."

Marie reluctantly answered the door wrapped in her blanket. When Downy saw her face he was alarmed, angry and empathetic.

"What happened Marie? He hit you? Tell me the truth." He stared at her as she made her way to the couch.

"Have some coffee Downy. I gotta sit." Marie slumped on the soft couch and pulled her blanket tighter around her.

"That son of a bitch." He looked over his shoulder as he put on water for coffee. He looked at Marie's swollen eye that was now purple.

"This can't be allowed, Marie. He's out of here. It stops now. Where is he?" His restrained anger made his hands shake. Downy grabbed a washcloth and filled it with crushed ice. "Here, put this on your cheek." Marie followed his directions.

"Did he hurt you anywhere else?" Marie dropped the blanket and lifted her pajama shirt to expose several livid welts on her rib area.

"That's it, Marie." Downy made the coffee and sat at the table. He stared across at Marie, his friend of many years and shook his head.

"What kind of person does this?" Downy took a deep breath and let it out.

Marie's eyes filled with tears and she began to openly weep. Downy went over and sat beside her. She cried against him. He patted her back to comfort her and thought of murdering Romeo and dumping his body.

"We're gonna have a council meeting. This stops now." Downy looked off out the window seething with disdain for that bag of useless skin called Romeo.

Chapter 46

Marie never really knew Romeo's background, it was thick with abuse and sadness. Romeo was born Rocco Ladro. It would be too easy to recount his abused childhood and indicate that it was the cause of his homicidal rages and destructive rampages. It would be convenient to rely on the psychological reports and test results from his occasional stays in institutions. Each of these approaches to an explanation would be reasonable and simplistic at best. It may be a more clear and succinct truth to say that he was born this way.

As the neglected middle child in a family of five children, Rocco, who later took the name Romeo in witness protection, was left to his own devices most often. He was free of the demands made upon the first born and the excessive affection given to the baby of the family. He was neglected and impoverished. To say that Rocco was lost in the shuffle would assume there was a shuffle. There was none.

His father was a merchant seaman who came into port once or twice a year and mated with his wife, Rocco's mother, until his ship was ready to leave. He gave her what meager money he felt she deserved, which was never enough. He ignored his kids. She hated him.

Upon his arrival home, Rocco's father's behavior, in today's world, would be considered grounds for removing all children from the home, if not outright imprisonment. Perhaps his violent conduct might be considered acceptable, in some yet to be discovered brutish subhuman culture, but not in any civilized society.

Rocco wanted to leave the house whenever his father arrived, but he and the rest of the kids were forced to stay and witness the urgent cavorting of his parents. No doubt this aberration had long term traumatic effects on all the children, especially Rocco, the most neglected of the offspring.

Rocco became a charming pimp by the time he was twelve. He knew how to manipulate his peers to behave as he demanded, especially the girls. And when they didn't obey, he used all the tricks in his repertoire to make them perform.

He would coax and cajole, encourage and compliment, chide and comfort, be affectionate and even kind. He would bribe them, deceive them, seduce them, torment them. And if, in the end, they refused, he would resort to outrageous force and violent coercion. It was his trademark. From the gentlest to the most hurtful methods were employed. Escalation could occur in a matter of minutes. Before he was 21, he had plucked out someone's eye, with his hands. He called it self defense at his trial. He only got three years incarceration, and with seemingly good behavior, he was released after a year.

Rocco charmed his way through everything. While inside, he recruited the most vulnerable of the inmates, forced them to dress like women, and had them service wealthy connected inmates. Every night, they performed in the steamy darkness of the privileged bosses' private cells.

Rocco's favors paid off. The day he left prison he was offered a place in a lower level organization as a pimp. He recruited women for brothels and parties by prowling for the lost and forlorn runaways that populated bus stations and transient motels. He promised modeling careers and acting debuts. And he gave them tryouts in all manner of performances, under the pretense of guiding them to success.

Unfortunately, for these young hopeful teens, Rocco's impatience and arrogance grew. Over a period of a year he became a vain, strutting specimen. He struck anyone who resisted him. His cruelty had no bounds.

One young woman showed a made-man a stab wound made by Rocco. She told tales of cruelty and how many of the girls were abused by him. Rocco was brought before the Mob boss, a goon named Itchy Palermi.

"You have to understand, I'm training wild horses. They have to accept that they will be ridden. It's not easy to whisper in their ear and have them attend to the wishes of their master," Rocco explained.

Itchy approached Rocco as if to compliment him. He stood before him and kicked Rocco hard in the groin. Rocco folded and hit the floor in pain. The entourage of henchmen chortled at Rocco's misfortune.

"Pick him up."

As one of the henchmen lifted Rocco from the floor, Rocco pulled a knife and repeatedly punctured the man in the lungs and organs. Blood was everywhere as the man fell to the ground. Immediately the other guards surrounded and grabbed Rocco. He continued to fight, stabbing them in the same fashion. The last guard pulled and aimed a gun at Rocco's head. Rocco dropped to the floor pretending to surrender, and in one swift thrust cut the man's Achilles tendon. The man fell to the floor and the gun dropped from his hands.

"Stop," Itchy shouted, "you are here only because I allow you to be, do you understand that?"

Rocco nodded from his place on the floor. He was given an ultimatum. There was no place for this kind of behavior in the organization. He had to behave or die. Rocco knew in his heart that he could never behave. His freedom to be his own violent self was what he needed to feel alive.

In the months that followed, Rocco reached out to the Feds. He requested to testify against Itchy Palermi and his crew in a major sex and drug trafficking case in exchange for witness protection. Rocco soon became Romeo Sporco, a permanent resident at Hidden Paradise. He was delighted when he took his new name Romeo. This was his childhood nickname, given to him by his beloved sister, Juliette.

Chapter 47

Every morning at 8am, Carol Shepp went to DiCarlo bakery to have a coffee and gossip with her best friend at Hidden Paradise, Kathy Fortuna, and maybe bring back something sweet for Shepp. But, something was clearly wrong today. The shop had a 'closed until further notice' sign on the door. This had never happened before. She called Kathy, who told her the news.

A minute later she rushed back into her own apartment. Shepp was just about to leave. He played golf twice a week with three FBI friends at a course favored by law enforcement outside of Tampa. His golf game usually included a long lunch afterwards in the clubhouse. He sometimes wouldn't get back until 3pm. He never discussed Hidden Paradise with his FBI friends if he could help it. They knew what he did. The golf course was his way to escape Paradise altogether.

"Thank goodness I caught you," Carol said breathlessly. "You can't go. There's a big problem. They're going to kill Romeo. He beat the crap out of Marie. She won't go to the hospital."

"Damn. Just what I don't want to deal with, a friggin lynch mob."

"The Grand Council is meeting now." Carol responded urgently.

"Oh great. The God damned Grand Council," he growled as he put his clubs back in the closet.

"Do you need your gun?"

"No. I don't need my gun. I'll just straighten it out. Where's Romeo?"

"He's tied up in the butcher shop. Apparently, Romeo beat her up real bad last night, and then left. He tried sneaking back in a little while ago, but they were waiting for him. Downy's ready to strangle him. You need to stop him. He's serious."

"I get it. I'd like to strangle him myself. At least Romeo is still alive. Maybe I can fix this." He looked at his watch. "I'll call my golf partners. Maybe we can schedule a later tee time, or maybe I can catch the back nine. If I'm lucky, saving Romeo's worthless ass won't take too long."

"They're meeting at Chez Roué, right Carol?" Without hearing her answer, Shepp was off to make peace at the Grand Council meeting.

Chapter 48

Outside on the patio at Chez Roué was the usual meeting place for Hidden Paradise Grand Council. Sitting around two tables pushed together, all looking quite serious, were the very baddest of the bad.

Shepp's timing was perfect, they were all here. Carmine Senzio, Nicolo Barare, Downy DiCarlo, Fat Tony Olivio, Gino Capresi, Tony Fortuna, Phil Buxley, Johnny O'Meara and Maury Caldo.

As Shepp walked up, their animated discussion stopped. Sitting back in their chairs they looked like naughty schoolboys who'd been caught by their teacher. Shepp grabbed a chair and pulled it to the table.

"I heard about Romeo," Shepp began, getting right to the point, a tee time waiting in his future. "I don't have to remind you. You know the rules: No crime, no violence, or I shut this place down."

He spoke this perfunctory speech perfectly aware that there was plenty of crime going on at Hidden Paradise–just not under his nose. The Grand Council was perfectly aware that Shepp was aware of their crimes. They knew he didn't want to see or know about any misdeeds, so they kept it hidden. Everyone saved face and life went on.

"I know you're angry. Romeo hurt Marie. I know you want to kill him," said Shepp. "I'm mad too. But, you can't do it."

The Grand Council members sat silently. They had no alternative plan. Of course they had been planning on killing Romeo. Now they couldn't.

"Anyone want to tell me your plan?" Shepp asked.

Nobody said anything. Their plan had been that Downy DiCarlo would strangle Romeo and then Carmine Senzio would make Leeray Bruce chop him up into little pieces and feed him to the gators.

"I figured you couldn't tell me," said Shepp. "How about this for a plan? Romeo gets banished forever. He leaves today and he never comes back. Banished this morning."

The Council members were silent for a moment.

"Can we beat him up a little first?" asked Nicolo.

Downy jumped in. "I can't be the one giving the beating. If I start hitting that piece of shit, I'm not gonna stop."

"Ok. Ok", said Carmine Senzio. "How about this for a plan. I'll have Leeray do a little damage."

They looked at each other and nodded.

"No hospital," said Shepp. "He has to be able to walk, and survive without hospitalization."

"Sure," said Carmine. "Leeray's a pro. Just a little carefully chosen pain. You know, we put it to him for Marie. Right?"

Maury Caldo jumped in, "We can't let him drive away. Romeo is as mean as a snake. He could easily come back and kill us in our sleep. You know he's capable of it".

"How about this," said Carmine. "He signs the title to his car over to Marie, as damages, for like, you know, pain and suffering. We put him on a bus to a distant city. What do you say to that Shepp?"

"Ok. But I need independent proof that he actually gets on the bus. And I need each of your solemn promises that you won't follow him, or call a contract on him."

"I can live with that, if I have to," said Carmine. "How about this for independent proof. We have the kid, Marco, drive Romeo to the Orlando bus station, put him on a bus to Atlanta. The kid's no killer. Is that enough proof for you?"

"That'll work for me," said Shepp. "A beating, his car title and a permanent exile from Hidden Paradise in exchange you don't kill, follow or put a contract on Romeo. Do we have full agreement from all of you?"

It took a couple of minutes with a bit more arguing and resistance, but finally they all agreed and promised Romeo would be exiled, and no hit squads would chase him.

Shepp completed by letting the Council know he'd be calling Marco to inform him he'd be driving Romeo to the Orlando Greyhound station, and he was to send a photo of Romeo, once on the bus. "Carol will buy Romeo's ticket to Atlanta." Shepp became very serious "If you're going to work Romeo over, do it now, but no hospital injuries. No facial disfigurement."

Shepp immediately took out his phone and called Marco to arrange Romeo's ride to the bus. He called his golfing buddies to say he'd be an hour late and would meet them by the 6th hole.

Better than the 9th, he thought.

Chapter 49

At the Butcher shop, Leeray Bruce, the most reluctant hit man in Florida, was hating his job for the thousandth time. Romeo was handcuffed to a chair. Plastic sheeting was draped over every surface of the shop. Romeo wasn't talking, he had been in Leeray's shoes many times. He knew what was coming. No words would make a difference.

Leeray was standing in the corner, looking out at the lake smoking a cigar with contemplative dismay. His cleaver sharpened, waiting for Carmine Senzio, his boss, to return with orders to butcher Romeo and feed him to the gators. Puffing hard on his Parodi he asked himself the same questions he'd been asking for years: *How did I get into this awful life? When will it all stop? How will I ever get out of this nightmare?*

Carmine walked in the door with Downy DiCarlo. DiCarlo walked directly over to Romeo and slapped him hard.

"It's your lucky day, shitbird." He slapped him again, and raised his hand for a third strike.

"Lay off him, Downy," yelled Carmine. "Come on. None of that. Let Leeray take over," said Carmine.

Downy stood back. "Your lucky day. You don't deserve one."

"What's going on?" asked Leeray.

"Shepp found out," said Carmine. "We had to promise not to kill this piece of crap."

Leeray breathed out a great audible sigh of relief and sat heavily in his chair.

"Don't get too comfortable, Leeray. We need you to inflict a little pain and damage."

"That I can do. What would you like?" Leeray was happy to do this for Marie. Everyone liked her. "I'm happy to make him pay the price".

"We'll get to that. First, Romeo, you need to sign this bill of sale and the title of your new Lexus to Marie."

"And why would I do that?" Romeo was still trying to be the bad ass.

"So we don't slice and dice you and feed you to the alligators." Carmine put the papers in front of Romeo, put a pen in his handcuffed hand, and Romeo scrawled a signature on the documents.

"Here's what's going to happen, Romeo. You're being exiled for life. Banished. We're going to put you on a bus and you are never coming back. If you come back or if you contact anyone here, ever again, or tell anyone about this place, I will personally cut your balls off. Do you understand?"

'Yeah. I guess. You're the boss. Right now anyway." Romeo snickered.

Carmine turned to Leeray.

"We decided that you would break a couple of fingers on each hand."

"Sure. I can do that."

Leeray went over to the cabinet. He took out some first aid supplies. He went to the refrigerator and took out a long, raw, beef rib bone. He went over to Romeo. "Open up." Romeo opened his mouth, and Leeray put the beef bone in his mouth."Bite down hard on the bone, Romeo."

Carmine undid the handcuffs and put Romeo's hands down on the chopping block. Downy and Carmine held Romeo securely.

Leeray pulled the bone out of Romeo's mouth. He took a pill bottle out of the cabinet and put two pills in Romeo's mouth.

"Swallow these vicodins. You're gonna need 'em." Romeo swallowed the pills. Leeray put the pill bottle in Romeo's shirt pocket.

"That should get you through the next few days." Leeray had more compassion than most other murderers. He put the bone back in Romeo's mouth and picked up the cleaver with the handle pointed down.

"Don't move, you'll just make it worse," he said softly, and almost gently.

"Look away. Now take a deep breath, that's right."

Just then Marco walked in the door.

"Wait outside, Marco. Go away!" ordered Carmine.

"We'll bring him out to the car."

Marco left quickly. *What's wrong with these people*, he thought?

Leeray took the cleaver handle and with the expertise of a lifetime of butchering, he brought the end of the handle down hard on Romeo's middle finger, and then his ring finger, then repeated this on the other hand. The entire finger breaking took about three seconds.

Romeo grunted, writhed, screamed and squealed around the beef bone. Outside, Marco heard the muffled cries of pain. *I hate this place.*

"Keep his hands still," Leeray ordered, then took out a spray can of freezing solution for athletes and sprayed Romeo's fingers.

"This'll help keep the swelling down." He picked up some first aid tape and carefully bandaged Romeo's hands, using the neighboring fingers as splints.

"He's good to go."

"Not yet," said Downy. "I want a broken rib. He broke one of Marie's ribs. I want a broken rib."

"I've got no problem with that. Do it, Leeray," said Carmine.

Leeray pressed his fingers on Romeo's shirt, feeling for the location of ribs.

"Which rib do you want broken, Downy?"

"Which one is going to hurt the most?"

"How about this one?" Leeray pointed to a lower rib on the right side, and looked at Downy.

"That looks good. Can you break two ribs?"

"Ok, Romeo. Look up," said Leeray. "Take a deep breath, then let it out, here we go." Leeray made a fist, pulled his arm back, and landed one mighty punch on Romeo's rib cage. Romeo's screams penetrated through the room.

"Are we done?' asked Leeray.

Downy nodded. Leeray took away the beef bone. Almost tenderly, like a parent caring for a child, he helped Romeo to his feet.

They walked to Marco's car. "It's over," Leeray said. "You're safe now."

"Thanks, Leeray. That was real nice work," whispered Romeo, teeth gritted against the searing pain with each breath.

Chapter 50

Romeo's vicodin kicked in within fifteen minutes after leaving Hidden Paradise. Head on the passenger window, a few groans and Romeo was dead asleep. Marco turned the music loud like he loved when he was driving. He was thrilled to not have to speak a word to Romeo. A beating, a banishment and a car for aunt Marie seemed not nearly enough punishment for his cowardly attack. The icing was, once out in the world, Romeo would be vulnerable to his organized crime enemies.

When they arrived at the Orlando Greyhound station, Romeo was still groggy, but functional. With his free arm, Marco held him up and together found the bus to Atlanta. Stepping in together Marco took a couple of photos of Romeo in his seat, head leaning against the window.

Good riddance you piece of nothing. We won't see your disgusting face ever again, how dare you hurt my aunt, he thought. Romeo didn't move, and Marco exited. Outside the bus he stopped for his last photos, one of Romeo slumped against the window, the other, a destination sign on the bus showing 'Atlanta'. As the bus was pulling out, Marco texted the photos to Shepp. On his way home he was relieved he had survived another crazy scene. He wondered again, if he would ever get out of his situation.

Back at Hidden Paradise, Vickie DiCarlo, Marie's oldest friend from childhood, was furious at her husband, Downy. Vickie was the reason Marie came to Hidden Paradise. 20 years ago, Marie had gotten divorced from Downy's brother, and was struggling to make a living. When Downy and Vickie went into witness protection, Vickie lobbied Downy to bring her best friend to Florida and subsidize her bakery so the two could be together. The two women had been inseparable for years. When they got together with their other friend, Bev Caprese, they called themselves 'The Three Musketeers.'

When Downy told Vickie about the terms of Shepp's deal of banishment instead of torture and death, she became unglued.

"How could you let that happen, Downy? He deserved to die. Marie is family. She's better than family. You know that. How could you?"

"I didn't have a choice Vic. Give me a break. I don't like it any more than you do."

She stormed into the bedroom and slammed the door. She sat on the bed and called her older sister Rose, the only relative she had trusted with the truth about Hidden Paradise. They talked every day. Rose was retired with her husband Carl, a retired machinist, in New Mexico.

Vickie told Rose about Romeo beating up their childhood friend Marie. Rose was aghast. "Poor little Marie. That bastard. I could kill him."

"Do you have any contacts with the outfit back in Chicago? I want to hire someone to meet the bus in Atlanta, and kill the bastard. I'll pay anything. I remember Carl once knew some of those guys."

"No. No. I'm sorry, sweetie. That was 30 years ago. I don't think he knew anybody. He just talked big. I can't do it. It would be too risky for you or me to reach out now. They'd ask questions. They'd want to know about you, and where you live. They could sell you out. You can't trust any of the new guys in this thing. No morals. They aren't like the good old boys. Sorry."

"Damn. Well, at least I tried."

"People like Romeo eventually find a way to get what they deserve."

"I guess that'll have to be good enough. Thanks sissy. I hate it, but sometimes we just have to let go and let life take care of it with karma."

Chapter 51

Romeo woke up when the bus was a half hour from Atlanta. A heavy woman next to him was pressing him against the window. He groaned. Maybe another vicodin, he thought. Then immediately he rethought, maybe not. The throbbing pain in his hands and chest were up to a 10. The hit men'll probably be waiting for me when I arrive. That's what I'd would do if I was hunting the prey.

He took stock of his wallet stuffed with money.

The pain worsened when they pulled into the Atlanta bus station. Romeo was the last person off the bus. As he stepped off, he looked for eyes watching him. It looked clear, but to Romeo that meant nothing.

Like a wounded wolf, he rolled his suitcase over to the ticket counter. The next bus to leave was for Birmingham, Alabama, boarding in 15 minutes. He got in line and noticed a special fare. When he got to the counter, he asked about it.

The bored ticket seller said "$499 gives you unlimited bus travel in the lower 48 states for two weeks."

"I'll take one of those specials, and I want to start with Birmingham." He took out his wallet and using only his thumbs, he fumbled out five hundred dollars.

I'll just keep traveling until it feels right to stop. I can always make pizza somewhere, he thought.

Romeo watched all the eyes in the bus station as he hobbled over to the bus to Birmingham. Nobody seemed to notice him. The bus driver was standing by the open luggage bay to take his suitcase. Once in his seat, he popped a vicodin into his mouth. Trying to take a deep breath of relief, he almost fainted with pain. He pulled the locket with the picture of his sister Juliet out of his shirt and kissed it.

Romeo was disappearing into America.

Chapter 52

It was 10 in the morning when Romeo pulled into the bus station in Jackson, Mississippi. He'd been wheezing all night from painful cracked rib breathing. He dozed on and off with his head slumped onto his chest.

Out of the bus, Romeo hobbled his way to the window and got his next ticket to Memphis, Tennessee using his bus pass. He had 45 minutes to grab some food and wash up before getting back on the bus. He was ready for another vicodin; his fingers were throbbing and immobile.

Romeo and his roller suitcase made their way to the seamy luncheon counter to look at the menu. He decided to purchase a couple of egg salad sandwiches for the road and grab an apple pie when he got back from the restroom.

He pulled out his hefty wallet with his taped and unbendable fingers and pried a twenty from the wad of green bills. He told the waitress to keep the change, and nodded with his head to indicate that he would be coming right back after visiting the bathroom.

From the end of the counter, a young man with short black hair sipped coffee and watched him. He was waiting for a ripe mark, someone easily separated from the herd, someone a little slow, hurt or infirm. When he saw Romeo's creaky walk and the difficulty he had getting money from his fat wallet, the young man's leg began to bounce in anticipation.

Romeo made his crooked way to the back of the bus station. When the young man saw Romeo enter the restroom, it took him all the patience in the world to count to twenty before he went in after him.

Romeo rolled his bag beside him and stood at the urinal. His impatience made him realize that he needed another vicodin very soon. He noted to himself that he would take another dose with the apple pie. Stepping to the sink afterwards he ran the water to get it warm. He splashed the water over his face repeatedly to wake up, cleaning off the smells of the long bus ride. With his eyes shut he grabbed for the paper towels.

At that moment, Romeo was hit from behind on his left side. He took a step forward to try to regain his balance and his right foot slid on the floor grime below the sink edge. Before he could turn and see the twenty year old meth addict, intent on robbing him, Romeo fell sideways and the right side of his head hit the protruding porcelain urinal. His head caved instantly with the force of his fall. He was dead.

The young man, facing the unintended consequences of his actions, said out loud, in a harsh whisper. "Oh Fuck!" He grabbed Romeo's wallet and considered taking the suitcase but it was too conspicuous. The glimmer of the gold locket around Romeo's neck caught his attention. He yanked it from Romeo's wet dirty neck, "You're not gonna need this where you're going." With that, he exited the bathroom and walked away unnoticed.

Chapter 53

Two days after Romeo's beating, Marco met Marie at the DiCarlo bakery at 4am to start on the day's baking. He was still haunted by the image of Leeray holding a cleaver over Romeo's hands on the chopping block. Marie was determined to open the shop as she had done every day for so many years. She sat in a chair in the kitchen with pillows around her and gave him instructions on mixing the dough, prepping the ovens, and doing everything necessary to run the bakery. Vickie DiCarlo and Kathy Fortuno came by at 8am to greet the customers and run the cash register.

Marco stayed at the bakery all day and he came back every day for the next week as well. During that time, Vickie DiCarlo bullied and badgered her husband to petition the Grand Council to allow Marie to hire a young man from the Boat Camp to work at the bakery. The council reluctantly agreed, and that is how Thiem became the first non-resident ever to be given a key to access the gate in the chain link fence, designed to keep out the Boat Camp people.

Thiem was a fast learner. On their first Thursday working together, Thiem and Marco arrived early. A lot of orders came in on Wednesday which meant lots of pizzas needed to be baked and delivered. Timing was everything. He and Thiem worked well together, making pizzas and delivering them to the Paradise residents on Thursday afternoon.

On Friday, Marco's last day of working at the bakery, he and Thiem were cleaning up at 5pm. He was just about done, and ready to meet Hannah, Rei and Kyle on the roof for their regular Friday night barbecue supper, when Vickie DiCarlo came by.

"When you're done, can you go over to Chez Roué for a minute? Downy and a couple others want to talk to you."

Oh no. What now? Marco texted Hannah, and told her he was

meeting Downy and the others at the restaurant.

As he was finishing the clean up, he had a sinking feeling in the pit of his stomach. A summoning never meant good news. *What could this mean? Nothing good, that's for sure.* His mind automatically went to the worst case. *What is it going to be this time: A body dump, witnessing a beating, destroying evidence, helping with some new awful crime?*

He finished up, walked outside, it was 95 degrees at 5pm. The sun's penetrating, searing brilliance, made Marco put his hand up to shield his indoor eyes. It felt like the sun could scorch every centimeter of exposed flesh in seconds.

Marco entered the restaurant to see a large fan set up next to the tables. It was blowing hot air onto the members of the grand council. Marco tried not to laugh. *What gavones*, he thought.

Gommeux got up when Marco arrived, and indicated that Marco should sit. He'd been conversing with the grand council. Excusing himself, he went back to the kitchen joining Cassandra getting ready for the evening meal. Marco sat next to DiCarlo, who held his Downy bottle closely.

At the head of the table was Johnny O'Meara with his oxygen tank attached to his walker beside him. The table went silent, with the exception of the loud fan. O'Meara cleared his throat signaling the beginning of the meeting. It was hard for Marco to read the mood of the men. Cassandra brought him a glass of water and left. They sat silently for a few seconds. Marco waited.

"Well, Marco," said Carmine Senzio. "Tell us what your dreams are. What is it you want to do with your life?"

Is this a trick question? he thought.

"I know where I would start," Marco answered slowly and carefully.

"I want to get my masters degree in teaching, while Hannah finishes her fourth year of college. I want to be with her. I want to teach school somewhere, and have a garden, maybe get a dog or cat. That's what I dream of doing."

They sat quietly, not betraying how they felt. Finally, Gino

Caprese spoke.

"I say he stays. He could be very useful. I haven't even asked him to do anything for me yet. I've got plans that could use some help."

"Yeah, I'm with Gino on that," said Fat Tony Olivio. "He's only been here a few months and I haven't gotten around to taking one of his tennis lessons. And he knows too much. He needs to stay."

Old Phil Buxley, who had rheumy eyes and a sagging bloodhound face, now added his two cents, "I could use some dog walking help. Keep him here."

Nicolo Barare spoke.

"Look at him and Hannah. Think of the beautiful children they're gonna have. There are no kids around here. It's wrong. It's unnatural! I want to be a grandfather. If he stays, Mysti and I can be God-grandparents. We need him here to make some kids. He should stay."

Marco felt his chances for a normal life slipping away. That's it. They want him to be a criminal assistant. They want him to be a breeder. He had a dark thought about simply jumping off the roof and ending his torment. Hannah was leaving no matter what. She had saved enough money. She was ready to go back to school. Staying meant no Hannah in his life, no college, no new life, only more of what he had grown to hate, prison in Club Rat. He said nothing. He had no say in the matter. He was trapped.

Finally Johnny O'Meara waved his thin, blue-veined hand. With great effort, he wheezed in as deep a breath as he could.

"He wants to be a school teacher." Several seconds, then another wheezing breath, and, "The world needs more school teachers." Another breath. "Not more goombas and wise guys like us." More wheezing. "Let him go." Wheeze. "If my old friend Caspar Melton were alive he would say that trusting Marco is a sound bet." Wheeze. "Let him go." He sat back, spent from the exertion of talking.

Carmine Senzio spoke next.

"Look. No matter how you cut it, he's a civilian. He's no

soldier. This isn't his life. But even so, he has been faithful. I know it. Leeray vouches for him. I say, let him go. Let him be a teacher."

"I agree with Johnny and Carmine," said Downy. "He has helped you all enough. Let him go to school. You'll come back, won't you?"

"Sure," said Marco, because this was the only safe thing to say.

The table went silent. Marco wondered how much clout Johnny, Carmine and Downy had in the council. Finally, Phil Buxley spoke. "What the hell. I don't like it one single bit, Johnny, but I can live with it. So I say, let the kid go."

"Ok, only because he's gonna to be a teacher," said Fat Tony Olivio.

"Yeah. Maybe if we had opportunities like that we wouldn't be here. Even though I did enjoy how I lived my life. Education is still better than crime," said Carmine.

And with that, they all nodded and Marco was a free man. He couldn't believe it. The mood of the table changed. The business was done.

Carmine shouted over to the bar.

"Hey Gommeux, bring that bottle of grappa over here. Bring glasses, and a couple of glasses for yourselves too."

Cassandra brought over a tray with shot glasses, and the bottle of grappa. She poured the shots and passed them around, except for O'Meara, who was too sick for alcohol.

Downy stood and raised his glass. "Santé." They all drained their glasses. Cassandra and Gommeux left the bottle on the table and went back into the restaurant. Phil and Tony got up to leave, saying goodbye to everyone but Marco.

Johnny O'Meara struggled to his feet, got moving behind his walker, and came over to Marco. He held out his weak, bony hand. They shook.

"Be good, kid. Take care of her." He patted Marco on the shoulder and rolled away.

"More grappa," said Downy. He refilled the shot glasses. "To

Hitman's Paradise." They drank. Laughed and refilled the glasses.

After four shots, they were flying high, becoming louder by the minute with drunken jollity, all hail fellow well met and life is good. One more shot and they were all steaming. The stories and the jokes started rolling, while Marco rested his elbows on the table like everyone else. Finally relaxed, he was enjoying himself for the very first time with the general population at Hidden Paradise.

It all seemed to be going swell until Downy looked at Marco, held out his Downy bottle, and said, "Here, have a drink with me."

Marco hesitated, then blurted without thinking, "Not on your life."

The whole table went perfectly quiet for a few moments. Marco became instantly fearful. But then, the entire table suddenly broke out into uproarious laughter, including Downy, who laughed the hardest.

Carmine shouted, "I wouldn't drink that either. I don't want trench-mouth."

"Leprosy in a bottle," said Maury.

Marco was drunk enough to add, "But it makes your mouth feel fresh and soft." They all laughed. Their brilliant quips seemed to be the world's greatest jokes. Downy put his arm around Marco, and gave him a friendly squeeze. "You passed, kid. Call me Downy from now on. Everybody else does."

With drunken Downy's arm around him, Marco could have cried with relief. Just then, Hannah appeared behind him. She put her hands on his shoulders. "Ah ha. The boys are having a little drink together, eh? I caught you." Everyone shouted out an affectionate greeting.

Marco struggled to his not too steady feet.

"I have dinner plans, guys. Thanks." He shook Downy's hand, waved to the others, and he and Hannah walked away with their arms wrapped around each other. Marco was glad for the support, as the world was spinning.

When they got near the stairs, Marco, drunk and excited

from his new freedom, grabbed hold of Hannah, "They're going to let me go. I'm going to college with you. I'm free."

"That's nice, Marco," she said.

He stopped. "Wait. You don't seem very surprised."

"Umm. I'm not too surprised. Maybe a tiny bit surprised."

"Did you know?"

"Well, let's say that for the last two weeks, I've been lobbying everyone who came into the salon to let you go. Some of the guys, but mostly their wives. There would have been a wive's rebellion if they had said no. So, yeah, I had a pretty good idea what was going to happen. They made me keep it quiet. They wanted to have a little bit of sick fun at your expense first."

Marco kissed her lightly. "You knew and you didn't tell me? You're terrible." He kissed her again. "You're treacherous."

She kissed him back passionately. Then she whispered, "Run away while you can."

Chapter 54

When Hannah and Marco arrived on the roof after the Grand Council meeting, Rei and Kyle were cooking barbecued chicken, and setting the picnic table. Marco was still reeling drunk. He was giddily happy.

"I'm free," he yelled. He was beaming. Then he tilted his head back and yelled to the swamp, "Freeeeeedom!"

"Wow, Marco," laughed Kyle. "What the hell happened to him?"

Marco went to the barbecue where Rei was basting the chicken. He draped his arm around Rei. "Rei, this smells like the best BBQ chicken ever. You are one very talented man, I love you and I'm free, Rei. Don't you love it, free Rei... Woo-hoo!"

Rei was laughing and perplexed.

"The grand council agreed to let Marco leave with me," Hannah bubbled. "He really is free."

"That is huge news. I am so happy for you," Rei said. He turned and embraced Marco.

Marco walked over to Kyle, and gave him a big hug.

"We had grappa tonight. Grappa grappa grappa. I'm a little drunk, in case you can't tell." he confided.

"Oh, really? I would never know. Here drink some water, it'll stabilize you." Kyle would know, after all, he was the health nut here.

"Chicken's ready," announced Rei. They sat down and piled their plates with salad from the rooftop garden and Rei's juicy barbecue chicken.

Marco told them the story of his meeting with the grand council, how scared he was, thinking for sure he'd never escape paradise. He told of his feeling of overwhelming relief, and how surprised he was to hear some of them express the belief that in the long run, education was better than a life of crime.

"Criminals said that to me. It makes me want to be the best teacher ever." Marco paused and in the calmest voice, "I will never forget that moment as long as I live. It's etched in time. It's like the clock on my life restarted at that moment."

Marco's phone rang. It was Shepp.

"Shepp! How are you? Hey everybody, it's Shepp!"

"Hi Marco. I heard about the meeting. Sounds like you're celebrating. Good for you."

"I'm going to put you on speaker phone." Marco fiddled with his phone. "Say hi to Shepp."

They all said hi.

"Come on up, Shepp. We're having a barbecue. It's a celebration."

"No, but thanks for the offer. Look. Congratulations. I'm happy for you. You deserve it. You earned it. But, I just called to get serious for a minute and give you some advice."

"Ok."

"You need to leave right away, Marco. Hannah too. You need to leave as soon as you can."

The rooftop party stopped instantly.

"Really?" said Marco.

"Really. Promises made by hyenas at this place tend to have a very short shelf life. What is promised today, can be taken away tomorrow. You need to get away -- I'm serious -- before somebody here thinks of a reason why you should stay, which then becomes a reason why you will never leave."

"Wow. Like, in a week, or in a month?"

"No. Tonight, if at all possible. Get out while the going is good. Remember, in the Hidden Paradise booklet, how Cole and Betty Bertram fled from the mob? Now it's your turn, just like them." Shepp paused, to let it sink in.

"So, goodbye Marco. Best wishes to you Hannah, and Carol gives you her love. Stay in touch." Shepp hung up.

The four of them sat dumbfounded. Marco's giddiness disappeared. Shepp was right.

Chapter 55

The next three hours were a blur to Marco. They cleared the roof of dishes and went down to Marco's apartment. Kyle suggested that Hannah should take the first shift as driver in Marco's car, so Marco could sleep off the last of his inebriation. Marco agreed.

Marco looked around his lovely apartment for the last time. He had mixed feelings of relief and sorrow. He would never again work in his beloved rooftop garden. The roof, his sanctuary and healing spot, would be gone. He felt a deep, throbbing pain at never seeing Rei.

"Let me help you pack, my friend," said Rei.

At hearing the words 'my friend', Marco almost burst into tears. He pulled himself together. Looking around, he decided he didn't need to take very much to Minnesota, nothing more than what he had brought to Florida, except for one thing... he wanted to take a houseplant. He asked Hannah for her opinion. She liked the idea, and they chose a small spider plant.

As he was leaving his bedroom for the last time, Marco had an idea. He asked Kyle, "Wouldn't you enjoy living here? The spare bedroom would make a great music studio. I think you'd like it. You could take over my share of the roof garden, if that would be alright with you, Rei?"

"Sure," said Rei. "Kyle could be on the lease for the roof. That would protect my rights from the others."

Kyle stopped. He thought. "Yeah. I'd really like that. I'll definitely take over the apartment. Wonderful."

Marco took the keys to the apartment and to the roof, and handed them to Kyle.

"It's a great place. It's all yours Kyle, and thanks for everything." They embraced.

Kyle and Hannah went back to collecting her things. In a couple of hours they boxed up the essentials, and made the first trip downstairs with Hannah's clothes. On their way back up the stairs, Kyle asked, "Can we stop down at my apartment, on our way out? I just want to play one more song for Hannah."

In Kyle's apartment, Kyle went to his electric keyboard. He chose a grand piano sound setting. Looking down at the keyboard, his chest heaving with emotion. His best friend was leaving. It hurt. He said softly, "This is for you, Hannah."

Hunched over, he began playing Claude Debussy's hauntingly beautiful Clare de Lune. He started with the sweet child's lullaby melody, hovering over the deep, luscious chords, and proceeded all the way to the rolling, thunderous arpeggios building to the ending with its single deep bass note, sustained until it was just a whisper until it disappeared.

Kyle stood and embraced Hannah. They cried in each other's arms.

"We'll talk every day," Hannah bawled.

Marco looked at Rei, who broke out into his own tears, and grabbed his friend for one last hug.

"Rei. I love you. You saved my life. You were my only friend. If you hadn't been here, I think I would have killed myself. You saved me. I was so lonely, so depressed. You gave me sanctuary. I'm so thankful for you. How can I ever repay you?"

"We are friends for life, Marco. That is enough. You helped me, too. I am treated better, now, by the others. I have this rooftop garden. My life is much better because of you, my friend."

Chapter 56

After they hauled the next load to the car, Marco wanted to say goodbye to Marie. The four of them stood in the open air hallway on the second floor. It was 2am. The night was warm and humid. Marco knocked on her door, and a sleepy Marie opened up the door wearing a bathrobe. Marco explained that they were leaving, precipitating more hugs and crying outside her door.

As they walked down the hallway to go up to fetch the last boxes, the door next to Marie's opened. Irving Slotzky stood in his pajamas.

"What are you doing?" he demanded.

"We're leaving," said Marco, unaffected by Slotzky's attitude.

"No you're not. You can't leave." Slotzky shook his head firmly.

"We're leaving." Hannah responded.

Slotzky pointed his finger, "You're staying. All of you. I say you can't leave and that's final."

Marco turned, walking away with Hannah, Kyle and Rei.

"Goodbye Irving," Marco said, as they continued to the car.

Slotzky went back inside, slamming the door behind him.

On their trip downstairs, laden with boxes, Slotzky, now carrying a baseball bat, and a very drunk Guy Marsh, all 6'8" of him, wearing a bathrobe and carrying five feet of heavy chain, met them on the second floor landing.

"Now, where do you think you're going, punks?" Slotzky bellowed, blocking their way. "You're not going anywhere," and with his chain, Marsh forced them down the hallway.

Slotzky stood behind Marsh. "You're not going anywhere!"

A door near the stairs opened. Arn Pekohr in his wheelchair peeked out. Marsh noticed Pekohr and pointed with his chain towards Pekohr's apartment. "Get inside Pecker's apartment. Now. All of you. Go!"

"You can't come into my apartment! No! I forbid it. Go away," shouted Pekohr, wheeling himself out to block the door.

Marsh walked angrily towards Pekohr. He stood in front of him, put a size 16 foot on Pekohr's legs, and gave the wheelchair a mighty shove backwards. The chair flew into the apartment and stopped when it hit the couch on the other side of the room. Pekohr didn't move.

"Shut up Pecker. I've had enough of you," he yelled. "Now get inside Pecker's apartment, all of you." Marsh slurred. He was drunk. He was enraged, weaving, brandishing his chain.

Marco knew they would be beaten or killed if they went into the apartment. Marco had one arm around Hannah as they backed away from Marsh down the hallway.

Doors started opening all down the hallway. The first people out were Downy and Vickie DiCarlo, wearing bathrobes. Carmine Senzio emerged, sleepily rubbing his eyes. Marie came out. Nicolo Barare and Mysti came out. Gommeux and Cassandra came out.

"Haw Haw!" laughed Fat Tony Olivio, leaning in his doorway and sporting an evil grin. "What do we have here? Having a little fun Marsh?"

He was the only one laughing.

"What's going on?" demanded Carmine.

Marsh pulled a pint of whiskey out of his bathrobe. He took a long pull, smacked his lips and pointed the bottle at Marco and Hannah.

"These two were trying to escape."

"Yeah? We gave them permission."

He belched loudly. "I didn't."

"Nobody asked you. You don't count. Now get the hell out of here Marsh."

"No. They know too much."

"You want to dance with Leeray? Is that what you want?"

Carmine moved in front of Marco. Downy joined him.

Shouting above the noise, Mysti Barare yelled, "I say let her go, but make Marco stay."

"What?" yelled Marie, walking over to Mysti. Kathy Fortuna joined her.

"Who asked you?" demanded Kathy. "They both go. It's been decided."

"I didn't decide. He should stay. He knows things," said Mysti.

This triggered a loud argument between a knot of angry women, Mysti arguing against everyone.

"Haw Haw Haw," said Fat Tony leaning in his doorway. "Look at the cat-fight! Go Mysti go! Woo hoo! Check out that chain!"

Carmine turned towards Marco, Hannah, Kyle and Rei. They were hanging on each other, wide eyed and paralyzed with fear.

"We're getting you out of here. Don't worry. Follow me." He turned to Marsh. "Get out of the way, Marsh. You're drunk." He and Downy led the way. Gommeux joined them.

"Nobody is going anywhere," Marsh repeated loudly, now swinging his chain in a vicious arc. It hit the iron railing with a brittle crack and the floor seemed to shake.

"C'mon kids, let's go. I gave you my word." They followed slowly.

D'Angelo Brown tried to make peace. "People. People. Everyone is so tense. Calm down. Let's all take a deep breath and relax. It's so important to allow your anger and concern to dissipate and be released. Breathe in with me. Nice and deep, just..."

Downy put a hand on D'angelo's chest and gently pushed him out of the way. "It's too late for that now." He moved forward with Carmine. Gommeux followed.

Carmine pointed to Marsh. "You're finished."

Marsh answered by swinging the chain and giving the railing another crack. Slotzky stood behind Marsh, tapping the baseball bat into his palm.

Marco watched the arc of the chain. He was sweating and felt like he might throw up. He put Hannah behind him. He felt like there was no way out. He was agitated, panicked, thinking they were all going to die. These puny old men couldn't stop a chain wielding giant.

The group, Carmine, Downy and Gommeux in front, followed by Marco, Hannah, Rei and Kyle, took another step forward. A grimacing Marsh swung and another bone chilling crack reverberated from the railing.

"STOP!" shouted a voice in a heavy Russian accent behind everyone. "STOP."

Everyone turned towards the man at the end of the hallway. He had pale, translucent white skin from never seeing the sun, and bony legs and a shock of white hair. He wore boxer shorts and an oversized wife beater tee shirt. All eyes rested on his beat up AK-47 with two long banana clips taped together. He racked a round into the gun.

"STOP. NOW", and took a step forward.

"Who are you?" demanded Mysti. "I've never seen you."

Nobody had ever seen Grigori in person except Marco. It was Grigori's first time outside his door in 30 years.

"That's Grigori," whispered Nicolo to Mysti.

"Really? That old man?"

Grigori started walking down the hallway, aiming the AK-47 at Guy Marsh's head.

"Get out of their way I said," peering down the gun sights. "They are leaving. Or, I shoot."

"Fuck you," said Marsh, not taking his eyes off the gun pointed at his eyes, but no longer swinging the chain.

Grigori took another few steps until he was even with Carmine.

"Go home. Last chance."

The two men stared at each other for a few very long, tense moments. Finally, Guy Marsh took a deep breath, released it, and dropped the chain to his side. "Fuck you old man." Then pointed at Marco. "You better not talk or I will hunt you down and rip you apart." He turned and walked to the stairwell.

"Are you going to let that old man talk to you like that, Guy?" Slotzky said.

"Shut up Slotzky," Marsh said, cuffing Slotzky on the side of his head as he weaved his way up the stairs.

Slotzky turned and walked past a gauntlet of murderous looks on his way to his apartment. Downy gave him a shove as he went by.

Everyone stood frozen in silence then sighed relief.

Grigori took up a position next to the railing. His eyes swept the area making sure he had a clear field of fire, covering the parking lot, the mall, the pool and the marina.

"Fun's over everyone," said Fat Tony, disappearing from sight.

Marie and Kathy Fortuna rushed over and hugged Marco, Hannah, Kyle and Rei. Downy and Vickie followed. There was plenty of crying.

Carmine went over to Grigori.

"It's good to finally meet you, Grigori." He put out his hand. They shook. Downy came over.

"Likewise, Carmine, Downy."

"Oh, you know who I am?"

"Yes."

"Well well," said Carmine. The three men stood together as the tension drained away. The night air became peaceful again.

"Do you like playing cards, Grigori?"

"I'm the king of cards, especially poker. Haven't played with anyone in over thirty years"

"Why don't you join our weekly game?"

"I would like that, but can you play at my apartment?"

Downy and Carmine looked at each other, "We could probably do that. Sure."

After a final hug, Marie went back inside and the four friends walked to the stairwell. When they passed Pekohr's apartment, his door was still open, and he was still in the chair where it had crashed into the couch.

"Let's go," Hannah urged, tugging on Marco, "Let's get the hell out of Club Rat while we can."

Maury Caldo, the insomniac, met them with his dog at the bottom of the stairs. "I'll walk you to the car," he yawned.

"Sure."

At Marco's car, the happy little schipperke stood on its hind legs begging for attention. Hannah and Marco bent down to scratch and pet it all over, and the dog quivered with pleasure. When the car was loaded, Maury joined in one last round of hugs, and then they drove off.

Standing in the parking lot, Kyle, Rei and Maury watched the car disappear up the road.

Kyle sighed. "Makes me think of all the people over the years we've known who have passed through this place, and yet here we still are. We've seen 'em come, and we've seen 'em go, haven't we?"

"That's the truth," said Rei, as the three of them started walking back towards the condo.

When the car reached the main road, Hannah said, "I'm running on adrenaline. I'll be good for hours."

"Great, let's get out of Florida," Marco murmured, "and never come back. We are going to make our own paradise." With those words ringing throughout his entire body, Marco leaned back in his seat, put his hand lightly on Hannah's leg to be sure she was real, and despite all the terror, tension and fear of their escape, a getaway that almost failed, he fell quickly asleep.

THE END

CODA

The Fountain of Scams:
Greed, Folly, Murder and the History of Hidden Paradise subdivision 1991

Unpublished manuscript by Caspar Melton,
former resident of Hidden Paradise
1988 to 1992.

PREFACE

The preface to the
FOUNTAIN OF SCAMS
Can be found at the end of chapter 16 in this book.

Chapter 1

The Ponce

Florida is the kind of place that's always been given over to one wild flight of fancy or another. The imagination of many people has been stoked by the stories this place harbors, and it's not bound to stop. It's possible that more than anywhere else in America, if one is to hear a whopper of a lie, it could originate in Florida. Here, more than just about anywhere, the lies that are told take on a life of their own and spread outward in the manner of a brush fire and never really die. One of the very first lies that we're taught as children, in whatever flawed system we're educated in, is the story of Ponce de Leon and his fruitless search for something called the fountain of youth. His explorations throughout Florida are still the stuff of legend, but they smell like what they really are —a fetid pile of horseshit.

People believe pretty much whatever they want, and like lemmings, they'll go running anywhere the mob is headed. They profess to want to know what's going on, but will bury their head in the backside of the person in front of them and just follow along out of habit. The bigger the lie, the further up that head goes, and one wonders how anyone can stand the smell of one shit lie after another that people are fed on a continual basis. I've used this truth concerning humanity to my benefit more than once, and I can tell you that people will follow any line of bullshit they want to believe, at least until the one feeding them is caught or otherwise removed. It was only after my near incarceration, when the wrong people caught on to my lies, that I had to stop the chow line.

To this day though, I'll admit that the reason I almost spent the rest of my life behind bars was my boss's dip-shit son. It wasn't my fault at all. I don't care what others say.

But, back to the point I was on, commenting on why a lot of humanity is doomed because of their need to follow. Ponce De Leon's legend had nothing to do with finding some damned fountain, even if the mythical nature of his quest was built upon a foundation of blood and bone that came from his real goal, that of conquest. The man came here for gold, and of course to make sure that no one could contest his right to take it, which meant exterminating any indigenous peoples he came across along the way. What's even funnier about this, is that Ponce's myth didn't even get draped over the real nature of his story until 14 years after his death, when Gonzalo Fernández de Oveida Y Valdés (ye gods what names) published 'The Fountain of Youth'.

Given how gullible people are, it's not much of a surprise that Gonzalo managed to get away with the idea that Ponce's quest was the fountain of youth. The lie was cemented into history again nearly three decades after Ponce's death. It was placed in Francisco Lopez de Gomara's 'Historia general de las Indias' back in 1551. This heaping pile of horse puckey managed to be unearthed a little over half century later in the memoirs of Hernando de Escalante Fontaneda, the survivor of a shipwreck who had lived with indigenous people of Florida for 17 years.

Everyone knew that Ponce's legend was a lie, built on a festering pile of worthless crap and a great deal of blood. But his myth had become too valuable to simply abandon. Consequently, each person in turn that translated the story, rewrote it and pushed it to the public with the primary idea that Ponce had been looking for the now-fabled Fountain of Youth that lay somewhere in the wilds of the Florida swamps.

Like most good scams—and I know what I'm talking about, so listen—a small kernel of truth can give even the most obvious of scams a great deal of staying power. There have been scholars that have guessed at the possibility that the Fountain of Youth was another name for the Bahamian love vine. It is a plant which, in its day, was used as the cure for male impotency, an aphrodisiac mostly. It's possible that aside from conquering and stealing everything, that Ponce could have been seeking the vine as an entrepreneurial venture to market back home, something for Spanish men who had trouble 'performing' when the time came.

One historian named, Arne Molander, has even gone so far as to speculate that the adventurous conquistador mistook the natives' word 'vid', or vine, for 'vida', which means life. That could have transformed the 'fountain vine' into an imagined 'fountain of life'.

I'd like to think that if the natives, those that knew about what their healing herb could do, hadn't been massacred, or been introduced to sicknesses and such things by Ponce de Leon and his land-grabbing bunch of thugs, they would have laughed their asses off. To think that a vine they'd probably forgotten more about than any scholar could learn, had been turned into a fairy tale by some uppity, pathological, self-important European liars, is just too much, in fact it's almost enough to make this old man laugh hard enough to soil himself. But, just think of what the natives could have made from that, and how they could have held that over the heads of their 'conquerors'. Ha, now that's damned funny.

The real Ponce de Leon, the guy the history books don't talk enough about apparently, came to the Americas as a 'gentleman volunteer' with Christopher Columbus' second expedition in 1493. They don't teach that much in history class, do they? They just make kids memorize that damned jingle about 'sailing the ocean blue' and then celebrate a holiday that's less than the pretty picture that's painted about it. Oh, I don't give two shits about what happened back then, it's so far back in the past that worrying over it is pointless. But, when one thinks about how Ponce became a top military official and crushed his indigenous enemies right and left without mercy, well, sometimes it's important to hear who people really were.

His king—that's the King of Spain for anyone having trouble keeping up—rewarded Ponce for his extermination efforts by appointing him to be the first governor of Puerto Rico. You could say that things were looking up at that point, and Ponce was finally ready to cash in on the chance to earn some serious plunder. One can only imagine how wealthy he almost grew, from the output of his plantations and mines, all of them more than a little lucrative.

Of course, as riches and fame are wont to do, his success

drew the attention of some little worthless punk by the name of Diego Columbus, whose father, Christopher, had been Ponce's superior at one time. Diego didn't know his ass from a hole in the ground, which wouldn't be a saying for a long time at that point, but you get the picture.

But, instead of taking lessons on how to acquire his own wealth by taking the time to learn how to pillage and plunder and earn what came his way, Diego decided to sue Ponce back in Spain to remove Ponce from his role as governor of Puerto Rico. Ain't that just like a little punk? He can't do the heavy lifting, so he finds the lowest way possible to get what he wants and thinks that he earned it. It's a shame that men like Ponce, who weren't perfect but at least worked for it, could be treated like shit even after being loyal to their superiors.

It's a familiar story unfortunately. Some lazy layabout doesn't want to work and he's related to a higher-up who decides they want what someone else has, and cries like a little sissy to those who will listen. And those who listen to the punk strip the loyal foot soldier with one hand and reward the shiftless punk with the other. In short, the fix was in, back in Spain, and justice wasn't on Ponce's side this time. The lawsuit that was brought against him kept Ponce busy in Spain for years, and when it was all said and done, he had his ass handed to him.

Diego managed to pull a fast one on Ponce, but this wasn't the end of the story for the poor guy, just an interlude in the continued bullshit that his life became. While Diego had managed to get what he wanted, and Ponce was left holding onto nothing but the clothes on his back, the king at least knew that Ponce was worth more than the lazy ass with the famous surname. That's why Ponce was sent back to Florida as an explorer, a map maker, and of course, as an exterminator.

Thankfully, Ponce did manage to make the trip back, but by that time the natives were a bit restless and more than a little wary of the Spaniards that had decided to invade their home. Sadly, the natives kicked Ponce's ass back into the sea, where the man's pride was left to sting as he had to come to the realization that he'd been screwed by the king, by Diego, and had nothing left to show for it.

One thing is clear though, and that's the fact that everybody has heard of Ponce de Leon, while very few, if any, have ever heard of that lazy punk ass, Diego Columbus.

Life isn't fair, is it? Sometimes we have to put up with the injustice of it all, and sometimes we have to just grin and bear it as life bends us over and goes to town. That's when it comes down to getting a hobby or just sitting around drinking. One person I met here at Hidden Paradise suggested I try fishing or tennis. But, I don't see the point of fishing when you can buy fish in a store, and tennis is a game for sissies, like my boss's useless son, the one who got me arrested. He used to brag about playing tennis before I helped the feds send him on "vacation" for 10 to 15 years. Tennis? Honestly, I'd rather drink.

Chapter 2

Cole Bertram Sr.

Back in the 1920s, Florida real estate was just getting hot when Cole Bertram Sr. first arrived. That was in 1923, and Cole was still a skeptic when it came to the real estate boom that so many others were depending on. Up north he was a junior banker from Boston and he traveled to Florida with his wife Betty for vacation, already disbelieving any and all claims that easy money was bound to be found in Florida real estate. As far as he was concerned there was no such thing as easy money and Florida's boom might have been a ruse meant to con the unwary.

Before leaving Boston that winter, he told everyone who would listen that anything to do with Florida real estate was nothing but speculative nonsense. He opined that it was built on dreams and dust, and would crash inevitably. Well, you can imagine that a lot of folks simply brushed him off or listened with half an ear. But, it's fair to say that a lot of those folks would have laughed uproariously had they heard that he was about to abandon all reason and jump right into the mix without another thought for the fiscal conservatism that he'd been preaching. He had no idea of course, that his New England ways and ideas, his safe cushy job, all of it, was already fading away the closer he came to Florida. Had he known that he was about to become one of the most shameless Gulf coast boosters, it's likely that he would have never left Boston.

But for all that he thought it was a bunch of humbug, fancy tales and nonsense. Cole managed to make his way down to Florida, where his life was about to be turned upside down. Along with his young, pretty wife he found his way down the Old Dixie highway, cruising in his Model T Ford, to New Port Richey on the coast, 60 miles north of Tampa. Cole was only 23 at that time, and while he was college educated and talked a great game, he wasn't exactly an imposing figure. He didn't stand that tall, maybe medium height, he was balding prematurely and overweight. In short, no pun intended, he was the kind of guy that valued security and a boring, humdrum life over everything else. That's probably why Betty married him, for security. She might have had a bit more ambition for life itself than Cole did.

The vacation was her idea mostly since she wanted to visit New Port Richey and see if she could catch sight of any movie stars, who were reportedly thick as flies there. Honestly, if anyone had ever told me to go visit a town just for the sake of meeting a few stuck-up, self-important fakes, I'd have told them to go pound sand the moment after. The only thing those overpaid Hollywood types are good for is a song and dance every now and then, and half the time they're not even good for that much.

Cole and Betty checked into the Sass Hotel for two weeks, but unfortunately, as they found out, there weren't that many stars in town at that point. Apparently, Miami was the hot spot in the winter of 1923. They did manage to catch sight of Babe Ruth, Casey Stengel, and a few ballplayers that had arrived early for spring training. The weather was pleasant enough and the hotel guests were all in a fine mood. This, of course, was opposed to the skeptical attitude that Cole had brought along with him, since a lot of the guests had one thing on their mind. They were all there to try their luck at Florida land speculation.

It wasn't until their third day in town that Cole and Betty met another couple, a young carpenter from Indiana and his wife, also on vacation. Herbert and Mildred Mays became quick friends to Cole and Betty and ended up dining with each other for every night of their stay. Cole continued to be rather vocal about his doubts over the Florida land boom for about a week, but it was lost on Herbert and Mildred, since they'd already been bitten by the land-buying bug and were in deep. They'd been in New Port Richey for a month apparently, and had used up all their own money, their parents' money, and even money borrowed from their bank back in Indianapolis. They'd taken that capital and purchased an option to buy ocean front property in Tarpon Springs, about 15 miles from New Port Richey. In other words, they were hanging everything on the hope that the Florida boom was going to pay out in a big, big way.

Every night at dinner, Cole would find himself arguing with Herbert about the dangers of investing in real estate, especially in Florida. Then, about a week later, Herbert and Mildred made it known that they'd sold their option for roughly $115,000, making a whopping $94,000 in profit. Herbert even showed Cole the check. He announced that they were headed back to Indiana without hesitation to pay off their relatives, the bank, and then use whatever was left to buy a big home and set up a construction business. In fact, they left the next day, still feeling the euphoric high from their sudden good fortune. One could say that Cole was flabbergasted as he waved goodbye, but that's the nice way of putting it. In his mind the wheels of his ruination were already spinning.

His first thought, well, one of them most likely, was if an unsophisticated sap such as Herbert Mays could make $94,000 in a little over a month, then why couldn't an educated man like himself, with proven financial experience, top that kind of scratch with ease? He didn't even consider that he might have answered his own question had he been paying attention. But, Cole was confused and conflicted at the same time.

Had he been wrong about Florida? He couldn't help but start thinking about the riches others were making, and how simple it seemed. It wasn't long until he became obsessed. He and Betty even went out and rented a small bungalow as their home base. He then went and called his place of employment in Boston and quit his banking job. You would have thought with this kind of risk being taken that his story would end with the kind of success that comes with grit and determination and putting your back into it. You would think that, but you'd be wrong.

Cole and Betty Bertram wouldn't make it back to New England again until 1926, when they were on the run from hit men that had been sent for Cole's second partner, Cyrus Haney. With bags of untraceable cash, they were on the run and needed a place to hide. But I'm getting ahead of the story again, since you'll need to know why Cyrus Haney was being hunted and why Cole was next in line for the executioner.

Chapter 3

Cole's First Real Estate Deal

After deciding to commit all his energy and all his savings into getting rich in Florida, Cole came up with what he believed was a fairly good plan. Did you get it? Mr. genius conservative banker decided to save the planning for last and take on the risk first. One thing you could say about Cole, was that he was one of the dumbest smart folks walking the earth at that time. But then, in my youth I wasn't all that bright either, and I might have signed on with Cole at that time. In fact, I'm sure I would have, and would have believed that he was pretty damned smart too.

But, I'm sure that I would have steered him back to the straight and narrow path rather than allow him to walk through one tripwire after another as he did in his own good time. One of Cole's biggest problems was that he'd been sheltered and privileged as a kid, and thought he had a good handle on how the world worked. He was guileless, but he was also clueless and all the wrong people noticed. Have you ever met a cocky teenager that thought he knew everything and was confident that the world would bow to their whims? Yeah, that was Cole Sr. But, he had no idea how to pick his partners, as he kind of just accepted whoever drifted in on the wind, be it a clear, airy day, or a foul wind that was best left to roll onward and out of sight.

When he and Betty arrived in New Port Richey in 1923, the future of Florida looked positively chipper no matter which direction one looked in. People were smiling, making money, and there didn't appear to be an end in sight to prosperity. The first few days after he decided to play the real estate game, Cole felt he had the playing field figured out. He was a quick study to be sure and he had an angle he could use for every situation. His clever plans were well established in his mind at least. It was kind of like shooting fish in a barrel at that time since there was so much money moving into the state that the local banks were swamped. Since Cole knew the banking business, he didn't have much trouble realizing that he could be of some help. After all, he did know something about the banking business.

So, he secured himself a job at First Florida Bank as a loan officer, a job that wasn't hard for him to get. But he'd also noticed that the state was suffering from a shortage of college educated, licensed real estate brokers. So guess what he did next... yep, he applied for his real estate brokers license and used his prior employment and college diploma as qualified references. Cole was granted his license the same day. You've got to remember the time period and the lack of quality, educated people made the need for expedience absolutely necessary at times. As the years went by the banks became a lot stricter about who could just waltz in and grab a job. A college degree might get you a smile today, but that's about it.

Anyway, the day following the issuing of his license, likely before the ink had fully settled, Cole went and applied to be a part of the local planning commission, again using his bank job as a reference. He might have thought he had the golden ticket, seeing as he was advancing so quickly. He and Betty moved into a larger bungalow and about a month later, perhaps shortly after a congratulatory moment between consenting adults behind closed doors, Betty announced she was pregnant. Now, the average person in his situation might have figured that he was in a good position to provide for his missus, himself, and for their coming bundle of joy.

Of course, anyone that figured that back then wouldn't have understood the avarice and greed that was slowly eroding the already flimsy bedrock that Cole's conscience had been resting against for many years. Capitalism was in full swing, speeding uncontrollably ahead and Cole had worked with great purpose to put himself at the center of a web of conflicting interests, and insider trading. Any or all of these scenarios could make money or could burn him down if he took one wrong step. But was anyone going to tell him that? Hell no.

It's a wonder why no one saw what he was doing sooner, but when he started making loans to people that would never get repaid, he helped to cause the First Florida Bank to fail spectacularly by 1929. After loaning out humongous sums of money to middle class folks for various speculative purposes, Cole and others like him, managed to amplify the worst aspects of the Great Depression when it hit later on. His malfeasance was worse than many of his peers, since, as a city planner he approved questionable subdivisions, and as a realtor, he hyped the selling prices of lots. This guy made every possible mistake he could and he kept moving forward. He kept the fever of greed roaring along when it should have been left to die from lack of common sense.

And yet, despite the conflicts of interest and insider trading that should have kicked him out of the game, the state of Florida didn't see fit to stop him. He was allowed to keep moving along his destructive path. He had no inkling that most of the loans he pushed would later be defaulted on when real estate took its inevitable nose dive. There were no ethical restraints set in place to even question his professionalism, let alone stop Cole from continuing to wreck the lives of others.

The truth was, the owners of First Florida Bank didn't even mind his double dealing, and went so far as to encourage it. In the late 1920s, Florida bankers often served the government as elected officials, in public relations, and as corporate board members. If anyone's thinking the mafia was bad during their run, just look to the government to see where the mob learned their methods. Like it or not, the US government isn't much better than any organized criminal group that's been seen throughout history.

Wearing multiple hats was a great way to keep the nation's money flowing uninterrupted into Florida, and into the banks. It maintained a fever pitch that served to keep up the momentum needed for the cancerous development of Florida.

Only a short time after he'd arrived in Florida, the skeptic in Cole had all but died out, and he was ready and willing to make his own real estate deals. The conservative banker was almost entirely gone, and the man he'd become shifted his savings from Boston down to Florida like it was nothing. The $25,000 that he brought down was another sure sign that the person he'd been was gone, since the old Cole would have never done such a thing, nor would he have arranged for a line of credit with his bank. Cole was determined not to miss out on anything and was getting primed and ready for his foray into real estate speculation.

Surprisingly enough, his first venture succeeded. Using his real estate connections, he found out about a new, previously owned, and largely unknown development opportunity near Tampa. He bought an option to buy the parcel for $25,000, which was ten percent towards the actual price, which was $250 large. Once the option was in place, he advertised the parcel without hesitation and one week later he sold his option for $110,000. Needless to say, he was elated. At that point he figured it was time to go big.

About two days after that he was bragging to a planning official by the name of Harold Decker, who worked nearby in Hernando County. Harold mentioned to Cole a tract of land that was coming on the market soon, and if you couldn't guess already, Cole was interested. After listening to Harold's sale pitch, Cole was ready to go in once again. It was a long, skinny, 237-acre property called Hidden Paradise that was just two miles off the Old Dixie Highway. It ran all the way to the gulf. You could say that Harold had seen Cole coming a mile away and was ready with a spiel about how Hernando County was the next big hotspot, an untapped area that would continue to attract developers for a long time to come. Harold made it clear to Cole that the seller was very motivated and best of all, the schmuck didn't know the real value of the land.

The trick was that Harold was the seller, but he wasn't about to tell Cole that. What he did tell Cole was that the seller would accept $25,000 for the plot of land, in cash though. That would trigger all kinds of personal alarms these days, but Cole jumped at the deal. That shouldn't come as much of a surprise at this point.

By the end of the week, he owned the land that would one day be the lovely subdivision called Hidden Paradise Subdivision, or Hitman's Paradise as some folks like me call it in low, whispered voices.

You have to imagine that by now he'd completed his abandonment of all of his conservative principles. The cautious, skeptical New England banker was gone, and the man that wanted to focus on making big money and finding the easiest pickings was in full control. This was no longer the guy that would talk your ear off about the high risk of playing in the Florida real estate boom. This was the guy that was leaping at every opportunity like a fish at a swarm of bugs on the water. The sad part was he didn't realize those bugs had some mighty sharp hooks buried in them, and destiny was just itching to reel him in.

One fateful night, when he was still giddy with his recent purchase of the Hidden Paradise tract (that he had not yet seen) and flush with extra cash, Cole made his first, and arguably one of his worst, mistakes: He met Mathias Farley, who became his first partner. The two connected at the local chamber of commerce meeting, where they both mingled with the several other deal makers, swapping inside information, and chewing the shit as people are wont to do.

During the socializing that took place after the meeting, Cole struck up a conversation with a handsome and personable individual who, as it later turned out, was looking for just the right investor for his next scheme. Con men had to be extremely charming during that period. Mathias Farley had an oily, slimy nature. A guy like Mathias wouldn't survive now since people are on to that kind of grift. Despite being a clever, highly literate, entertaining, and smooth talking, blackmailing son of a gun, he was also as dishonest and crooked as the letter S. Of course, Cole wouldn't learn this until Mathias had driven him nearly to bankruptcy, and fled in the night for greener pastures in Hollywood, California.

Sounds like a comedy, doesn't it?

Chapter 4

Mama's Little Chickie Boy

To really get the most out of Cole's story it is necessary to realize who Mathias Farley was, especially since he became such a destructive force in Cole's life. The man was born in 1878 in Albany, New York, and was the youngest of four children. He was also his mother's favorite, as she called him "My sweet little chickie boy." When Mathias was about 18, he traveled to the Klondike to take part in the gold rush with his older brother, Thomas, who would later become a famous architect in New York. Thomas tried his hand at prospecting and was fully dedicated to it, but Mathias quickly found he wasn't enamored of the hard work and effort that mining required.

Instead, he dedicated his time to playing cards and running 'badger games' on the other prospectors. He would lure miners that were just in from the bush into sexually compromising liaisons with prostitutes and secretly photograph them in order to blackmail them later. Now to be sure, it's a miracle that no one ever found Mathias with a pick, or some other implement buried in his skull or in other parts of his body, since the things he decided to do to earn his money weren't at all nice. Not a single miner stopped his endeavor.

About a year later, Thomas gave up on mining and along with Mathias went back to New York. While Thomas went his own way, Mathias spent the next two decades ingratiating himself and mingling with the New York elite. To his credit, he exhibited a great deal of skill when it came to writing plays. A few of his works went on to be produced, which gave him greater credibility and access to performers, producers, and writers. At one point he became a low-level celebrity, and with his ready wit and risk-taking demeanor he was more than capable of maintaining his status. He worked occasionally in advertising, and continued to perfect his gambling and blackmail scams. All that talent and opportunity to do something legit, and he ended up being just as scummy as ever, oh well.

When the Florida land boom picked up steam and reached his ear, he made his way southward in 1922, following the scent of money. Mathias spent some time in Miami, trying to latch onto whatever deal he could find, but with little luck, surprisingly. He managed to talk himself into an advertising and promotion job for the fancy new subdivision of Boca Raton though, so he obviously found a place to start. At first, amazingly, he played everything straight down the line and didn't pull any scams or cons. His promotional ads and the accompanying pictures of fun, wealth, and high society appeared in hundreds of newspapers back north, but it wasn't bound to last. As you can guess, after a few months of the honest life, Mathias became bored and started dipping back into his old habits.

The falsehoods and lies came easily to him and in his promotional prose for individual lots in Boca Raton, he started to magically turn drainage ditches into romantic Venetian canals with gondolas that were designed to make one feel as though they were on a romantic cruise. Mangrove swamps that were an unmanageable mess became spacious yacht clubs that one could navigate effortlessly, and so on and so forth. Plans for the eventual development of hotels on empty lots of sand became luxurious hotels that had already been built and were ready to serve the public.

Boca Raton, which at that time had just constructed its first few buildings, was described as the "Jewel of the Gulf Stream" and "The sun porch of America", and even "The world's most beautiful playground." Because of this, lots sold sight unseen quickly and without pause to people that were never there to see them and might have demanded their money back if they'd been given true to life pictures of what they were purchasing. But, as long as the money kept rolling in, the board of directors of Boca Raton took no legal action. In fact, the only action they might have taken was to look the other way when this scam was going down. And when they looked back, they might find that their wallet had grown a little heavier.

Unfortunately for Mathias, his lies and ballyhoo caught up to him eventually, as things tend to do. His final ad included the names of all the major financiers of Boca Raton, which was a big error on his part. The Vanderbuilt's, the DuPont's, the Morgan's, and many others were listed in the ad, further, the ad boldly proclaimed that these wealthy families personally guaranteed that anyone joining the Boca Raton venture would see their money doubled in no time at all. The ad went on to encourage buyers to attach the ad to their deed before finalizing anything as proof that the profits were certified. As you can imagine, sales managed to soar once again. However, the other shoe eventually dropped.

One financier, Coleman DuPont, became so alarmed at the liability risk that he attempted to chase Mathias out of Florida. DuPont dug up an old article claiming that Mathias had once owned an old gambling house on Long Island in 1919, but Mathias responded by producing a salacious document of his own. After making his way to the local jail he spoke to a female inmate and convinced her to write a letter to DuPont claiming that she was about to have his love child. If you can believe this, Mathias tried to use this letter as leverage against DuPont in order to keep his job. It shouldn't be too surprising to figure out that DuPont had way more pull than Mathias, since not only did his leverage vanish, but his job went with it.

After that, he drifted for a while as he made his way to the western part of Florida, near the Tampa area. Seeing as how the east side was closed to him, there were few other directions to head, and he wasn't ready to give up on the state just yet. For a while he supported himself with an occasional badger game. He even went so far as to see if he could make any legitimate money working in real estate. That's how he came to be in New Port Richey in 1923: he was looking for real estate opportunities while falling into his old habits seeking celebrities to blackmail, and deals he could find that might make him a few extra bucks.

The biggest problem is that to run a clever scheme it takes money, and he had none, and no one was about to loan him so much as a penny. But it wasn't long after making his way into town that he stumbled onto a tract of 25 acres of beach front property near Clearwater. He finally found something to sink his teeth into, so to speak. It was beautiful, but he needed one more thing to make it complete – a money partner. Mathias attended one Chamber of Commerce meeting after another all over the Tampa area, looking for just the right person to become his financial partner. He needed someone that wasn't overly knowledgeable about the business but someone who was eager. In other words, he needed someone he could control. And wouldn't you know it, one night out of all nights he spotted a chubby, respectable looking individual by the name of Cole Bertram. It didn't take Mathias long to realize that he'd found his perfect target.

Striking up a conversation with Cole was easy, as Mathias knew how to talk a good game no matter who his audience was. They went out for dinner the next night and talked mostly about vaudeville and their favorite stage plays. All the while Mathias was setting his hook, regaling Cole with stories of Broadway and prospecting in the Klondike.

But the real interest he was sharing was the desire to make a killing in real estate while still in Florida. Soon enough Cole was bragging about his one successful deal that had netted him 237 acres, an area he hadn't visited yet. At that point one could almost imagine that Mathias was drooling on the inside as he thought of how he could take Cole for all he was worth. It became even more likely that Mathias might fleece him blind when Cole made mention that he was looking for other high quality investment opportunities. If ever Cole Sr. needed a good solid thwack upside his head, it was then.

Beg pardon, I need another drink just thinking about this; grifters like Mathias make my blood boil, but a cool drink will help.

Anyway, Mathias had his mark, and he pounced. It was

over coffee and desert, or so it's said, that he showed Cole a map of the 25 acres near Clearwater he wanted to buy and develop. Cole loved the idea, especially since Clearwater was close enough to Tampa to be a sure thing in his eyes. Mathias then told Cole they could buy an option to purchase the property for $45,000 with the balance of $450,000 due in 90 days.

Is your head spinning with these amounts yet? Just think of what that would be today, and it might.

Cole went for the deal and the two made a plan to buy the tract, subdivide it as quickly as they could into lots, promote the hell out of it, and then sell their options to a rich individual before the option came due. They were planning on wheeling and dealing the hell out of this, and once they shook hands and made their partnership it was a done deal. Cole went and bought the option with his own money the next day, with only his name appearing on the contract. Mathias had everything worked out, as they would advertise in a big way, using binder boys (rhymes with 'cinder' not 'grinder') as much as possible.

To give you an explanation, binder boys were college students that had come south in droves. They sold options or 'binders' to potential lot buyers and were unlicensed intermediaries that would do deals for several property owners and real estate brokers while accumulating real estate deals for themselves. The only way a binder boy got paid was when the deed transferred to the actual buyer. These fellows would often sell their binders to other binder boys, or to realtors, or to speculators. The problem with this scheme was that if the actual land sale failed to go through, the chain of failure would touch everyone that had purchased the re-sold binders. If you want a good example of shit flowing uphill, there you go.

Most binder boys often worked at undeveloped subdivisions, which was part of the scam. The landowner would set up a putting green or a tennis court at the edge of the subdivision, that way when people visited, they would see prosperous young folks happily playing tennis or working on their stroke. The plan was simple; make things look as good as possible to get people interested, and it worked.

Back in 1924 it seemed as though everyone was making money on all sorts of questionable land deals. A lot of folks believed it would never end. Never in the history of the United States had the gap between pure idiocy and brilliant genius been so narrow. Mathias's plan was sound in most regards, except for one critical detail. This was something that Mathias failed to disclose to Cole before his new partner bought the option to the land. The barely used roadway through the property ran right along the beach. If you're wondering why that's a problem, just think about it.

None of the lots had direct beach access, and for the type of money that this project was meant to pull down, keeping people happy was a key to success that couldn't afford to be lost. Ergo, the value of the land would go down significantly without beach front ownership and access, which was not good, not good at all.

Still, once he disclosed this fact to Cole, Mathias told his partner not to worry, that they would simply move the road inland. He needed $5,000 to hire the heavy equipment that was needed, and voila, they would simply move the road. It was only a quarter of a mile inland that the road was moved, so it shouldn't have bothered anyone, right? If you're getting the gist of this story, then you'll know by now that this wasn't the case at all. By moving the road, even a short distance, Mathias and Cole ran afoul of another landowner that was none too happy. This is where the Swedes came in.

Chapter 5

The Swedes

Moving the road onto someone else's land was audacious to say the least, but it was also their immediate downfall. The land they'd moved the troublesome highway onto had been owned for the last 15 years by a family of Swedish farmers that had been working their own coastal farmland since they made their way to Florida. To say that they weren't happy would be a gross understatement, especially since they were quick to hire an attorney who ended up suing Cole, not Mathias, since his name was the only one on the legal papers. The legal fees mounted quicker than Cole could read them as time kept running out on the option that he and Mathias had purchased. Eventually, Cole was forced to pay to move the road back as a condition of settling the lawsuit.

It was almost right after the lawsuit was filed that Mathias abandoned Cole, no doubt seeing little to no future in this scam as he left in the middle of the night like the thief he was. He was already on to greener pastures and even managed to get in touch with W.C. Fields, his old drinking buddy from his days back in New York City. Fields was already a Hollywood celebrity at that time, and he urged his pal to come out west. Fields promised screenwriting work, women, and all the fun he could handle. In fact, he quoted a man named Mizner as stating that a trip to Hollywood was akin to taking a trip to a sewer in a glass-bottomed boat, which meant it would be Mathias's type of place.

As you can imagine, the option ran out on Cole, and as a result he lost everything but $19 grand. He still had his job at the bank, his real estate license, and his position on the planning commission. But he was dealing with a lot of bleak prospects at that time and was only a few licks away from being a beaten and downtrodden individual.

The way he saw it, there was one last opportunity in Florida for him, and that was the 237 acres known as Hidden Paradise in Hernando County, a place he still hadn't visited yet. You can almost get the sense of group-think idiocy that these folks succumbed to back then, can't you? These days buying anything sight unseen is a good recipe for disaster and a good way to get a reputation for being eccentric, or a bumbling buffoon.

So, Cole finally went to see his land in Hernando County. It took him a while to find it, but when he did finally lay eyes on the destination, parking on the side of the Old Dixie Highway, he saw that there was no road to the property, not even a dirt or gravel path, or even a set of well-worn ruts in the landscape to mark the passage of anything. The land itself was still two miles from the highway but getting there was bound to be rough riding. All he did see was a mosquito-ridden, fetid mangrove and palmetto swamp. You know what he did then? I'm sure some people could guess.

He sat in his car, and cried.

Now there's nothing wrong with a man crying when he's been pushed to his limit, since everyone has a breaking point. But Cole had been stupid, there's no other way to say it. And the worst part was that he knew he'd been stupid, and he'd been played. He had no idea how to face his family and friends back in Boston after all his boasting and idiotic dreams. A part of him realized then that it was time to forget Florida and go home to take his lumps. But it was going to get worse before it got better, since he had to face his wife first, and any man that's done something stupid knows that a wife can make it better, at least a little, by supporting him and helping to get him back on his feet, or she can make it worse with four little words, those being "I told you so". I believe if Betty had said such a thing, Cole might have found the highest point in New Port Richey and jumped.

But of course, that's not what happened, or I wouldn't be bothering to tell this story.

Cole drove back to New Port Richey, and was working up the nerve to talk to his wife, but decided to take a small walk to calm himself down. This became a long walk, and then a longer walk, until the afternoon had passed into the evening. At some point he came to a local playhouse where a vaudeville review was in progress. Standing outside the stage door as the happy, upbeat music played, Cole couldn't help but feel a little bit better as the laughter of the people washed over him.

He was approached by a man smoking a cigarette not too long after this, as the stranger was also listening to the music. After offering Cole a cigarette, which Cole declined, the two of them stood by the door together and listened until the review reached its end. That man's name was Cyrus Haney, and he was about to change Cole Bertram's life, but if it was for the better or worse is hard to say.

Chapter 6

Cyrus Haney

Cyrus Haney was the patriarch of a clan of bootleggers and small-time criminals. He was born in 1881 in a sharecropper's shack near the rural area of the Gulf coast, just north of Tampa. He was born to a hard life, as there were very few pleasures to be had. But he had a great passion for life and a real talent as a singer. Haney was blessed with a strong, vibrant voice that could carry any tune from tin pan alley to opera.

Growing up in rural poverty kind of limited him to singing church songs and playing fiddle tunes on his banjo. He was married at the age of 16 and had three sons in quick succession. It was the kind of life in which he was expected to be productive and do what he could for the family, and surviving in a rough world was what he knew.

Haney had big dreams of making money, and when prohibition became law, he went into bootlegging with a side job trapping fur animals and alligators in the swamps along the coast. It was small money to be certain, but it was better than chopping sugar cane. His sons grew up to become trappers and bootleggers. Soon the father and sons branched out into a new direction, theft. They were an uneducated, proud, and sometimes violent family, but they stuck together. This bunch would rather beat a person to the ground for a minor, imagined slight than suffer a word of disrespect, no matter if it were obvious or not.

After a while they had a well-deserved reputation in their area as one of the most dangerous clans around. Cyrus had always wanted more than life had seen fit to give him, since he felt that he deserved it. He wanted the type of respect that he saw rich folks getting. One night in February of 1924 he was standing outside the stage door at the Scripps Brothers vaudeville house in New Port Richey, listening to the various acts with a great deal of enjoyment. He couldn't afford a ticket, but he saw another sad-looking man, a bit chubby, approach with a defeated look on his face. This was how he met Cole Bertram Sr.

After offering the sad-looking man a cigarette, which was politely declined, the two men stood there without saying a word to each other as they listened to the gay frivolity inside. When Cyrus recognized a song he joined in singing, often performing better than the people on stage. The other man complimented him when it was all said and done, and afterwards they exchanged pleasantries and began to talk about music. After a while, Cole invited Cyrus to join him for a cup of coffee. Cyrus accepted.

At the restaurant they traded more small talk, and it was then that Cyrus took in the sight of Cole's suit and his well-coiffed hair, no matter that he was a little disheveled from walking for so long. After asking what Cole did for a living, he was rewarded with the truth, but it was then that Cole announced he was picking up stakes and heading back to Boston.

Cole told Haney his sad story, from start to finish, somehow thinking that this rough-looking, rawboned man with the hard, calloused hands wearing his beat-up floppy hat was worth trusting. Haney's appearance didn't appear to bother Cole. He went straight from explaining his early skepticism of the real estate boom to the abandonment he'd suffered at the hands of his most recent partner, and the worthless land he'd bought thinking it would be a gold mine when in fact, it was nothing but a worthless swamp.

You can just imagine the way the gears were turning in Haney's head as Cole laid out his woes to him, and what he must have thought when being told that Cole was ready to pack it all in and head back to Boston. If anyone was thinking that Cole was a dunderhead before, what happened next will likely confirm it once and for all.

It shouldn't be too much of a surprise to learn that Cyrus asked where Cole's parcel of land was located, and when Cole told him it turned out that Cyrus had trapped and hunted up and down that coastline. He knew the area very well and agreed that building houses there was anything but feasible. However, he did quickly think of a better use for the land. It didn't take much for Cyrus to trust the mild-mannered and naïve Cole. In fact, the question he posed to Cole about wanting to make a fortune using his land would have likely been music to Cole's ears if his recent failures hadn't brought his skepticism roaring back. He'd been humiliated already and had no intention of having it happen again. He still wanted to make money, and to recoup his lost pride. So really, he felt like he had nothing to lose. If you're rolling your eyes, you're not the only one.

When Cole asked about the details of this new plan Cyrus was forthcoming for the most part, and to his own credit, Cole didn't go running when Cyrus told him about his plan to smuggle illegal liquor into central Florida. It was a plan that he'd been dreaming of for years before that point, and he had all the contacts he needed for bringing in the booze and the know-how to deliver it. All he needed now was capital and a base of operations on the coast. That plan impressed Cole so much that it's easy to think he was ready to say 'sure' before even thinking it over. But the skeptic he still was, realized that Cyrus was a schemer, and a smart one to boot. That attracted and repulsed Cole at the same time but considering that there was a fortune to be made in rum running, you can bet which way he was bound to decide.

Cyrus knew everything there was to know about the boats and the operation, and as they talked and talked, they pored over every little detail, closing the restaurant as they took their conversation to a park bench, where it was finalized with a handshake as the sun was coming up. Back in the day, this was, at times, the best way to finalize any deal. You couldn't get a lot of people to agree in that manner these days.

Cole agreed to invest $4,000 into the building of three 'Bimini boats' and $7,000 towards the financing for liquor purchases. The boats in question were shallow, draft smuggling boats that could navigate the narrow, shallow creeks that dotted the region, and they were designed to be seaworthy enough to make it at least 15 miles into the gulf to meet the faster rum running boats that picked up the booze in the Bahamas or in Cuba to deliver to the waiting Bimini boats. Cyrus knew every key person that could help to make this work since he had plenty of contacts in many of the clubs and speakeasies from Tampa to New Port Richey. The customers were already there and were ready for the kind of liquid fun that he and Cole would deliver.

The next day Cole withdrew his funds, $11,000 total, and gave it to Cyrus. In turn, Cyrus put his three sons to work blazing a well-hidden trail roughly four miles long from the Old Dixie Highway to the Gulf. They bought four sturdy pack mules and hid them from sight in the swamps, which could have gone terribly wrong if one understands what kind of critters roam those swamps. After that, they built a rough, hidden warehouse within the mangrove swamp to store the liquor.

It was decided that Cole would stay in the background of the operation and launder the money. Keeping his job at the bank helped maintain his low profile, as he continued to make mortgage loans and kept up the act as a regular, law-abiding individual. He also remained active in the chamber of commerce to keep up appearances.

Cole's wife Betty, who was busy with their infant son, Cole Bertram Jr., was told the truth at last, and while she was worried about what could happen, she finally agreed when Cole explained his overall behind the scenes role, acting like a law-abiding citizen to keep up appearances. By the time a month had passed, Betty's concern hadn't faded much, but the profits that came rolling in, $8,000 to each of the partners in the venture, made Cole's past failures as a real estate developer appear almost silly by comparison. For a while their elation was enough to eclipse the worry, but hell, there's always a reason to worry.

Chapter 7

Satchels Full of Cash

Over the next two years Cole laundered Cyrus' money through the bank without fault. He didn't put any of his own profits into a bank account. He kept all his money stacked in bricks of currency that were stored in a giant safe deposit box in Tampa. He maintained his respectable appearance and practices and made sure to distance himself from Cyrus and the smuggling business. Whenever they met it was always someplace discreet and far from the smuggling base. Betty met Cyrus only once in the entire time that he and Cole were partners.

In 1924, Cole Bertram Jr., my eventual source for this tale, was born, and he kept Betty happy and busy as one could imagine. Cole Sr. and his small family lived on his earnings from the bank and from brokering real estate deals, and for the most part they kept a low profile. They did buy a cute little house on a quiet street and even upgraded their car. But they lived a life that was safe from scrutiny since Cole was careful enough that no one knew what he was up to, or who he was connected with.

Following the first six months after Cole Jr.'s birth, Cole Sr. had more than enough cash to think about moving some of it back north. When he found the time, he would hop the train with satchels stuffed with cash. He would make his way to Boston where he rented several safe deposit boxes, placing them in his name, Betty's, and Cole Jr.'s. Over the next two years he had roughly $585,000 stashed in Boston safe deposit boxes, all of it the illegal earnings that had come from his partnership with Cyrus Haney.

Also, during his first trip back to Boston he'd decided to hide any evidence of his ownership of the tract of land in Florida.

Cole went and hired the largest, most respected law firm in Boston to create a partnership that would include him, Betty, and their son. It was called "The Holmesworth Partnership," and as soon as it was formed Cole had the law firm draft a deed transferring the tract of Florida land to the Holmesworth partnership. This effectively hid the ownership behind the lawyer's covenant of confidentiality. In other words, Cole pulled a fast one to make sure that no one knew what he had. To finalize things his lawyers created an escrow account owned by the partnership to automatically pay all Florida property taxes into the future for years to come. Cole then socked away $27,000 of his rum running cash into the escrow account, figuring it would be a good emergency fund to have around if things went badly for him once again.

Back in Florida the partnership with Haney was still flourishing as the two men genuinely came to like each other and had become committed to treating each other fairly and with respect. Because of this, the riches kept pouring in, which answers the question of why greed and avarice are such popular methods of business for some.

But about a year after they started, an event occurred that drew the mild-mannered Cole into the uglier side of rum running. One shipment of rum that originated from a warehouse in the Florida Keys turned out to be nothing but colored water. You can imagine how each one of the partners responded. Cyrus flew into a murderous rage, while Cole was furious but not quite the match for his partner. Why anyone would think to cheat and ruin a good thing is beyond me, but hey, people in this kind of business aren't exactly known for being honest. And some people, like Cyrus, aren't known for being calm when they're being cheated. The same day the swindle was discovered, Cyrus and his sons rented a large fishing boat and armed themselves accordingly. Against his better judgment Cole decided to go along.

When the boat got near the warehouse in the Keys, Cole was handed a sawed-off shotgun that no doubt felt a little heavy in his otherwise clean hands. It was in the middle of the night that the small group, their faces blackened with soot and boot black, went ashore to commit mayhem. The guards they encountered were left beaten and tied up. Despite being there for revenge, it was decided that the brutality they'd committed was more than enough to send a message, as was the bonfire that torched what used to be the warehouse. But first the group emptied the warehouse of its booze and cash supply, leaving Cole with $24,000 for his part in the lesson. As it would happen, the lesson was learned without fail, since no one ever sold Cyrus a single bottle of watered-down booze after that night.

Chapter 8

The Bubble Bursts

Two years after the rum running success had started, in early 1926, two events occurred that popped the happy bubble and put Cole into a serious tailspin that would eventually cause him to take his family and flee for their lives.

The first event that happened was the catastrophic crash of the Florida real estate bubble. By 1926 there were millions upon millions of speculative Florida lots for sale, but there were almost no people interested in living on the lots. A momentary drop in sales became a complete drop when new suckers stopped climbing on the speculation merry go round. The market for real estate options dried up quickly. If a person could sell their option to another buyer and make a little profit, everything was fine. But as soon as it slowed down, there was nothing to stop the crash. When a real estate option or binder came due the last person in the chain had to pony up the dough to actually buy the land, which was 25% of the overall value, leaving three additional years to pay off the balance. They didn't use 30-year mortgages in those days, just a 3-year balloon payment that would stick the last person to grab it with the check.

If a person holding an option didn't manage to put up the money to buy the property, then they lost their option money, and the option went down the line to the next person. If that person also welched and lost their option cash, then the obligation just kept moving down the line until the final sucker was tapped.

The bubble created by the Florida land boom started bursting everywhere in 1926, but the biggest players and the newspapers kept telling those who were panicking that this was just a momentary blip, a bump in the road so to speak, and that things would even out. But a lot of people could feel the end was near, even as the tragedy was happening. The magic they'd come seeking was gone, the fountain of opportunity had dried up, and anyone who stuck around was going to be left with little more than dust and debris when it was all said and done with.

But, why did the bubble burst? Well, the sellers and promoters overplayed their hand, plain and simple. They ran out of suckers to sell to, and realized that before they knew what was happening, they'd been taken as suckers too. The results were more devastating than you could believe since when the bubble burst, buyers stopped buying and people walked away from millions of dollars in lost investment capital. It had flown south from all over the country, representing the dreams and hopes of millions of small-time investors, each of them chasing what were essentially dicey land speculation bets that had looked, from afar, like a shining city of gold no doubt. It all vanished overnight. Poof, like a magic trick, only the trick was that the magician had robbed them with their eyes wide open and made off with everything.

The July edition of *The Nation* magazine, described the overriding fear of so many as "The world's greatest poker game, played with building lots instead of chips, is over. The players are now cashing in, paying up, or finding a nice quiet hole to hide in."

There was even worse to come later in 1926, since in September, a hurricane topping out at 140 mph brought in a 15 foot storm surge to Miami's shore, killing hundreds and injuring thousands. Roughly 18,000 were left homeless, and by that point the optimism that had been present in the early part of the year had been firmly squashed.

One could easily say that most of the nation was perplexed, dazed, and confused. How did this happen? During the boom, developers had created literally millions of excess lots and homes in Florida, but no one had answered the hard questions, such as: Where were the people going to come from to live in these homes? What were they going to do? How would they make a living? No one wanted to ask or answer these questions during the boom, likely because there weren't any real answers to be had.

As the United States reeled and the price of Florida real

estate started becoming valued for pennies on the dollar, the speculation ruined many lives across the nation.

Florida weakened the nation's economy to the point that for a long time afterwards, there was no chance that the US would ever just breeze through the second big crash that was looming just over the horizon, that man-made societal cataclysm known as the 1929 stock market crash. For example, during the boom, cities in Florida were issuing millions in municipal bonds to pay for roads and infrastructure. Once real estate values plummeted, the tax base of the cities failed, and the value of the bonds evaporated like smoke. The cities defaulted on their bond obligations only shortly before they defaulted on the rest of their obligations, like employee salaries. Lots stopped selling and the demand for building materials also dried up. Mill towns around the country that had relied on the boom were decimated. Huge swaths of the country were affected. Workers nationwide found themselves laid off as wages went down.

The prices of steel and lumber went down, and the downward deflationary price spiral continued around the nation. Then the banks failed. Imagine how foolish businessmen and politicians felt at that time, as they realized how badly the Florida real estate bust devastated one bank after another across the nation.

When word got around that options for lots were crashing the banks panicked, and you couldn't blame them really since many of the options had been purchased with borrowed bank money. You couldn't even count the number of people that went bust almost all at once. The Florida banks floundered without direction and started failing left and right as newspapers gleefully, then glumly, ran stories of banks shutting down, which only increased the panic. See? Even back then, the news was set to swing on a pendulum, delivering whatever it had to–to stay afloat.

The real estate crash was a financial disaster worse than the stock market crash if you could believe that, since the stock market involved mostly the rich and their money, however they'd gotten their grasping hands on it. Only about 1% or less of the US population owned stock at that time. On the other hand, around 15% of the US population owned some form of speculative real estate, not just in Florida, but around the nation. That is an astounding percentage. These investors were primarily middle class, so when real estate started to become a massive catastrophe in the 20s, it was the middle class that saw their savings and hard-earned wages drift up in a puff of smoke. Thus, the middle class of America was weakened and already reeling when the Great Depression hit.

The savings of many upon many people didn't recover until WWII. The Florida real estate collapse only made the Great Depression hit even harder.

Cole quit his banking job in early 1926, and I can't say I blame the guy. He got out before the bank failed, and advised Cyrus to get his money out too, which he did. In fact, Cyrus went and did something that might not have been wise, he buried it on his family's property. That might have been a mistake, but it's hard to figure what people were thinking back then, other than how to stay alive and what might come next.

Chapter 9

The Getaway

The second event that changed Cole Sr.'s life forever was that their profitable little smuggling operation had been gaining attention over the two years it had been running, and they'd been noticed by none other than Al Capone's outfit in Chicago. Back in the 1920s, at first all the easy money that came from gambling and liquor was controlled by common local folks, small fry criminals like Cyrus Haney. But it wasn't bound to be long until such an enterprise, small as it was, drew the eye of an organized crime syndicate moving in to Florida's shores. When everything was going well, colorful and social criminals like Capone were tolerated and even welcomed. Capone openly owned a few clubs in Miami, and he'd become part of the celebrity culture of the era. It was no big deal at first. But things have a way of getting serious rather quickly.

Capone quickly made his move to control all illegal activities in the area. He bought out the largest smuggling operations, but the smaller ones, like Cyrus', he allowed to operate independently, provided they kick back a 12% peace offering to the mob from their gross receipts every month.

Unfortunately, Cyrus did one of the worst things that anyone could think of, he refused to pay. In fact, when Capone's agent, a well dressed, soft spoken man, came to Cyrus' house to inform him of Capone's desire to let him operate freely for a small fee, Cyrus grabbed the little man by the back of his shirt and his belt and gave him a rough heave off his porch. If you're thinking that was a mistake, then you're an instant genius.

Haney should have paid. I certainly would have after learning about Capone's reputation. The odds of disobeying someone like Capone and surviving were incredibly small in those days, and I know all about the odds. After all, I successfully, and profitably, shaved the odds at several racetracks in New York and New Jersey for over three decades. I'd probably still be doing it if not for the boss's stupid, greedy pig of a son, a smarmy, smirking punk that belittled my 9th grade education for 25 years. Eventually that little puke got what he deserved.

But back to Cyrus.

When Cyrus told Cole about the visit from the mob, Cole was understandably worried and likely scared stiff while holding the phone in a cold grip. But Cyrus assured him that he was the king daddy around those parts, and that Cole shouldn't worry. He even bragged about the weak little man that had been sent to his door, before telling Cole that he was running things before the 'Chicago wussies', his words, arrived, and he'd be running things after every last greasy-haired one of them were gone.

Unfortunately for Cyrus, the mob wasn't used to being treated with such disrespect, and they didn't like it one bit. They already had a fearsome reputation to uphold after all, and in their way of thinking, country crackers like Cyrus didn't have the right to belittle even the least of their representatives. The mob stories that have been carried forward into Hollywood today aren't entirely accurate, but they're not inaccurate either.

The next day, a Sunday, saw Cyrus, his wife, and their three sons going to church. One would have thought that Cyrus would have at least kept his head on a swivel and been willing to engage in a little healthy paranoia. But this wasn't the case obviously since on a deserted country road, their car was ambushed, and as you can guess, there were no survivors. The killers were methodical in their approach and left the bodies of the Haney family in the road as a message to anyone that might have passed by.

No one was arrested for the crime, as there was no one willing to come forward, and there were no witnesses. There wasn't even enough evidence to say who might have done it, since a firearm wasn't as easy to trace back in those days, and while fingerprints were a thing that had been used for years at that point, gloves were still pretty effective, especially when the killers touched nothing but the bodies. Like it or not, investigative methods weren't quite up to the level they are now.

Around 10 years later though, a federal grand jury spearheaded an investigation into the corruption in the police force that served Hernando County, and a witness testified that she saw two police cars leave the scene of the massacre. It was written that there were no witnesses when the murders happened, but no one had ever bothered to interview this woman. Plus, everyone had known the police were corrupt at that time and controlled by the mob, so no one wanted to risk the chance that they'd be the next body found on a lonely stretch of country highway.

When Cole heard the news of the massacre on the radio the day after the murders, he panicked, as most people probably would. He was certain that he, Betty, and Cole Jr. were the next in line for an old-fashioned shooting gallery. So terrified was he that he convinced Betty that it was time to go, and she didn't argue. Cole Sr. emptied every safe deposit box he had in Tampa, and they packed up and fled to Boston. Cole told Betty everything, the whole story, on the way north, but she'd already guessed at most of it, as she'd heard the news report of Haney's death as well. From the day they left to their last day on this earth they never saw Florida again.

Upon arriving in Boston, Cole was able to take his job as junior bank manager once again, if you can believe that. He went on to show Betty how to access the money he had stashed in various safe deposit boxes throughout Boston just to be certain she could access it, but in the panic and fear that had followed them from Florida, he forgot to mention the escrow account with the $27,000 in it, or that he had transferred the ownership of the land to the Holmesworth Partnership, which was owned by all three of them. As far as he and Betty were concerned, they were done with Florida, so it never came up.

One might think that it's a stroke of good luck that Cole managed to escape the mob, but only six months later that worry was over and done with, as were his concerns about pretty much anything. It was January of 1927 when Cole Bertram Sr. was cranking his car to get it to start, as he was on his way to work, when he likely felt an excruciating pain in his left arm. All that's known of that final and tragic day was that a neighbor discovered Cole lying in the snow, dead of a heart attack at the age of 32. But hey, life went on for everyone else.

Chapter 10

Cole Bertram Jr

Cole Sr.'s heart attack could have been the end of this story, except for one thing, the forgotten escrow account. It had been created to automatically pay the property taxes on the swamp land that had been left behind when Cole had fled from Florida. Betty didn't know about the well-funded escrow account, and she didn't know the name of the law firm that represented the family and paid the taxes. Each year the lawyers dutifully paid the property tax without informing her, and thus did the years fly by.

Cole Bertram Jr., who was born in New Port Richey, Florida in 1924 and grew up in a modest home just outside of Boston with his mother, Betty. When they moved to Boston from Florida the Great Depression hadn't fully hit yet, but it was on the way. But before it did, Betty managed to get her job back at her former place of employment, hiring on as a bank cashier once again. This was the job that she would work at for the next 15 years while she raised her son quietly and unobtrusively. Times were tough when the Great Depression hit, but Betty, who was far smarter than her late husband Cole Sr., had learned how to be both resourceful and frugal.

The first thing that Betty did after Cole's passing in 1927 was to draw up a financial plan that would allow her and her son to live comfortably on their illegally gained fortune as she started to launder the cash in the banking system, slowly so as not to attract attention. Over a period of 13 years she did this, slowly drawing out the cash that her husband had earned in Florida and putting it little by little into the bank, and then into a few safe investments she'd researched.

In 1939, with all the cash successfully laundered, Betty could almost sense the feel of war in the air. She had a hunch that American corporations would once again flourish from the upcoming war profits, and as a result she invested everything they had into blue chip stocks. It was pretty obvious that Betty had better investment sense than her late husband, since during the war year and afterward she saw her investment of $500,000 grow to the tune of four-million and more as it kept growing.

All through his childhood, young Cole Bertram Jr. was obsessed with airplanes and flying despite his youth. He confessed to his mother that he had dreams of being a pilot. Given that she had the money to indulge his fantasy, Betty went ahead and purchased flying lessons for her son. While his friends were out playing sports and being rowdy, Cole Jr. had, at age 16, already gained his private pilot's license and touched the sky more than a few times in celebration.

It might have worried Betty plenty, but at the age of 19, Cole Jr. joined the US Navy as a pilot and went on to fly dozens of missions in the Pacific, including during the battles of Iwo Jima and Okinawa. When the war ended, he went off to college to study aircraft engineering at MIT. By 1950 Cole Jr. was 24 and had found the woman he wanted to marry and was hitched with twins on the way.

After that he moved his family to Seattle, Washington and started working as an engineer for Boeing, which is one of the smartest things that anyone could do really. It was his dream job, and to say that he was loving life was kind of redundant at that point. His mother remained behind in Boston, proud of her son but not ready to pack up and move again.

One day in 1957, Betty received a strange and unexpected phone call from a large law firm in Boston. They claimed to represent her and her son, as well as the interests of her deceased husband. They asked her if she wanted to continue putting money into the escrow account that had been paying the property taxes on a parcel of land in Florida. For Betty, that call was likely one of the most confusing of her life.

Chapter 11

Draining the Wetlands

The news that she and Cole still owned Hidden Paradise shocked Betty without any doubt. Her late husband had never told her about the escrow account or the Holmesworth Partnership. Betty had been certain that she was done with Florida, and good riddance. Really, could you blame her? There'd been nothing but lingering fear for her and Cole in that state, and she was done with it.

She called her son in Seattle to tell him the news, and for the first time she told him the entire story of their ordeal in Florida, the legal and illegal portions of it. That is pretty astonishing. She had been prepared to die keeping the Hidden Paradise away from her son, but for some reason, she changed her mind and she told him everything. She even went into the details of what had happened when she and his father had learned of the mob hit on Cyrus Haney clan. After telling him that they'd fled with bags of illegal money, she finally concluded her story, waiting for his response.

Of course, it was kind of a shock for Cole Jr. to find out about his parents' past, and it took him a couple of days to get used to the idea. But then, a new idea took hold, and he called his mother back as soon as this inspiration struck. He told her that he'd decided that he wanted to see the property before letting the escrow fund run dry.

So in March 1957 he took time off work and hopped on a flight to Florida. Upon arriving at the Hernando County planning department, he studied various maps of the undeveloped tract of land known only as Hidden Paradise. It was obviously low-lying swampland, but Florida in the 50s was in the beginning of the second great land boom, and this one would prove to be a lot more sustainable than the first one, which had ruined so many people. There was less hype, less speculation, and this time people were actually moving to the state to occupy the new houses that were being built.

It took a little doing, but Cole Jr. concluded that the land would need a serious amount of dredging. He contacted the local planning department and found that they had no problem letting him dredge the area. Back in the 1950's the regulations on what one could and couldn't do with the environment, especially if one owned it, were far more lax than they are today. These days one can barely put up a fence without being cited for altering the environment in some earth-shattering manner. But back then, one could do what they wanted on their own property. It wasn't until around the late 70s I believe, that wetland conservation became a thing.

Cole Jr. went and hired a marine engineer and surveying crew next, and he and the engineer walked the whole tract. They also viewed it by boat from the Gulf. The engineer took his notes, ran some calculations, and a few days later informed Cole Jr. that it would be possible to create just enough dry land for a new subdivision. You've got to remember, lots around this time were selling like hotcakes and it was a seller's market.

The engineer's plan was to dredge two wide and deep canals on each side of the parcel of land. By then throwing all the debris from the dredging onto the middle, in-between the canals, they could then create 200 dry and usable acres that would sit a good 27 inches above the high tide mark. The cost for this was high, around $500K. Back in his hotel in New Port Richey, Cole ran the figures and drew a rough map of the plan. Even as he was drawing this up, he'd already decided to keep the name of the place, figuring that Hidden Paradise was still a worthwhile moniker for this location. The way he figured it, if he could divide 175 acres of the land into ¼ acre lots, he could sell those resulting 700 lots for around $5K apiece, which would net a total sum of around $3.5 million.

The next step was to call up his mother and let her in on the plan, to which she heartily agreed, with two conditions. One was that she never had to set foot in Florida ever again, and the second was that she wanted Cole to sell the entire subdivision as soon as the dredging was finished. He had no troubles with this and agreed readily.

It wasn't long after this decision that the bulldozers and dredgers went to work. When everything was finished three months later Cole had a flat, empty, sandy tract of land that was 725 x 10,000 ft. It was uglier than sin to be certain, but the planning department approved the selling of lots in the Hidden Paradise subdivision, that's all that mattered. And the timing was perfect since the boom was on and people wanted to buy.

Cole put the entire project up for sale and in a week, he had two bids, with the higher of them coming in at $1.1 million, which was less than he was thinking about by quite a bit, but was still money in hand. He sold Hidden Paradise before a single house had been built to The Pettigrew Development Company, an outfit that was based in New Jersey.

He then went back to Seattle to resume his life and his career, eventually becoming lead engineer for the 747 Boeing aircraft. Betty passed on in 1984. Always the shrewd investor, she'd managed to amass an estate worth seven million dollars. Not once in the years since Cole Jr. had first visited the site in Florida had they returned. To be honest, they spoke of it very little, if at all. It was a part of their lives that they simply didn't want any longer, and that was best left in the past. In fact, that might have been the end of the story as well, except for Hurricane Elena, which made landfall in 1985.

Chapter 12

The Happy Years

Over the next 27 years following the sale of Hidden Paradise in 1958, Pettigrew Development built the land up into a thriving and happy subdivision. They even kept the name as you can see, and people loved living there. The corporation arranged for fruit trees to be planted all over the place, and to make it a livable space that promoted safety and joy for those that found it. The money that was made on that place came quickly and in plentiful amounts as well, as people couldn't get enough of the place. Those were the good times obviously. Eventually the corporation petitioned the state of Florida to rename the nature preserve surrounding the subdivision Smuggler's Point Bayou Nature Preserve, which they believed would highlight the colorful nature of Cole Haney's rum running that took place back in the 1920s. Did you get that? They wanted to honor the memory of a rum running hard-ass like Haney. Ain't that a kick?

While Pettigrew was selling lots, they were also building a three-story condominium near the entrance to the subdivision. They also built a marina, a swimming pool, and two tennis courts. Four years later in 1962, when all the lots were sold, they built two more stories on top of the existing three-story condo. Unfortunately, they didn't bother to take steps to strengthen and improve the concrete footings, which rested on sand and dredged up muck. The planning commission made it possible though, and Florida was in a boom. No one wanted the land boom to stop.

An unfortunate problem came from the addition of the last two stories since the added weight made the entire building start to sink about an eighth of an inch per year. The corporation discovered this and did their best to cover it up, which worked. They also made the decision not to put any more money into the condo, so they never ended up finishing the elevator to the 4th and

5th floors, cheap bastards. No one in the local government, not even the buyers of the upper rooms, appeared to mind, which was odd but not unheard of. It was just an exciting, giddy time to be in Florida, being that it was a land boom and all.

On one side of the lake that was next to the condo they built a nautical and pirate-themed shopping mall. The 'Smuggler's Cove Mall' they called it. The place was built on wooden and concrete pylons, so the shops were suspended on a boardwalk over the water. This was a modern and exciting bit of fun for the people that came around, and in those days, there wasn't much trouble at all with the wildlife, since the alligators had nearly gone extinct. But since the 1990s the gators have been protected by the federal government to get their numbers back up, and oh yeah, they've been rising. Once their numbers did start rising though, people managed to put up chain-link fences around every inch of the lake, just to be safe.

For thirty years, it was a wonderful place to live, as the 1960s to the 1980s represented some of the best times for this location. But Hurricane Elena came to visit in 1985 and everything kind of went to hell.

Chapter 13

Hurricane Elena

By Florida standards, Hurricane Elena wasn't anything special. But, Florida's 'nothing special' can still get pretty deadly in a big hurry. In 1985, Elena moved inward and became a two-day national news event. It was forgotten soon after since nobody died, and Floridians even admitted that it wasn't that big of a deal. But, those within the confines of Hidden Paradise weren't quite so lucky, since Elena snuck ashore right over the subdivision and came bearing gifts in the form of 110 mph winds and a powerful storm surge ten feet high that made its way inland and did its own damage. You might not think that ten feet of water is a big deal, but when that ten-foot wall of water has enough force behind it, the damned thing can flood and swamp everything and wreak the kind of havoc that ends up costing an arm and a leg and maybe a hand to fix.

The only good part here was that people had advanced warning, which means no one died since they had a chance to evacuate. But, the subdivision was hit hard. Nearly every house was damaged or wrecked in some way, roofs were torn off, and trees planted around the houses were toppled left and right. The Pettigrew Corporation had managed to get the windows boarded up on the condo on the Gulf side, which meant everything above the ground floor came through alright. But, the shopping center was a god awful mess. Much of it was ruined and left no easy solution as to how to fix it.

Once the storm was over and the property owners started filing claims with their insurance companies, the companies decided to be dickish enough to refuse payment. They claimed that the damages came from flooding, and floods weren't covered by normal property insurance, meaning that the residents were shit out of luck. A lot of folks gave up and took the loss, abandoning their homes and apartments, and even the condo apartments. A few thought to take the fight to the insurance companies in court. Unfortunately, the business-friendly Florida courts made certain that these lawsuits were extremely expensive.

In the end, amidst the wreckage, the Pettigrew Development Corporation had to declare bankruptcy. They had to walk away from everything, as did 99% of those that owned homes, most of them with nothing but what was in their pockets, which might have amounted to air at that point. And, as if to be extra petty, the insurance companies issued a statement that they would never again issue property insurance covering any building within the Hidden Paradise subdivision. It was the kiss of death to be sure, and once again, it might have been the end of this story if not for one man.

An obscure budget analyst named Warren Digby working inside the justice department, trying to fulfill a mandate handed down by the president of the United States at that time, Ronald Reagan, managed to keep this story going. That's either a kick in head or the nuts, I'm not sure anymore.

Chapter 14

Warren Digby's Plan

In the 1980s, the Reagan administration declared government to be the problem, not the solution. Extreme cost-cutting measures were mandated all over the US, except when it came to defense. I guess killing and bombing was fine, but taking care of ordinary citizens at home was a Godless slippery slope to communism. It was also the time for getting tough on crime. There would be no more coddling of criminals and drug dealers, and the justice department was taking this to heart. "Save the taxpayers money" was the common mantra heard around the nation. It almost brings a tear to the eye unless you're a lifelong skeptic.

One day back in 1986, this budget analyst named Warren Digby, who grew up in Tampa, Florida, was looking for places to cut the budget for the Witness Protection Program when he came up with a novel idea.

Being from that area of Florida, he'd heard about Hurricane Elena, and he'd also heard about the extreme damage that had been done to one certain location, a low-lying subdivision that should have never been built called Hidden Paradise. The owners had declared bankruptcy and the insurance companies would never consider covering it, but when Warren looked at the photos of the damage the storm had left behind, he was intrigued.

It was at that moment that he had a great cost-cutting idea. The government could buy the place and put the high-value criminals in the condo. That way they could save millions and use it to make bombs and build prisons.

So he pitched the idea, and as usual it went up the chain and he had to wait for a while before it finally made its way to the oval office, and then it had to be placed in front of Vice President Bush, who pushed for the idea and pushed hard. Once it was accepted, the Department of Justice quietly bought the area known as Hidden Paradise for a song and maybe a little dance. They cleared out the condo area, the marina was rebuilt, the pool was fixed up, and the mall was cleaned out and declared open for business. It was a return to something that the next residents would see as a haven, and some of us would see as a gilded cage that was better than a hailstorm of bullets or whatever other horrors our killers would offer us.

Chapter 15

Club Rat

So, that's how Hitman's Paradise came to be, from Ponce to the sorry putzes that now call it home, yours truly included. It's a place for turncoats, traitors, squealers, stool pigeons, criminal outcasts and cowards that couldn't face what was coming to them. That's why I'm here. I was the third resident to enter Hidden Paradise under WitSec's less than mindful eye, and at this point I know I'm not that important, I'm just here to be out of the way and off their radar so they can catch the bigger rats. It was lonely here for a while, but since the population has increased, I've made a couple of friends, you know, those folks that say they've got your back and are looking for a good place to stick a knife.

In case you haven't guessed it yet, or I lost track and didn't tell you (did I tell you?) I learned this story from Cole Bertram Jr. Out of curiosity I called him up after seeing his name in the planning records for this place. I didn't tell him I lived here, because all of us in the program are supposed to be in hiding. I'm also a wanted man and have a big enough price on my head that it's not wise to go out walking in the city anymore. What I told him was that I was living in a senior retirement development in New Port Richey. I made up a story about being old and bored and how, on a lark, I did some research on an interesting spot called Hidden Paradise that I'd heard about somewhere. He bought my story.

He was kind of reluctant to tell me the whole story at first, in fact it took a while to get the story of how he and Betty used his father's rum running money to get Hidden Paradise up and running. But he wanted to talk, and finally he loosened up. Apparently, he'd been obsessing over Hidden Paradise and the father he'd never really known for over three decades at that point. Over quite a few phone calls we became real friendly and managed to talk about all sorts of things. I found out that his mother only told him the whole truth after the law firm had informed her that she still owned the land, and after he found out the truth he never told anyone until I came long.

At this time, he's retired and living in Arizona and still flies small airplanes now and then. When the subject came up about the writing of this story he asked if I'd ever publish it, and I told him that writing was just a hobby, which is true. About a year after we first spoke, he called me up and in a friendly way asked if he could see my book. I had already completed it by then, but since it makes mention of the Witness Protection Program, I decided that I couldn't risk it. I told him that I'd abandoned the project, and sadly, that was the last time we spoke.

As I've said before in my life, this is my last stop. With my advanced diabetes and heart disease, and the price that's still on my head thanks to the gods-cussed mob that won't just up and die finally, there's really nowhere else to go. But to hell with it, I don't mind. I've had a surprisingly good run up to this point, but all that nonsense is another story. Who knows, maybe I'll think about writing that one if there's still time.

Or maybe, just maybe, I'll walk down to the end of the subdivision, next to the Gulf, and meet the hardscrabble squatters that are moving in with their boats, taking over the hurricane wreckage and whatnot. The residents of Hidden Paradise have already taken to calling the place "Boat Camp". From what I can tell, the folks living in Boat Camp are about as hardy and rugged as any gypsies that anyone in Florida has ever seen. They're the types that'll survive a nuclear holocaust if only because they are kind of like roaches, they're used to living on shit.

I hear tell stories that these folks have been living on boats all over the Gulf of Mexico and Caribbean Islands, squatting here and there, people with no country, no state, and no real home to speak of. I'll bet they have some dynamite stories. Maybe one of these days if I can get them to tell me about themselves, I'll learn a thing or two.

Looking back on my life I can own the fact that I've been a cheater and a criminal as far back as I can recall. But it was fun when I was still at the top of my game. Believe this if you will or don't, but I wouldn't change a thing, not even when it came to sending my best friend Rico Stanucci to prison for a 30-year stretch. I don't even mind that I ratted out Joey the Hat, who was the best boss anyone could ask for, just so I could save my own skin. I did that, and I'm not proud of it, but I wouldn't change it. Joey's snot-nosed punk of a son, Dominic, was the one that caused the initial trouble and made it necessary for my self-preservation instinct to kick in. I danced a jig when he went to prison.

But, what the hell. We all knew what we were doing. We weren't in the Boy Scouts, and what happened to us goes with the territory. It's all a part of the life we chose, kind of like The Ponce, like Cyrus Haney, and yes, even like Cole Sr. One way or another, everybody's got to pay in the end.

The end